The Darkness of Myth

Emma Bradley

Beyond the unknown is the deepest truth.

For Debbie and her relentless proofreading – thank you for being so gentle on my sensitive ego!

CHAPTER ONE
SANNAR

"The nether feels off today."

It was the convenient excuse used for every minor misdemeanour, grouchy mood and accident that happened at the Nether Court.

Sannar Hollowbark was more than used to hearing it many times a day, especially in his capacity as Chief Attendant to the court's ancient lady, but not usually from the Lady Aereen herself. She had her foibles as most lords and ladies did, but she didn't usually deign to speak randomly in his presence, only to bark some vague instruction at him.

She turned her head away from the window that overlooked the court's central courtyard, the sounds of folk ambling around in the sunshine and stopping to chat filtering in on the breeze. Set high up in the mountains of their realm, the court was a haven for scholars, with low buildings rambling around the large platform that led into the mountain and the vast tunnel network that formed the fabled Nether Court archives. When Lady Aereen's gaze fixed on him, he knew from the wistful expression on her face something wasn't right.

"Does it?" he asked, forcing himself to focus on the paperwork in his hand. "People are always saying it feels off."

She wrinkled her nose, the many lines across her wise face deepening. Her long white hair was pinned back, and she rubbed a hand over it with a distracted air.

Great, last thing I need is her waning sanity on my plate.

She flicked an irritated look at him so suddenly he almost apologised for his thoughts, even though she couldn't read them. Not that he knew of anyway.

"I suppose they're all sizing me up for my box already," she said, her gaze returning to the window. "Vying over who will take up the mantle when I mumble my last words. Shame you're too young really. You're very amenable."

"I am seventeen already," Sannar protested.

She let out a soft chuckle but didn't bother to look his way.

"So you are. Too young. What are you here for this time?"

He took the papers over to her complete with pen, ignoring the sinking of his ego. He definitely didn't want to be Lord of the Nether Court, because even being assistant to it was more than taxing enough. Lady Aereen might enjoy the opulent room they were in, her grand office decked in the court's colours of brown and muted purple, and she might benefit from having two fireplaces in her bedroom adorned with antique draperies and linen that fitted her noble status, but her role was a dangerous one. There had been more than one attempt to overthrow her rule in the last fifty years, and one assassination attempt almost succeeded twenty years ago. Sannar had no desires to climb that particular burning rope to nobility, but it still hurt to know she agreed with his inadequacy for the role after all he did for the court, and for her.

"Signatures," he said, holding out the papers and a pen. "The approval for extending into the south rockface, the confirmation that we're going to host the open day for the town again, not that anyone bothers to come up this way for it. Oh, and I've penned a letter to the queen's court in response to their request for a-"

He trailed off as she snatched the pages from him and the pen. He reminded himself that she was ancient and therefore wise in the ways of the nether itself, which was more important than her people skills. Many drifted to the Nether Court because they preferred silence and darkness to people, but Sannar had realised too late that he wasn't one of them.

It had been such an amazing opportunity for him to swear his service to the Nether Court at thirteen years old. The other new initiates had welcomed him and he was quickly chosen as someone who would be useful to the court. But more often than not, his gaze would drift to the edge of the mountain inlet the court was built on. His feet would take him to that edge, his gaze drifting down to the heaving town below. To its people and those he'd left behind.

As the lady signed the papers, and reviewed them with suspicious 'hmm'ing noises that suggested he would likely have to rewrite all of them *again*, he stared out of the window.

Across the neat grass courtyard, beyond the simple one-level buildings that served as court housing, meeting rooms and the various discovery centres that investigated and monitored the nether, was that edge.

I'll sort these papers out and go take my break, he decided. *Nobody will miss me for a little while.*

They probably would miss him, because several of the higher court members wouldn't do something themselves if they could offload onto someone more junior, but the restlessness that had plagued him lately was getting harder to ignore.

"There." The lady placed the papers back in his hands. "Off you go."

Sannar took the papers and didn't even bother to ask if she needed anything as he left the room. It only took a few moments to sort the paperwork into the relevant trays on the office desk outside and finally he was free.

With a deep sigh, he left the lady's chambers and walked around the edge of the grass, drinking in the blissful heat of summer sun on his face.

The mountain towered above the wide ledge the court was built on, with a steep hill tumbling down to the town far below. It was walkable to town and back in an afternoon, but on the rare occasion any of the nether brothers would venture down there, they took one of the free-to-use bicycles.

Sannar pushed swiftly past thoughts of his family whenever his thoughts strayed down to the town. His parents owned the local inn, but they'd always been very clear to him and his siblings that they were parents in biology only. He'd gone down once or twice out of duty to visit when he first joined the court but quickly gave up. They hadn't once come up to see him.

He gazed further on, past the boundaries of the court and the ledge to the mountain ranges in the distance. He'd heard great tales from travellers of their realm, but never once had he seen the deserts beyond, or the grey hills that were rumoured to be speckled with valuable pink granite that sparkled during a full moon.

Joining the court had been his ticket out of the town, a gateway to the realm and even the wider world of Faerie beyond that.

And like a fool, I believed the whole lie.

He shook his head, knowing that at any moment

someone would come bounding up with some question or task he needed to do. But in those tiny moments of irritation, refusing to move felt sadly liberating.

Perhaps if he'd been going at his normal pace and rushing along to his next task instead of dragging his feet, he'd have missed the girl walking on the other side of the courtyard.

She had her long dark hair loose, which was unusual for her. Most days it was in a ragged bun somewhere in the vicinity of the back of her head, errant strands escaping every which way. Her skin was tanned from what he assumed were still days spent helping her father on the harbour, but she'd been sneaking up to the court more often of late.

Odella Dewlark.

Once, long ago, she'd been his best friend, or one of them at least. Now she was a stranger, barely even stopping to give him more than a cold glance. He'd never told a soul that he thought she was beautiful, and many of the other nether brothers that were court-sworn had often called her too 'hearty' when discussing the rare few girls from town that ventured up to the actual court. Sannar didn't think she was hearty. She was strong and graceful, each movement effortlessly powerful. Even looking at her made him feel inadequate whether she cast those wary green eyes or not.

He wondered what had happened to make the previously cocky, good-natured girl he'd grown up with turn into a polite but cold young woman. The moment he'd been accepted up at the court, she'd distanced herself. Those early days had been a whirlwind of initiations, and he'd asked her to keep her distance for a bit while he made new friends, but at as time went on he'd noticed her absence more and more. Until it eventually became the norm and the odd glimpse of her set his heart racing with nerves.

He raked a hand through his shaggy red hair and straightened his brown nether brother robe. The hem barely covered his jeans now because he'd had too many growth spurts fairly late, but with everything else he had to manage, his appearance had taken last priority recently.

Although he'd intended to go to the wall surrounding the edge of the cliff-top inlet, his feet seemed to be on some other track entirely.

Odella looked up as he approached, her pace slowing as her back stiffened.

"Sannar." She nodded with no hint of a smile.

He gulped. "Hi, Odella."

"Hi."

He had absolutely no idea what to say next. He couldn't ask after his parents because even though they lived down in town he rarely saw them, and Odella of all people knew he wasn't too keen on them anyway. She probably already drank in the local tavern they ran, his mother flirting too much and his father drinking half their profits. His older brothers and sister had all fled elsewhere and his parents made no secret of the fact they were glad to be childfree on the rare occasions he did have to see them.

He opened his mouth to ask Odella how her family were instead, but he saw her mother every day because she worked at the court, and her mother told him all their latest family news.

"How are you?" he asked.

It was either that or continue standing there with his mouth hanging open. Odella raised her eyebrows, the iciness of her expression not lifting with them as she pushed her glasses up her nose.

"We don't do small talk," she reminded him, pushing her glasses up her nose with her finger. "What do you want?"

Ouch. Sannar took a tiny step back.

"I… honestly? I have no idea. The nether feels off today."

That at least earned him the tiniest of smirks from her which was something. Emboldened by this triumph, he glanced at the buildings behind him.

"Are you here to see your mother?"

She nodded. "Do I come for any other reason?"

"No…"

She might have pitied him because he could have sworn her eyes warmed the slightest amount.

"I'm helping her more here while Dad's off on the boats for a bit. But don't worry, I won't cramp your style or anything."

Sannar frowned. He certainly couldn't imagine her cramping anyone's style but he wanted to reassure her all the same. Before he could find a way to say something eloquent and helpful, his orb burned in his pocket. Huffing under his breath, he pulled it out and held it up.

A familiar face loomed between them as a pearlescent grey vision and he forced a smile as the Lady of the Illusion Court caught his eye. She was relatively new to her post, but she'd taken to it surprisingly well by all accounts.

"Hi, Sannar. I won't keep you," she said immediately with a grin. "I know how undervalued you are over there."

He rolled his eyes. "Flattery will get you nowhere, Lady. But as you've helped us, what can I do for you?"

Though the sharp image of her face he could see the hazy imprint of Odella, her brow ever so slightly narrowed. Aware he shouldn't technically be having this orb conversation out in the open, especially in front of someone like Odella who wasn't court-sworn, he hoped Lady Reyan wouldn't say anything damning and stayed put.

"I'll be along for another visit soon," Reyan said. "But I've heard from the queen that the Forgotten have been reported trying gather favour from a few of the big noble houses and also a couple of the courts. They know not to bother with us but they might come for your lot next."

Sannar glanced around. The courtyard was empty and he couldn't see a single soul. Except Odella, but for some reason he was loathe to move away from her or excuse himself.

Instead he gave Reyan another mandatory smile in the hope of hurrying things along.

"You know I've little control over what our lady will want to do, but the queen has my support for what it's worth, for the good of the court and Faerie."

Reyan nodded. "Ah she knows that. But things are kicking off so consider this a warning to be ready. I'm just saying that next time I visit it might not only be to keep the shadows happy."

"Noted. Will Lord Kainen be visiting with you this time?"

He waited, a tiny tinge of hope growing. He liked Reyan because she was kind and friendly, and rather unladylike. She'd been visiting recently to check on the beast slumbering beneath the Nether Court mountain, but his favourite part of her visits was when she brought Lord Kainen with her. He had a devilish knack of flustering all the nether brothers by being charming and suggestive, and Sannar found it hilarious.

"Yeah, he's accompanying me this time." Reyan

laughed. "But you two need to play nice and not antagonise your entire court, okay? See you soon."

She disappeared before he could reply. He replaced his orb in his pocket with a smile lurking on his lips. Then he remembered Odella. She stood frowning at him, but he couldn't tell if she was intrigued by what she'd heard or worried.

I don't know her well enough to decipher her looks anymore, he thought, his insides sinking.

He wondered if his decision to randomly approach her today was something to do with the nether being off, or maybe him being off instead, but he couldn't ask her that without her thinking he was deranged.

Then Odella's expression cleared and she folded her arms across her chest, one hip tilting as she eyed him.

"You shouldn't have said any of that in front of me," she said with a smile.

His insides lit up with fluttering relief and he grinned wide.

There she is.

CHAPTER TWO
ODELLA

Odella couldn't help teasing him. She hadn't spoken to Sannar directly since the day he'd sworn service to the Nether Court, not more than a dismissive word or two in passing. He'd not spoken to her either, but today he actually made an effort.

Even if he did blame it on the nether like everyone else does around here.

But now he stood beaming at her and she had nothing else to say. She knew everything about him and his progress from her mother already, and he probably knew she knew it, so any mundane questions would be fake for both of them.

She took an awkward step back.

"Right, I have to find my mum." She hesitated but he didn't move to fill the pause. "Bye then."

Ignoring the unexpected heat covering her face, she set off toward the court buildings. She never blushed. The last time she could remember blushing had been when she was a lot younger and embarrassed herself at the harbour trying to jump from boat to boat. Now even her normally easy stride felt forced and unsteady as she crossed the courtyard.

Maybe the nether really is off.

Okay, so Sannar had grown up really well with the longish red hair swept behind ears that he'd finally grown into, along with the extra few inches in height to his lithe frame and the strange way his brown eye complimented his grey-blue one. Not that she was staring at his eyes or anything.

She shook her head as she peered into her mum's empty office. Not seeing anyone in the office next door to ask either, Odella ambled across to the large gap in the inlet that led down into the mountain. Perhaps her mum was somewhere in the tunnels where the scrolls were kept.

She often wondered why the court, so protective of their secrets, let a townsperson wander around their court. Her mother had taken the job years ago but Lady Aereen had been in place as ruler of the court back then as well. In her mother's eyes, nothing much had changed since. The elitism of court-folk v.s. townspeople was often veiled but always there. It lingered in the dismissive looks, the inner jokes and the bragged about secrecy the nether brothers clung to. Nobody would dare call her mother a 'town-rat', which was what a lot of the nether brothers called them when they thought nobody important was listening, but Odella knew they thought it all the same.

How many of them even bother to look down when the meadows are singing, or speak to traders like Dad in the harbour?

Not many, she knew that. Nether brothers weren't often seen in town either, not unless they were running some kind of errand. No, they were happier dashing about their court feeling superior.

She frowned. The square of grass in the middle of the court's platform needed watering. One of the nearby fenceposts was wonky. Several of the banners looked like they could do with a good clean. And yet for all her scurrying around the court, doing odd jobs for her mother and chatting to the maids and attendants in service there, she had learned one thing: when in doubt, tell Sannar and he'd sort it. But she didn't want to go back for another awkward conversation, and she could sort herself out perfectly fine on her own.

As she approached the two guards blocking the entrance to the mountain, she pushed her glasses up her nose and squared her shoulders.

One of them, a broad-shouldered young man who she recognised as a friend of Sannar's, smirked and blocked her way, one hand out between them.

"Your mother's gone to the upper archives," he said. "Long way up. I *could* give you a lift on one of the trundles, for the right price."

Odella pulled a face as he looked her up and down before winking. The trundles were weighted trolley lifts that took large goods and those who didn't want to walk the long tunnels through the mountain. Nether brothers would no doubt be able to use them at will, but since she wasn't a nether brother or in any way sworn to the court, she would have to trade for a lift. Because she helped her mum most would give her leeway but Sannar's friend, whose name she couldn't remember, clearly had some kind of issue with her.

Unable to use the trundles without him or his silent companion, she ventured back outside. Most in town knew of her gift but she doubted the nether court would pay any attention to people outside their hallowed walls.

Sannar's friend looked at her like she was crazy as she walked up to the cliff wall nearby and peeled off her boots and socks.

"What are you doing?" he asked.

She gave him a look. "Getting up to the upper levels, what else?"

He stared at her for a long moment before laughing and turning to his companion.

"She thinks she's going to climb the mountain! It's virtually flat rock up there, you'd slide straight back down and don't think either of us is going to desert our post to catch a town rat."

The other guard looked uncomfortable, his hands in the pockets of his robe and his shoulders hunched, but he managed a weak smile when spoken to.

Odella rolled her eyes. "I wouldn't let you close enough to touch me. Besides, you're deserting your post to fling insults at me, so that says all it needs to about you."

He realised she was right and took a step back as she put her socks inside her boots and knotted the laces around her shoulders. She slid her glasses into one of the zip pockets on her jeans and breathed in deep.

Calling the Fae essence of her gift to her hands, Odella placed her tingling palms against the rock and let the connection flow through. She wasn't entirely sure how it all worked but the rock and bare earth would respond to the heat from her hands, like butter might do as it melted in anyone else's fingers.

She sensed that sudden snap, the taut structure of the rock yielding and becoming soft to her touch. Digging her fingertips in, she started to climb. The gasps of horror from the guards fell away as she concentrated on creating each hand and foothold, careful to smooth the rock back into place when moving on further.

That had been a lesson she learned early, that leaving climbing holes to solidify for others to find only resulted in other people using them, falling and getting hurt. No need to tell those two nitwits that she'd done this many a time before either. Let them worry a while.

Her muscles warmed as she climbed, the rush of chilly air stinging her face until her nostrils hurt from the cold breaths. But she climbed on. It was still quicker than walking up through the winding dark tunnels and she could take the trundles down with her mum.

A while later Odella hauled herself over the lip of the viewing deck that she could use to get into the upper levels. She needed some moisturiser on her face and something hot on her aching limbs, but the climb had at least calmed her irritable thoughts, which she freely admitted were irritable more often than not. People rarely made sense, and she'd learned that being polite and unassuming meant they paid less attention to her so she could escape quicker.

That never applied to Sannar though, or our other friends he left and replaced so easily.

She shook her head as the thoughts began to circle. She wouldn't let them take hold, wouldn't let them overcome the mental calm from the climb. Despite the physical effects of aching and dryness, nothing was able to settle her thoughts like a brisk climb did.

Letting herself into the upper levels through the viewing deck door, she hurried along the firelit tunnel with her fingertips brushing the smooth rock of the nearest wall to cool the rough scrape on her fingertips.

Odella hesitated in the middle of the long corridor. If her mum had already taken a trundle back down while she was climbing, she'd be stuck there. She wouldn't put it past those dimwit guards to say nothing about her going up either. She'd have to wait until someone else came up, which could be days unless she climbed back down again.

Worried at the thought of being stuck waiting until she was strong enough to climb again, with going down needing more care than going up, she hurried on and took a random turning.

She stumbled to a halt at the corner, her breath making

a startled whooshing noise.

A man stood hunched over in front of a door with his face pressed up close to the lock. She blinked and cautiously unzipped her pocket to pull her glasses out.

His short brown hair was fuzzy as though it had been recently shorn off, and his simple khaki shirt and brown trousers were ideal for blending against the rock.

Odella frowned. *No robes so he's not a nether brother. He's not sworn to the court either or I'd have seen him around.*

She guessed he could be new or someone who'd been away from court a long time, but even then why was he taking an interest in a door that was obviously locked without anyone to guide him around? She had no idea if she should creep away and get help, although she wouldn't be able to get down on the trundles if her mum had left already, or if she was safe enough to demand he explain himself.

When she cleared her throat, he jumped and stumbled backwards.

"Can I help you?" she asked.

His eyes darted over her and he straightened up, a smooth expression washing over his face. A mask of a wolfish smile that sent warning shudders over her skin. She got the feeling he was hoping to charm or scare her, and that he didn't really care which.

"And who are you to help me?" he countered.

She folded her arms, the Fae-like answer setting her irritability on edge.

"My mother works here and I help out. I don't recognise you though."

He nodded, his face becoming mockingly understanding.

"Very wise. I need to get into this room and you can help me."

Odella had her hand outstretched and a protection warding cast before he could finish his second sentence. He lifted a hand but the sharp needling sensation of whatever gift he was sending to attack her prickled against the form of her warding. She'd been one of the kids who actually paid attention in school and her protection stood firm against his gift. So many people she knew had learned the hard way, being bombarded with spitballs in the schoolroom or tripped and tricked by other people with various gifts.

"Nice try," she said. "But no."

She marked out the way back to the viewing deck. She was a fast runner but the man was older than her by a couple of decades, and given the fitted fineness of his clothing fit for sneaking in, he looked like he might be the high-born type to have many gifts bestowed by fancy relatives.

"So, are you going to tell me your name at least?" he asked.

She shook her head. "No, but you can go first if you want."

He laughed and took a step forward. She took one back, keeping him in view. She had no skills to fight him with, the climbing ability her only gift. She might be able to take a chunk of the wall out and firm it into a ball to throw at him, but if it actually hit him in the head she could be looking at damages, or even a murder charge knowing her luck.

Keep him talking, get him as close to the viewing deck as you can then vault over.

Unless he had a levitation gift like Sannar did then she

was absolutely done for.

Trying not to let that thought add to the chaotic heap stirring her adrenalin into a frenzy, she kept up the steady process of inching backwards, drawing him with her.

He swept out an arm and sent another wave of power flying toward her, the sheer strength pushing against every essence of her protection. She gritted her teeth and held firm, but the ache in her muscles told her she wouldn't last long.

She reached the corner and stretched out a hand against the stone. Pushing her gift into the stone, she fought every instinct telling her to run and gouged out a handful of rock, letting it solidify in her palm. She lifted her hand and threw.

The rock arced through her protection and hit the man in the chest, his power so laughably dominant against hers that he hadn't even bothered to ward himself.

He staggered back a couple of steps. Odella dodged around the corner and stumbled down the next hallway.

"That's a mighty useful gift," he called after her. "We could come to some agreement."

She forced herself forward with her blood pounding in panic.

If I can get to the viewing deck I can try to block him off, but I'm in no state to climb down now.

"'Della?"

Her mum's voice floated toward her. She lifted her head to find her mum ahead and stumbled to a halt, spinning around to see the man stopping a few metres away. He pressed a finger to his lips, gave her a wink and vanished.

Odella rounded on her startled mother, her breathing ragged and her legs shaking.

"Did you see him?" she demanded.

Her mum nodded. "Yes, and that is really worrying. Come on, we'll go straight to Sannar and you can explain everything to him. No sense going to Lady Aereen these days."

So relieved that someone had at least seen the random man so nobody else could accuse her of making it up, Odella said the first glib thing that came to her mind.

"Not to the lady of the court?"

Her mum grabbed her wrist and hustled her along the hall toward the trundles at the far end.

"Of course not." She rolled her eyes. "You and I both know Sannar runs this place these days, bless him. I wish you two would talk again. He's such a lovely boy."

Odella let her mum manhandle her into the nearest trundle cart and firmed up her stance. The trundles were sturdy and safe, but fast and not much more than a metal floor with a waist-high railing and some thick pulley ropes.

"I did talk to Sannar actually, right before coming up here."

"You did?" Odella didn't like the way her mum's face lit up at the sound of that. "Lovely! What about? Did he bring you all the way up here in the trundle himself? It's nice to hear you two are speaking again."

Odella tried to remember. "He said hi, so I said hi. I asked what he wanted and he said he didn't know. Then Lady Reyan of the Illusion Court orbed him, and afterwards I said bye and climbed up here-"

"'Della! You know not to climb this far up."

"I know, but the guard on the gap is a buttface-"

"Language."

"-and he was goading me. He's actually part of the reason Sannar and I don't talk anymore, apart from today, so you can blame him for everything."

Her mum huffed, a clear sign that she knew neither of them would get what they wanted from the conversation. A long moment passed between them, silent but for the rushing of air as the trundle shot downwards.

"He didn't do anything to you, did he?" her mum asked.

"Who, Sannar?"

"No dear, but interesting to know he's the first 'he' your mind goes to. No, I meant the man upstairs."

Crud, I walked right into that one.

Odella shook her head. "No, I had my warding up when he tried to compel me. But the fact he tried is worrying, I mean, it's just old scrolls up there isn't it? Old records? What could he want? And who is he?"

The trundle came to a stop and her mum didn't answer. Odella followed her out into the sunshine, blinking against the light and using it as an excuse not to look at either of the guards on the gap. Her mum led the way across the courtyard and into the network of buildings that formed the main hub of the court separate from the nether study block and the lady's private chambers.

Having to speak to Sannar twice in one day after four years of stiff silence didn't exactly register on her 'it's a good day' game card, but she took a deep breath as her mum knocked on his office door.

"Yeah?"

His voice echoed through the wooden door and he sounded as exhausted as she felt. Her mum pushed the door open, but at least had the common sense not to announce Odella or say anything. She gave her a rather insistent shove on the back though which didn't help.

Sannar looked up, his eyes widening when he saw her as her mum shut the door behind her. When she didn't speak immediately, a nervous smile spread across his face.

"Twice in one day," he said. "Have I done something wrong?"

She snorted. Not in a delicate, amused way. Not like a genteel lady might. The noise bounced around the room like a rumbling gunshot and that only made him smile wider.

Get a grip. She walked toward his desk, taking comfort from the fact his smile dimmed and he leaned back a bit. *As fun as tormenting him would be, this is serious.*

"I climbed to the upper levels to see my mum because your mate on the gap was being a total butt-wipe and there was a random man trying to get in one of the doors."

Sannar stared for several moments. Then he rubbed his forehead and blinked back at her, bemused.

"I'm not used to your babbling anymore. One more time?"

She glowered down at him. His hair looked like a ball of wool after the cat had been at it, no doubt because he kept raking through it, but the short beard around his mouth was trimmed.

Weird, none of his other friends have really grown into their facial hair yet.

She shook the thought off, mainly because it made her feel uncomfortable and also she wanted to get out of there and back to down the mountain to civilisation where people didn't treat her like a town rat oddity.

"I climbed the mountain," she said, exaggeratedly slowly. "I went to the upper levels to find my mum. Instead, I found a man trying to get into one of the doors. When I asked him what he was doing, he tried to attack me with some kind of gift. When my mum appeared, he vanished. Like realm-skipped out on the spot. I didn't even think you lot could do that."

Sannar rubbed his eyes with his thumb and forefinger.

"We can't. I mean the lady can, but the rest of us can't. So that means it was someone powerful, and definitely not one of us."

"You don't have anyone away from court who I might not have recognised that's returned?"

He shook his head. "None that would be trying to get into the upper levels without clearing it with me first. The fact an outsider has managed to get past our wards is worrying enough, but he tried to attack you? Are you okay?"

"I'm fine. I can ward better than most."

"I remember." He smiled again. "You know I got that orb message? Lady Reyan warned that the Forgotten might come calling, but for them to sneak in and all the way up there too, it's not good."

Odella eyed him for a long moment until he noticed her looking. Again that aggravating heat spread over her cheeks, and she couldn't for the life of her remember if it was visible on her face or not. Jolly Merrytree went red as a bush-mouse, but then Sammy always talked about this boy or that girl making her blush and Odella could never tell. Perhaps if she was really lucky, she'd be one of the non-visible blushers.

"You look a bit flushed," Sannar said. "Are you sure you're okay?"

Crud.

That only made her face heat more and she backed up to the door.

"I'm fine. You should probably go and tell your lady and ask her what to do. Or ask you what to do as apparently you're the one running things here."

He chuckled. "Yeah right. I don't get to make the

decisions, I just do the work."

Odella might have joined in the laughter if it were anyone else, but before she could gather herself together and figure out what in the name of Faerie was wrong with her, the surface of Sannar's large desk orb started swirling purple.

She reached behind her to find the door handle, relieved beyond belief to be escaping. Sannar bit his lip, his eyes on her as the orb-vision began to materialise.

"Odella, can I-"

He never finished the sentence as the image of the Queen of Faerie loomed between them.

Sannar shoved his chair back from his table and dropped to his knees. Odella had no idea if Sannar was familiar with Queen Demerara or not, but she certainly had no business being in the presence of royalty.

Odella found the door handle and froze as the queen was cast into pearlescent grey view. Even from the diagonal angle she had, Odella was stunned again at how young the queen was, only a year older than her. Everyone in Faerie would recognise her even without being able to see the dark hair or the pale skin through the orb-waves. The royal face scrunched into a look of momentary indignation as a floating grey hand rammed a circlet crown of holly onto her head like an afterthought.

Realising she was still on her feet gawking, Odella struggled to open the door behind her back. When it wouldn't give, she dropped to her knees and pinned her chin to her chest. The queen rotated to scan the room and stared at her, then the spun until she was staring at Sannar.

"There you are," she said with relief. "I was worried I'd have to orb your lady."

Odella choked down a derisive snuffling noise that

snuck out of her nose, although the queen's head turned her way momentarily.

"My queen. How can I serve?" Sannar asked.

"Why are you still on the floor? I can't talk to you down there. Also, I have things to ask of your court so you might as well call me Demi. Everyone else does."

Odella knew Mr. Sticker-For-Rules Sannar wouldn't be doing that, but he did stand up and meet the queen's gaze. Odella stayed where she was but risked peeking up through a strategically draped curtain of hair.

"We're more than happy to assist," Sannar began. "I am worried as we've literally just had a security breach. Someone we think might be the enemy was trying to access our old scrolls in the upper levels. He was found at a locked door, then he tried to attack someone and realm-skipped out again, which suggests it's someone fairly powerful."

The queen frowned. "This info is from someone you trust?"

"Yes." Sannar caught Odella's eye. "One hundred percent."

He turned his attention back to the queen and Odella fought the increased pounding of her heart. He had no reason to trust her now after so long not knowing each other, and he'd asked her so few questions about the strange intruder before vouching for her.

"Right. I'm afraid I need to impose on the hospitality of your court a while. Given you've had an intruder, I can at least add an extra level of protection which should suit your court for the time being."

Sannar nodded. "We'll be only too happy to host. I'll have your special quarters prepared immediately."

"Cool thanks. That's not the awful bit though. I need to host a meeting of all the courts, and Arcanium is an absolute zoo at the moment, no peace and quiet whatsoever. So I need to ask that the Nether Court hosts instead."

Odella lifted her head at the resounding silence that followed. Sannar's face was a picture, wide eyes and mouth slack with shock. He couldn't say no to the Queen of Faerie, although she knew it would put everything else into absolute bedlam. Even the lady of the court wouldn't say no to either of the two queens. But half of the nether brothers would flee into their homes and take most of their research with them to avoid being disturbed. Those down in the town would want to swarm up and gawk if they found out.

Odella frowned, wondering if Sannar could persuade the brothers to move their research into the mountain, or maybe host the meeting itself in the mountain, although if the strangers were sniffing around it might not be safe.

Either way, not answering the queen wasn't going to solve anything. She made a sharp huff, a meaningful noise of impatience, and Sannar flinched into action.

"Of course, my queen. We'll be only too happy to host. I'll have lodgings prepared for the other courts also. May I ask when exactly?"

Queen Demerara pulled a face. "Tomorrow I'm afraid. Not much time but I've told the others that we're being a huge pain and to rein it in. Not that they'll listen but still. I don't think we've actually had all the lords and ladies of the courts in one place for a very long time, but we'll have to hope it's not a complete slaughter."

Odella bit both lips between her teeth to hide a grin. The rumours and gossip about all the courts were known throughout Faerie. While working distantly in tandem to trade various specialities, they rarely got on. Several of the lords and ladies and the more prestigious members of nobility sworn to the courts were related and often held the pettiest and most spiteful grudges. Odella wouldn't admit it but she often relished a night in watching the latest dramas on the *Faerie Net*'s society coverage through the orb-waves.

"We'll ensure there is adequate space between the courts too," Sannar insisted. "I'll put it to our lady, but I'm sure she won't have an issue with hosting you and your guests."

The queen nodded. "Thanks. I hate to ask, but- yes, I know Milo, but I do. Sorry, my right-hand man thinks I shouldn't admit I feel bad asking people for stuff. He just hasn't got the habit of *not interrupting my orb calls*."

She glared sideways and Odella tried her best not to laugh out loud.

"Your genuineness is one of the many virtues your people love about you, my queen," Sannar said diplomatically.

"Ha, not likely with Fae but nice try. I'll see you tomorrow. Also, start practicing calling me Demi for the sake of my sanity."

Sannar nodded. Odella guessed he would probably get around that request by not calling the queen anything at all when she arrived. But it seemed like she was waiting for something so he had to go against his instincts.

"Thank you, my quee-" he grimaced. "*Demi.*"

"Good, boy catches on quick."

The vision of her vanished and he was left smiling at his empty office.

Except it wasn't empty.

Odella lifted her head and clambered to her feet, Sannar doing the same. No doubt he would give her some lecture about not telling anyone what she'd seen, which of course she wouldn't anyway, but her heart sank when she realised she wouldn't get a chance to see the queen given that she wasn't sworn to the court.

"Are you any good at taking notes?" he asked.

She frowned. "No, why? What are you going to do about the queen's visit? It'll take nothing short of a miracle to get everyone into form here by tomorrow. Your scholars are going to get really grouchy and there isn't enough room to host all the courts if they bring whole entourages and-"

She paused mid-breath as he pinched the bridge of his nose.

"I know," he muttered. "Trust me, I know. Which is why I'm asking you, a non-sworn townsperson, to help me so I don't go raving mad trying to sort it all out."

He sounded so irritable and the urge to smile tugged at her lips. He sounded exactly like her thoughts in that moment. Plus he'd asked her to help. How many townspeople could say they'd actually been near a Queen of Faerie, maybe even caught a glimpse of her? Despite the fact she knew it was a kindness on his part, and she was unnerved why he was suddenly talking to her and being kind, she wanted to see the queen.

"At least you said townsperson and not town rat. Okay, but I'm no good at notetaking. I try but my mind goes faster than the people I'm taking notes of, so it gets bored and wanders off."

Sannar pressed his hands onto the top of his desk and closed his eyes. Odella forced herself to stay silent, wondering if he was having a breakdown of some kind or thinking things through. When he straightened up, she watched him with great intrigue.

"You'll help? Thank you. Right." He pointed to a

notepad and pen on the desk which she grabbed. "The brothers will move into the mountain as best they can. We'll put up the nether day tents for us lot and move everyone out to make room. The queen has rooms in the lady's quarters already and I think I can muster up enough space there for the rest of them. Their entourage can then take our rooms in the normal block. Some brothers will possibly venture down to town as well, so I'll need to remind them all to be discreet about why."

Odella scribbled, focusing on keeping her mind on the task as he issued lengthy instructions. It amazed her that he could invent all those ideas almost immediately, that he was so in tune with his court and already had a plan.

Drat, I missed that bit. She pulled her mind back to what he was saying. *Food by kitchens. Send note to courts to ask for any allergies or requirements. Lady's ceremonial gowns out of storage. Remind the lady not to say anything controversial-*

"What do you mean by controversial?" she interrupted.

Sannar sank into his seat. Still concerned about her run-in with the mysterious stranger, Odella gave up trying to be polite and perched on the opposite edge of the desk. Sannar glanced up at her, but they would be working together for the next day or so by the sounds of it, so he'd have to get used to her again.

"She has a habit of saying odd things," he said darkly.

"But like what?"

He sighed. "Like Fae weren't always land creatures and sometimes she asks where the second sun has gone. A lot of the brothers think her prolonged proximity to the nether has detached her awareness of Faerie, like she kind of forgets what is real and what she's dreamed."

Odella pulled a face. Sometimes she felt like that, as if

dreams she had were real, but the sensation always passed and she'd never started harping on about missing suns.

"Maybe the nether's feeling off every day," she offered, keeping her expression innocent.

Sannar stared at her for a moment before tipping his head back against his chair with a groan and a chuckle.

"I've been thinking that more and more myself lately. By the way, I can't exactly pay you for a couple of days work, so start thinking about what I owe you."

Odella slid off the desk as he stood up. "Owe me?"

"Yeah, I'm not expecting you to help me for free. But unlike your mum I don't have access to court finances, not for my own ends anyway so I can't technically hire you, and I wouldn't want to get her in trouble by asking her to run it through. So I'll owe you a medium-sized favour instead if that suits."

She grinned. "You'd risk owing me a favour? What if I ask you to embarrass yourself for my amusement."

Sannar walked to the door of the office and paused with his hand on the handle, smiling at her wearily.

"I'm hoping you at least like me enough not to torment me, or can be kind for old time's sake."

For old time's sake. Odella's insides chilled at that. *Doesn't he remember why they became 'old' times?*

He caught her expression and managed a sheepish smile.

"I guess we were once friends is what I mean. I don't have many of those left, not since I got the Chief Assistant job. Never mind. I owe you a favour and I'll take what I'm given. Come on."

Odella watched him as he opened the door, then she followed him out and down the hall to the courtyard. The sun was beginning to wane for the evening and she still had to walk down the long path to the town. Usually she'd meet the others in the tavern, but tonight all she wanted to do was go to sleep. That was assuming she was even able to go home given the amount of work she was now supposed to be helping with.

Sannar eyed the deserted courtyard, perhaps gathering strength for the onslaught of preparations. With her arms folded, Odella stared at the edge of the inlet and decided she'd let the past go if he was willing to as well.

"We can be friends," she offered grudgingly. "If you really want."

CHAPTER THREE
REYAN

"Ladies of courts shouldn't be hiding in cupboards. Not alone anyway."

It wasn't the jump-start Reyan Roseglade expected first thing in the morning, but then she probably shouldn't have been hiding in her wardrobe.

Reyan rolled her eyes at the face hovering above her. Even though Kainen Hemlock, actual Lord of the Illusion Court, knew her position as court lady was a fake, as was their engagement, he'd taken to teasing her about it at any opportunity.

But she had tasks to tie up back at the Nether Court and should be getting on with them, so she accepted Kainen's outstretched hand and let him help her out of her wardrobe. It wasn't the most likely scenario, a court lord hauling her out of a wardrobe, but she'd been at the Nether Court a lot recently since putting the void inside their mountain to sleep a month ago. She only came back home to try on her re-fitted 'appropriate attire' for the upcoming inter-court meeting.

"Meri wanted me to try that infernal dress again," she explained. "I've said most will be going in normal clothing, probably even Demi despite her being a queen, but she huffed at me. I came so close to telling her that I wasn't actually going to be lady of this court after all, that our engagement was a complete fake, but I managed not to."

Kainen's lips lifted in devilish amusement. He swept his

free hand through his dark brown hair, shovelling the errant strands back. Reyan noticed he hadn't let go of her fingers even though she was now well free of the wardrobe.

"It's tradition," he teased. "You have our court's reputation at stake."

"Are you dressing up?" she asked.

"I've also been *Meri'd*." He pulled a face. "Jacket, flouncy shirt, freshest jeans that have no give in them. If you're going to see her now, I'll escort you."

She nodded. "I need to pop back to the Nether Court to check one last thing, but I've orbed Sannar already to let him know we'll be visiting to check in. He didn't sound overly stressed so I assumed Demi hadn't had a chance to tell him about the courts meeting yet."

"We'll make a quick appearance to the court first," he said. "Best they see you as often as possible while you're here, keep them from thinking I'm potentially up for grabs."

He held up his free hand. A subtle tinge of glittering black smoke curled on his palm and she tightened her fingers around his. Each time he realm-skipped her to the Nether Court for her research on the queen's behalf, she had a strain of awkwardness over having to hold his hand. He didn't seem to feel any similar weirdness. Add on that she was supposed to be the prospective lady of his court, even if it was a pretence to fool the whole of Faerie, but he didn't seem in any rush to discuss or cancel that either. While he seemed content with pretending, she tensed each time she had to return from the Nether Court and greet him in front of people like they were madly in love. She blushed with every kiss to her cheek and couldn't bring herself to look him in the eye after, something she'd never had to worry about much with anyone else before.

If my insides wouldn't go all fizzy every time it might not be so bad.

But after so long being tied in service to his court, she needed some freedom from it. She'd agreed to continue pretending to be his future Lady for his benefit to keep the arranged matrimonial unions from knocking at his door, and he'd gone to great lengths to secure her freedom. Now she was determined to enjoy being her own person, finally able to make decisions for herself and to not fear that one wrong step would ruin the fragile balance of her service. Doing research at the Nether Court for the queen of Faerie was a great way to start.

The air shivered around them, a wisp of purple and grey nether swirling and obscuring everything from view before the scenery resettled into that of the main hall in the Court of Illusions, their court.

Several gazes turned their way and Reyan forced herself to hold her head high. She knew that several of those in service who used to be friends of hers now looked at her with suspicion. She'd been a nobody from an all-but-extinct Fae lineage until Kainen had chosen her for his plans. Now in all their eyes she was to be Lady of the Court. They whispered about her and gave her the same faux smiles they always gave him. She could well imagine what was said behind closed doors and in the service dormitories.

"You're leaving us so soon again, Lady," someone called out.

It wasn't said with any disappointment, only pointed accusation. It sounded like Glennoria, someone Reyan would have once seen as infinitely above her own level socially. Now the woman was expected to bow to her.

Kainen's hand tightened around hers, but he knew better than to speak for her. She took a deep breath and let the shadows gather around her shoulders. Having a shadow-merging gift was unusual, but considering the Illusion Court was based around mischief, trickery and the illicitness of dark corners, she was in the right place.

"The Court supports our queen," she said silkily. "My excursions are a part of that. You're more than welcome to demand an answer of *her* the next time she visits."

Easy, sweetheart. Kainen's amused voice echoed in her head. *Glennoria holds grudges like FDPs hold wardings.*

Reyan smiled back at him, letting the shadows surround her face. She'd quickly gotten used to his ability to speak into her mind, and her own freedom to speak back.

I should kick her out then. Or you should.

He laughed, the Court held in place around them. Whispers and the low buzz of frustrated conversation picked up, but given that Kainen had appeared before them, until he released them to go about their business they were stuck waiting to see if they were needed.

It would create more problems than it solves, he added.

Reyan let the situation slide as he turned his attention back to the waiting crowd, the hum fading instantly.

"The courts have been called to a meeting by the queen," he announced. "I'm taking this opportunity to remind you all of where our allegiances lie."

Reyan marked out the derisive looks from several highborn courtiers. Many were sworn to the court, others were frequent guests for revels or matters of business. But some were loyal and devoted, and they were the ones that would follow the court into the new age and help it prosper.

"Go, make mischief, cause some mayhem and have some fun," Kainen drawled. "If I need any of you, I'll summon you."

Given the dismissal, the court dispersed like water raining downhill. The hall picked up a lively chattering, but Kainen had made it clear he wasn't in the mood to be approached.

Out of habit, Reyan took a step to go about her own business, forgetting that her business was now essentially him when at court. He tightened his hold on her hand, drawing her to face him. She stared up at the deep brown eyes and swallowed against the catch in her throat.

"We need to go and see Meri," he reminded her. "It can't be avoided I'm afraid. Then I'll take you back to the Nether Court."

His subtle inclusion of her ran through her mind but she didn't dare call him on it. Sometimes she wondered if the political game he played really was as ruthless as he pretended. Other times she wondered if perhaps there was the slightest part of him that truly cared for her.

Both options were unnerving at best.

When he didn't move or skip them anywhere, she realised he was waiting for her to agree. As if she really were his equal. She'd goaded him a lot in those first few days of their pretence, refusing to let him dominate her even though in terms of hierarchy he had every right to. But the new age of Faerie had dawned, and his ancient family line and his court title didn't hold the same kind of dominion that it would have done before, not with Holly Queen Demerara being so progressive.

She nodded and the nether folded around them in an instant, dropping them right in the middle of Meri's office.

"Well, there you are." Meri tutted, rising from the chair behind her long sewing desk. "I have enough to do as it is without waiting around for you two to deign to show up.

Lord, Lady."

The titles were dripping with sarcasm but Meri had minded the court for a long time, and she had cared for Kainen longer than Reyan had been there. Kainen rolled his eyes and dropped Reyan's hand to pull off his sweatshirt.

Catching her eye as his t-shirt followed next, Meri gave Reyan a prim look.

"Your dress is behind the screen." She pointed to the far corner. "Let me know if you need a hand. I've modified it slightly."

Reyan slouched across the room to the wide wooden privacy screen and wriggled out of her cardigan and jeans. She couldn't see any difference in the ancient dress since Meri had made her choose it the day before, but apparently all ladies of courts would be in dresses. At least this one was strapless and therefore not likely to pin her arms to her sides. She tunnelled underneath the smoky grey satin skirts lined with black lace and tiny gems, holding her breath to wriggle up through the bodice.

It slid over her easily, a far cry from the faff she'd had with trying it on before.

"I elasticated parts of it," Meri called out.

Reyan could only assume she was talking to her and not Kainen, but she was too busy marvelling at how breathable the dress now was to answer. Skimming her hands over the grey satin folds of the bodice, she wondered if there might be some elbow-length gloves to go with it.

A small click echoed through the room and shoes appeared in front of her, slipper-style and dark grey to match the dress. Reyan slipped them on and ran her hands through her flat blonde hair to try and give it some more life. The only hope for change she had was putting it up in a ponytail but that left her with a tiny spike of hair at the back of her head, not exactly in keeping with a ladylike style.

"Ready?" Meri asked, as if she was psychic and knew Reyan was beginning to doubt herself.

Reyan nodded even though nobody could see her and stepped out from behind the screen. She was used to walking around in leggings and long shirts, or jeans and cardigans, but several of the court ladies still opted to wear dresses or fanciful fashion pieces like suits made of expensive material. But she wasn't a real lady. Even if she had been, she'd have insisted on wearing the same clothes. Although some nicer leggings and a better array of shirts might have made her feel more confident moving around the court. Maybe some fitted jeans instead of ragged baggy ones. Kainen had asked her if she wanted some new clothes but embarrassment and pride had forced her to refuse.

Now she stood in front of him in a fanciful dress with barely any make-up on and unfluffed hair and she felt like the urchin from the old fable.

"Though my borrowed shoes are fancy, my feet are still poor. Without the shoes, I am but a simple urchin."

She shook the thought from her head, focusing on Kainen instead. He of course looked effortlessly powerful, his charcoal grey shirt flickering with hints of shimmer in the firelight. His jacket fit him like a second skin, his jeans moving easily as he shifted to one side. He at least had to keep the reputation of being casual in his power.

What does the fable have to do with it? His voice echoed in her head, his tone drenched with confusion. *Are you saying I'm poor?*

That was another flustering thing; lately she'd been

thinking to him without realising instead of keeping her thoughts to herself. She couldn't see any sign of indignation on his face, his eyes dark and fixed on her.

I think if anyone is the urchin dressing in finery here, it's me, she snapped back. *Don't get your sensitive ego flapping.*

He smiled at that while Meri dropped her focus to something on her desk, no doubt to give them some illusion of privacy. She knew everything that went on at court, but even she hadn't been officially told about the pretend engagement between them. To all eyes except theirs and the queen's, Reyan and Kainen were blissfully in love.

"We have to consider what our stance will be before the meeting tomorrow," he said after a long pause.

Reyan frowned, risking the necessary steps to stand in front of him. Her skirts swished around her legs but even with the satin bodice it felt like walking freely in a bathrobe.

"We support the queen, don't we?"

"Yes, but as a court. You've been finding out more about what the Forgotten are planning, and the whole 'finding a way into the Prime Realm' thing sounds dangerous enough as it is. But we need to consider they might attack us first."

Devoted as he was to his court, Kainen's worries had been on her mind as well. She figured she was fairly safe at the Nether Court, a group of Fae that kept to themselves and researched things to do with the nether that permeated the fabric of Faerie. The Nether Court realm was difficult to get to without realm-skipping in, which most Fae couldn't do at will. Only lords and ladies of courts, the royal family on occasion and a few un-courted Fae with very rare gifts could do so. For the rest of Faerie, they had to rely on communal skip-ways.

"Rumour has it that the Forgotten are now calling themselves the Blood and Bone Court," Meri said. "It's not a verified rumour as such, more sensationalist mutterings but still."

"Sensationalist mutterings tend to have at least a grain of truth though," Reyan added.

Meri nodded. "They do indeed. So please be careful. We've increased our security but all courts are on alert for intruders nowadays."

Kainen rubbed a hand over his face with a sigh. Even though he'd sorted Reyan out her own room that connected to his when she agreed to remain playing his fake bride-to-be, she often hung out in his before going to bed. He had more space and she knew he was lonely. He had friends who wanted advancement, acquaintances who wanted his favour, and Meri who treated everyone like an entire court full of errant children. But he had nobody he could trust and relax with, so she filled that role.

Carrying a court at eighteen was no trivial thing but Kainen had enough charm and confidence to make it look easy. Nobody saw the strain it put on him, and nobody had to worry with him around.

"We'll be careful." She answered for them both. "The court has protection too, and Kainen won't be gone for long."

"You should come straight back with me," he grumbled, a well-worn argument.

She smiled. "And disappoint the queen?"

"She wouldn't be disappointed, she'd understand. You've been combing those tunnels for ages now and you've already discovered most of what's there."

Reyan fought the urge to grin wide. Teasing him as much as he taunted her had become one of her favourite things, not that she'd ever admit it to him.

"But once I'm done with the Nether Court, then where would I go?" she asked, pretending to frown with worry. "I suppose I could introduce myself to the Flora Court, or the Lord of Revels. The Word Court has its merits. I'm not too sure about Fauna, but I bet they're lovely too."

His expression never faltered but she'd learned to recognise the subtle tightening of his features.

"You could." That was all he ever said, ending the discussion. "Or you could come home."

That second part was new, and he'd never referred to the court as her home before.

"To my father's?" she asked, her tone light and her entire being panicking inside. "I don't think I want to see that place ever again."

Kainen took a shuffling step to stand right in front of her and the absence of Meri suggested she'd skipped somewhere else in the court to give them privacy.

"Reyan, I said you can call this court home whenever you choose to. That will always stand. What does the Nether Court have that we don't? Or any of the others?"

She shook her head. "I didn't say they had things we don't have here."

"You've only just gained your freedom, I know." He sighed, glancing away. "I'll stop, sorry."

He looked so tormented suddenly, his mask of indifference slipping, that her chest squished and she couldn't help smiling.

"Anyone would think you wanted me to come back," she teased.

He eyed her for a moment before letting the matter go,

his usual wicked grin returning.

"Ah yes, my fake bride, how do I cope without you? Are you ready to do it again? To pretend to all of Faerie that I'm actually somewhat loveable?"

She nodded. "Where you lead, I'll follow. Unless I'm actually doing stuff, in which case you'll have to run around after me instead."

She left him with that suggestion while she changed out of the dress again and left it hanging on the screen. When she emerged, Kainen was also dressed in his more casual black jeans and grey t-shirt, looking no less sinful for the effort. Unwilling to be caught staring, she held out her hand to him as a suggestion they should get going.

Kainen took her hand. "Whatever happens, we stick together tomorrow, okay?"

"What are you expecting to happen exactly?" she asked.

"We're going into a meeting with every court lady and lord in Faerie, plus the queen."

Reyan wrinkled her nose. "So?"

"So, sweetheart, that hasn't happened in an age, mainly because the bickering and axe-grinding will be endless. But also if you were the Forgotten, what better opportunity would there be to attack all things good than that?"

She grimaced. "When you put it like that. Come on then. Into the nether we go. Can you take us to the iron door though please to avoid being seen?"

"I can do that."

The nether wisped around them once more and she frowned the moment the familiar underground tunnel at the Nether Court appeared.

Kainen frowned. "Is the beastie door meant to be open?"

The enormous iron door that usually blocked the tunnel

was still in place, but the smaller hatch door cut into it was wide open. Given that there had been a soul-sucking, gift-stealing void on the other side until recently, Reyan's panic surfaced. If the *Maladorac* was awake again that would be awful, but then it would have gone much further then opening the door.

"No, it's not. Carelessness or worse. Wardings up?"

Kainen's hand tightened around hers and he drew her closer to him.

"Already on it, sweetheart. We go in carefully and have a quick look, nothing more."

She nodded and set off through the hatch door and into the gloom beyond. Where the labyrinthine halls had once been blocked off and in total darkness due to the *Maladorac* being awake, now fires burned on the walls to light their way.

Reyan summoned the shadows around her and fed into them, sensing calm and quiet.

"It's still asleep but someone's either down here or they have been," she confirmed.

"Could have been someone who just forgot?"

Reyan didn't answer, picking up the pace through the tunnels she now knew from memory. A subtle flicker down one corridor caught her eye as she passed it. Veering back, she turned and pulled Kainen along the hall toward another open door.

"This one shouldn't be open either, but I don't know what anyone would want from it. There's nothing but old papers and some mouldy old paintings. Ouch."

She stared in alarm at the chaos. The room had been neat and orderly only days ago when she'd left it behind, her research there concluded, but now there were piles everywhere.

"They need to do a serious clear-out," Kainen said.

"It was much clearer when I left it. And tidy, I made sure to organise as I went through. Someone's been ransacking since."

She ran the fingertips of her free hand over an open book on the table and leaned her nose right down to the page.

"Someone's had a finger here, look there's a print in the dust." She frowned, twitching her nose to ward off a sneeze. "Why take the trouble to look this up though? It's just a basic inventory of the Nether Court archives."

Kainen peered at the page under her fingertip, holding out a tissue from his pocket moments before she sneezed loudly into it.

"Thanks," she sniffed.

"Any time. I live to be useful. Maybe they wanted to see where other things were? Whatever Demi's got you looking for, the Forgotten will likely be after it too. Do you want to go up to the court and ask Sannar if anyone's been allowed down here?"

Reyan shook her head. "No, I can speak to them both later. Whoever was here is gone now."

Kainen led the way back out of the room, hovering while Reyan shut the door.

"I just need my notebook from down here," she pointed, hurrying further into the gloom.

As Kainen kept pace with her, she wondered if she should be honest and tell him that her time at the Nether Court was basically done, and that once she collected her notebook, she had little reason to return after the court meeting.

"So what's the plan?" he asked. "Are you staying here tonight?"

Good question. She took a deep breath.

"Not unless you're ditching me here. Everything is pretty much done anyway, so I could do with a good night's sleep."

He raised one eyebrow, his lips curving with undisguised delight.

"You don't sleep well away from me, sweetheart? I'm touched."

She snorted. "So humble. No, after so long at our court I find it weird sleeping somewhere with a ground floor window. I keep waking up thinking someone will have come in, which is silly because the window in my room overlooks a really sharp drop down the mountain."

His languishing posture straightened slightly, a subtle gleam lighting in his eyes.

"You can't get better than our court anyway, window or no window. Can I tempt you to an evening of good food, whatever ridiculous film you'll end up choosing and some relatively passable company tonight then? We can get our story straight before the meeting tomorrow."

Reyan stepped through the iron door and waited for him to follow before hauling it shut. If someone who had permission to be inside was still there, they'd be able to get themselves out. If they weren't meant to be in there... well, she would check tomorrow to see if there were any captives banging to be freed.

None of that did anything about Kainen staring hopefully at her as she pulled the door bolts across. They'd spent time in each other's company either watching films on his orb-viewer or reading in silent company, but something about the lack of humour in his tone caught her attention.

Is he hoping this is a date?

She pushed the possibility aside straight away. With a court full of social climbers and maniacal Fae wanting to use him for advancement, Kainen tended toward her because she was kind to him and treated him like a person instead of a court lord full of potential treasures for the taking.

"Our story is very simple," she teased. "But if you need to practice far be it from me to deny you. I happen to have nothing better to do. Sad really."

Kainen lifted her hand, holding her gaze all the while, and kissed the back of it, which sent a ridiculous explosion of fluttering through her insides.

"You honour me. But no nagging me about how messy my room is."

"I haven't done that in weeks!"

He grinned. "No making me get up in the middle of the film to go to the kitchens."

"No stopping the film to ask me what's going on," she countered, folding her arms and trying not to smile.

"No falling asleep halfway through."

"No waking me up to moan at me for falling asleep when I fall asleep halfway through."

"Deal." He lifted their hands between them. "Home?"

She nodded. "Home. Wait…"

A subtle beat echoed through the shadows. Kainen tensed as she twisted from side to side, sending out her gift to sense the unexpected thrum of life from the otherwise still tunnel network.

"There's something down here," she murmured. "Not the *Maladorac*, that's still asleep. But something. Come on."

Kainen huffed out a breath as she dragged him back down the tunnels, the shadows skittering along in front of her like excited children leading her to a prize.

"Can you tell what the something is?" Kainen asked.

She shook her head. "No, but the shadows aren't scared of it, not like they were before. Oh, there look."

She pointed to a small arch cut into the rock ahead, the shadows dodging the firelight as if leading her straight to it. On top of a ledge below the arch was a spherical object the size of a desktop orb.

"That wasn't here before." Reyan frowned. "First the door is left open, now someone's left an egg here?"

A loud crack rippled through the still air. When Kainen tried to tug her back, she relaxed her hand and slithered out of his grasp.

"Don't get too close," he warned, although he kept right behind her.

"It's hatching!"

A pointed curl of darkness wisped out of the crack in the shell, followed by the flick of a forked tongue of shadow.

"What in the name of Faerie is that?" Kainen asked.

Reyan rolled her eyes at the quiet horror in his voice. She'd heard rumours before about shadow-snakes but she'd never thought to see one herself. She let herself become the darkness itself, her gift firing through her body until she became the outline of a body swathed in shadow.

Hello little one, she whispered. *It's okay.*

Dark eyes blinked back at her as she tried to sense what exactly it was. The tiny scaled face had no sense of malice about it like the *Maladorac* had shown, and shadow-snakes were almost a legend.

Reaching out the shadowed outline of her finger, Reyan nudged the top part of the ridged shell aside to reveal the serpent's head. The snake uttered a soft hiss and blinked against the firelight before curling it's thin, wispy body around Reyan's hand.

Taking care to keep the change subtle and slow, Reyan let her body reform to flesh and bone, leaving her finger until last.

"There, not so scary, is it?" she murmured.

Kainen cleared his throat softly.

"Just so I'm clear, are you talking it or me?"

Reyan wrinkled her nose in disgust. "Shh, lower your voice. I can't believe it! The chances of finding a shadow-snake are so unlikely."

"Uh. Sure. I thought shadow-snakes were a myth though, something from the ancient tales."

"Well, clearly not. People used to think shadow-weavers were a myth too, many probably still do, yet here I am. And here she is. Isn't she beautiful?"

The shadow-snake clung to her skin, slithering between her fingers as it tried to hide from the light. Reyan cupped her hands and watched the body curl between her palms.

"Is this what whoever left the door open was doing down here?" Kainen muttered.

Reyan had forgotten him and frowned at the echo of his voice, but the shadow-snake didn't seem to mind. If anything, it pressed its head into her hand closest to the vibrations the sound made.

"No way of knowing, but we can't leave her down here."

"Her?"

Reyan sent her senses out but she'd learned to trust them over time and she was getting a distinctly feminine vibe from the little spiral of shadow in her hands.

"I think so. Feels like it. She's nothing like the *Maladorac* though and we can't leave her down here to

46

fend for herself."

Kainen sighed as she looked up at him. Realisation registered on his face a second later, his jaw dropping.

"Wait, you want to take it- *her* with us?"

"What else can we do? We can't leave her here on her own, and if anyone else found out about her, they'd likely trade her!"

She dabbed her thumb-tip gently against the snake's shadowy head and received a slow blink in reply.

"What if they're breeding them?" Kainen asked. "We can't steal without consequences. Don't give me that look- *Orbs alive*. Fine. But if anyone mentions it, we bring her back, agreed?"

Reyan nodded. "How much trouble can shadow be?"

She wanted to promise that the snake wouldn't cause any trouble at all but she didn't know that. From what scant information she remembered, shadow-snakes couldn't take on flesh and bone form, but she'd need to do more research first.

"Do you need to take the shell?" Kainen asked, his tone dripping with doubt. "What if she grows up and eats half our court?"

"No, leave it, and don't be ridiculous." She couldn't be sure, so she word-tangled a hurried question. "She's made of shadow so how could she eat people? If whoever put the egg there comes back, they'll assume she's escaped into the tunnels."

Kainen groaned softly. "Which means less chance you'll be told to give her back, right?"

Reyan gave him her most withering expression, which only made him smile.

"Who better to look after her than me?" she countered. "And where better to raise her than the court of illusions and shadows?"

He grinned. "The Court of Illusions and Shadow has a great ring to it. We'll see if we can fit it on the stationery. Can I see her?"

Reyan turned fully to face him and lifted her hands closer to his face. The shadow-snake's eyes were closed, the poor thing apparently exhausted by the hatching process.

"She's kind of cute," he said. "With your permission?"

He hovered his hands either side of her hips. Realising he couldn't hold her hands when both were occupied with the snake, she nodded. His arms wrapped around her waist and his chin settled on her shoulder as they cocooned the snake between them.

"Hold her tight now," he murmured in her ear. "Or you'll lose her in the nether. Then we need to figure out who left the door open and who is hatching rare creatures under the Nether Court."

CHAPTER FOUR
SANNAR

"We can be friends."

Sannar huffed to himself as he lugged the last of the fold-out tables across the courtyard, sweating and muttering under the late afternoon heat. For some reason, Odella's offer of friendship bugged the life out of him. No matter the fact she smiled at him when they moved around the court after, both trying to smooth ill tempers and reassure panicked brothers to give up their research spaces temporarily.

It was as if her deciding they should be friends had lifted a weight off her shoulders, so that should have been a good thing. A great thing. He'd often thought of her and the friends he'd left behind in town, wishing he could stroll down the mountain to sit and laugh with them like old times. Now he finally had an opportunity to re-establish some hope of her acknowledging him again, but something about it irked him all the same.

He stood in the middle of the courtyard to survey their efforts and a trickle of pride leaked into his chest, warming the exhaustion and irritation lingering there. Banners in the court's brown and purple colours fluttered from every flagpole, not only in place after the poles being bare for so long but also somehow more sparkling clean than he'd ever seen them.

The tables were laid out ready to be heaving tomorrow with food and drink for anyone who felt like gathering to chat, a pointless exercise as all the court lords and ladies would probably go straight to their rooms until hauled out for the queen's meeting.

But with the sun shining down on their efforts, he could at least be proud of the court he'd maintained for four years, even if he wouldn't get the actual credit for it. He couldn't have managed the whole thing without Odella though and wondered what favour she might extract from him as payment.

As if he'd thought her into being, Odella crossed the grass toward him with her shoulders slumped and her eyes half-closed. He couldn't remember the last time he'd eaten, which meant she would probably be ravenous by now.

"Right, we need to go and check in with the kitchens," he announced.

A radiant grin spread across Odella's face as she unearthed a length of green ribbon from her pocket.

"Great, I'm starving," she said.

He had to laugh. She'd been surprisingly good-natured with the other brothers, women and men alike, cajoling them with how irritating he was for upending them and how she was sure it wouldn't be long. They took to her as he remembered everyone else taking to her, like she was their best friend.

She moved in front of him in a rush to get to the court kitchens and he noticed how haphazardly she'd tied up her hair with the ribbon.

"Hang on, you're all lumpy," he said.

She turned slowly and he realised too late what he'd said.

"Lumpy?!" She scowled at him, her cheeks tinging pink. "When I said lets be friends, I didn't mean feel free to mention the products of puberty-"

"Your hair! Your hair is lumpy! Bumps! I haven't even

noticed the rest!"

He flapped his hands in the direction of her head. He hadn't thought about the rest of her. At least, not beyond the things he couldn't shove quickly out of his head again in the name of not mucking up the fragile friendship she'd offered him.

She narrowed her eyes at him, her lips pressing thin.

"You haven't?"

He wanted the mountain to swallow him whole. If he knew of a sure-fire way to wake up the nether void slumbering inside it, he would have considered it a worthy calamity to cause if only to escape or distract from this very moment.

"I haven't! I mean, I have, I imagine most have noticed, you know, *that*, but- no! I didn't mean like that!"

When she started laughing he wanted to cry. Leaving his family behind in town, not being really wanted by them in the first place, knowing everyone around him at court saw him as a commodity to be utilised, none of that gave him the amount of panic that facing Odella did.

When she noticed his face, hers sobered too although her lips were still twitching at the corners.

"I'm sorry," she said, folding her arms around her middle. "I went too far. Mix and Sammy always say I take it too far."

Sannar eyed her face but she was staring back with worried wide eyes, her teeth now rolling over the edge of her bottom lip.

"It's okay." He took a calming breath. "I meant it when I said I had no friends, so that kind of teasing will take a bit of getting used to."

She frowned as he joined her side and they started walking toward the kitchen.

"What about the tall one with dark hair? Permanent sneer on his face like the whole realm owes him a favour." She looked across the courtyard and pointed. "That one."

Sannar followed the line of her finger and noticed Arno staring back at them. Memories of his first day leapt to the front of his mind and a long-ago-buried shame surfaced. He'd forgotten about that day, when he'd been so desperate to find acceptance among the other initiates. Arno had been one of the main instigators then, but Sannar couldn't use that as an excuse for his behaviour.

I'd forgotten about that. He grimaced. *Is that why Odella stopped speaking to me? I thought she'd understand, but of course she wouldn't.*

He couldn't believe he'd forgotten, let alone assumed back then it was okay. Memories of her smile fading leapt into his head, long since buried down deep so he could convince himself she just didn't want to associate with him.

I turned her away because I wanted to make a good impression. Orbs, I was awful to her.

Arno noticed Odella pointing and muttered something to the guard next to him. Sannar groaned under his breath as Arno started toward them.

Odella's shoulders shot up near her ears, her posture stiffening and any sign of emotion draining from her face in an instant.

"I hear you're kicking us all out of our rooms, assistant," Arno said. "And you brought your town-rat girlfriend to help, how nice."

Sannar noticed the subtle glance Arno gave Odella, attention hidden as dismissal.

He fancies her. Sannar slid his hands behind his back, clenching them together.

"Charming of you to notice." He failed to hide the seething note in his tone. "But *townspeople* are welcome up here when invited and you know that. The queen has requested we host and any insolence will look bad on the court. She's also very pro-human and anti-elitist, so I doubt calling Fae in our realm 'rats' would go down well. Mind your tongue and learn some manners."

He turned toward Odella, hoping that she'd trust him enough to take his lead and follow him as he brushed past her and continued toward the kitchens. A tense moment later, she appeared at his side.

"I'm sorry I embarrassed you that day," he said quietly. "You know, my first day here. I only said what I did because they were goading me and saying court Fae couldn't have townspeople as girlfriends. Not that we were ever… you know."

Odella huffed but he couldn't bring himself to look in her face.

No wonder she ignored me for four years after that. Orbs alive, I wouldn't have even given me the time of day earlier if I'd treated me like that.

Guilt swelled, racing to the front of his mind after being squashed down for so long, the excuses he'd made to himself for his behaviour suddenly ridiculous.

"It doesn't matter now," she said, her voice quiet enough to tell him it mattered to her a great deal more than she'd ever let on.

And it mattered to him. A lot.

"He's not my friend, as it goes," he added. "Hasn't been for a long time."

"Since you got your assistant promotion I'll bet. One boat overtakes the others or breaks and suddenly the rest are fleeing. And they call townspeople rats."

Sannar pushed open the door to the kitchens and stood aside to let her pass. His stomach growled as the waft of *kaprike* stew floated out, but he caught Odella's sleeve in hesitant fingers.

"I really am sorry."

She nodded, a small smile resurfacing. "I know. Thank you. But if you keep me from the food any longer, no more friendship I swear."

He laughed at that, relief making him dizzy. Or maybe that was the hunger because he'd skipped lunch, but having her smile at him went a long way to giving him happy hormones.

"Allow me to do the talking then," he whispered over the clanging coming from the kitchen at the end of the hall. "I might not have many friends, but I am good at what I do."

Odella raised her eyebrows at that and the urge to prove himself right sent him charging down the hall.

He hurried past the mismatched tables rammed against the walls and stood in front of the enormous block of wood in the centre that had many cubbyholes for storage hewn into all sides of it. The low, beamed ceiling had all manner of culinary wonders hanging, from pots and pans and unnerving-looking blades to herbs and straggles of what looked like drying pastry. A fire at the far end threw out a cosy blast of heat and the urge to nestle down beside it sank tempting claws into his to do list, threatening to tear it to shreds.

"Sannar!"

The cheerful voice of Lindy the troll filled the air, and she hurried up to the wide table that covered the length of the kitchen between them. Past the serving counter on the far side, he could see the mess hall was empty, but soon it would fill up with hungry brothers all baying for his blood for kicking them out of their research spaces and rooms, even if it was on the queen's request.

"Hi, Lindy. We're after food and to let you know that there's going to be a very last minute visit from the queen's court tomorrow, and all the other courts as well, I'm sorry."

Lindy eyed him and Odella with a huge grin before flexing her long fingers.

"And you want me to tell the old grouch so he doesn't decapitate you and serve you to the already grumbling precious darlings that have no doubt been ousted from their pits for the occasion?"

Sannar gave her a sheepish smile. "Um… maybe."

Lindy roared with laughter and set off across the kitchen at speed.

"I'll tell him, but you might want to warn her ladyship he's in a mood."

Lindy's partner was technically head chef of the court, but other than cooking he had zero skills. He shouted at the brothers and often managed to make the new initiates cry. He refused to leave the court so Lindy would often realm-skip out to pick up the supply deliveries. He never discussed money for said supplies, and woe betide anyone who asked for something different to be served. But orbs alive, he could cook.

"Now, I'll sneak you some of the *kaprike*," Lindy said. "Technically not for today, but the old brute will never know. I'll discuss a menu fit for the queen with him when he wakes, but if there are any dietary requirements please try to let us know before lunchtime tomorrow."

He would know and they both knew it too, but Lindy had some kind of 'chef-whispering' skill that turned him into a sweetheart whenever she asked him for anything.

Lindy rushed off to get them some food and Sannar glanced at Odella, who was looking at him accusingly.

"You said you don't have any friends but she seems very fond of you."

Sannar smiled. "I guess I have one then. Lindy loves everyone, but don't go anywhere near her husband. He's um... let's just say people skills are a no go."

"You say 'um' a lot."

He bit down the automatic 'um' that immediately started brewing and shrugged instead.

"Turns out my people skills are a 'barely go'."

Odella snorted. "You're not so bad really."

"Oh thanks, I think."

"You're welcome. What's next on the to do list?"

Sannar took the bowls that Lindy passed over to him and nodded to the small table set in the far corner of the kitchen.

"We eat. Then we check everything's ready."

"Or..." Odella hesitated before lowering her voice. "We could go and check the upper levels, see what exactly that man was looking for."

Sannar's insides washed with icy nerves and he glanced around to check they were still alone. He wouldn't have put it past Arno to find an excuse and sneak in to eavesdrop on them.

"We can't do that," he protested.

Odella huffed and dropped onto one of the stools at the table.

"Why not?"

He placed the bowl down, weighing his response carefully. Too much dismissal and he'd lose the fragile hint of friendship they'd re-established. But she wasn't exactly supposed to be wandering around the upper levels either, alone or escorted.

"You could check the security," she added. "Then have the quickest look to see what door he was trying to get through."

Sannar frowned and took the stool opposite her.

"I don't know. Let me think a minute."

She folded her arms and leaned back in her chair. Sannar had a fleeting flicker of panic as she fixed him with a determined frown.

"Fine, you think, I'll ask questions. Why is the queen visiting? Do you know?"

"Not exactly," he said. "She came here when we had all that trouble with the *Mala*- um..."

His face burned as the words tumbled away. Odella had a scary ability to get him babbling all sorts of secrets with just a look.

She leaned forward. "The what?"

"There was a situation recently, involving that big iron door in the tunnels-"

"Oh. I caught the Lady of the Illusion Court down there not too long ago and escorted her back to the courtyard but I didn't think much of it after that. So is that what caused all those big rumbles coming from the mountain? We figured as much down in town. The queen was here for that?"

Sannar nodded. She'd given him a reprieve from the incessant questions, but that only made him more tempted to share things with her.

"It's a tricky one," he admitted. "First the rumbles started and then everything happened with that, and now you're finding strange men wandering in our archives. It's no secret that we have half the histories of Faerie and the nether squirrelled away here."

"So they're after information. What for?" She glanced around and lowered her voice. "He asked about origins, what can that mean?"

Sannar rubbed his thumb over his eyes, digging the pad into the socket to ease a cramp of pressure there.

"We can only guess. There are legends about how Faerie originated, and rumours of some hidden realm it sprang from filled with treasures of the land and bountiful power, but those are just myths."

"Myths always have a grain of truth." Odella arched one eyebrow at him.

He smiled, her gesture so familiar that he hadn't realised how much he'd missed it. Or her. He cleared his throat and shrugged before she could catch him staring.

"Well, one definite fact is that there hasn't been a meeting of all the courts together for a long time. It means something is coming."

Odella nodded. "There are rumours coming off the boats about the Forgotten regrouping. Might have something to do with that. What do we do next then?"

Sannar watched her close her eyes as she ate her first spoonful.

What next was a good question. He still had to go and see Lady Aereen and explain the situation to her, although she would have heard the commotion and no doubt received a selection from the ceremonial wardrobe by now ready for the queen's arrival. If she wanted him, she would summon him, so he would continue planning the whole thing on her behalf until told otherwise. But Odella, he was finding it alarmingly enjoyable to have her around.

Almost enjoyable enough to let her accompany me to the upper levels while I check the wards are in place.

"Desperate to get away from us already?" he teased. "You can go whenever you want to. I don't want you to think I'm holding you here."

"What about my favour?" she asked, her mouth still full with remnants of roll.

He shrugged. "Honestly? I just wanted someone sane to speak to, and I can hardly ask your mum to knock around with me all evening. But you don't have to stay if you have better things to do. You've already helped a load."

She laughed and the sound of it, hearty and lively, made him grin.

"I've not done that much really."

He shook his head. "You kept people calm so they didn't yell at me so much. Trust me, that's more than worth its weight in a favour."

"Worth two favours?" She wiggled her eyebrows.

"Don't push it, Squish."

CHAPTER FIVE
ODELLA

Squish. The nickname threw her completely.

She hadn't heard that in four years, mainly because Sannar was the only one who'd ever called her Squish, and he only called her that because of the time she'd sat on a buckberry so hard the tough outer shell had split.

He'd noticed the sudden awkwardness swelling between them too, his lips parted as though he could suck the nickname back in.

Don't make it weird.

She dropped her gaze to the almost finished bowl of stew but her hunger had fled.

He cleared his throat. "So um, we'll go up to the upper levels next then. If you promise not to get into any more scrapes."

She nodded, forcing herself to raise her head until her gaze met his. He managed an apologetic smile which made her feel a bit better.

They would find their way back to being friends but it would take time.

Perhaps I'll take him down to town and he can see Mix and Sammy again.

"I won't cause trouble." She pulled a face as he shot her a disbelieving look. "I won't!"

"If you say so. After we've done that, it'll be more court matters. The rest will be dealt with by the housekeeping team. The favour's yours for helping me today, but if you still want to help tomorrow, you might even get a glimpse of the queen. Finished?"

She nodded. "Yeah, let's go."

He swiped her bowl and napkin before she could offer to clear it herself. She watched as he hurried past Lindy's indignant protests and quickly washed them up. Only when Lindy threatened to go and wake the chef to chase him out did he return to her side.

They passed Arno, who gave them both a snooty look, and ventured into the firelit darkness of the mountain, leaving the dimming light of the dusky evening sky behind. Sannar nodded to a couple of nobles that drifted past, their conversation hushing until they were out of earshot. A couple of nether brothers lounged against one of the far walls flicking through books as though they had all the time in the world. Given how frantic Sannar always seemed to be, she wondered if anyone else ever bothered to do anything more than lofty musings about the realms and the nether.

"Do you mind telling me exactly what happened up there earlier?" he asked.

Odella sighed as they got into one of the trundles and Sannar set it whistling upwards.

"I asked him what he was doing and he asked me the same, I think." She frowned, wracking her memory for the exact details. "He didn't want to tell me anything, usual Fae trickery, but then he tried to, I don't know, attack or compel me. So I ran."

He gave her a disapproving look. "This could have ended much worse. No more sneaking into the mountain without someone with you, please."

She nodded. "If you say so. Before I could get to the viewing deck and find the strength to climb down again, Mum turned up and he vanished."

Sannar rubbed a hand over his mouth and she took his distraction as an opportunity to get a proper look at him. He'd grown into his ears, but also his facial features were rugged and well-defined now. His hair needed a brush but the strands looked like molten lava in the firelight. He was a few inches taller than her, but she had a feeling it was because he slouched. Curious to test it, she prodded him in the ribs.

He jumped like a scalded cat, almost flinging one elbow out of the trundle to be scraped on the back wall.

"What was that for?" he gasped.

She had to choke back the urge to giggle. "You slouch."

"So?!" He gaped at her, scandalised. "You just go around poking random people when they're not expecting it?"

She shrugged. "Not usually."

"Just me then, great. How would you like it if I said 'oh, you frown' and prodded you in the forehead?"

She leaned closer, still fighting giggles as he veered back in alarm.

"Try it, I dare you."

He eyed her, a small smile breaking over his face as the trundle came to a stop.

"No, you scare me."

She nodded. "Good."

He opened the gate and let her out first, taking the lead once they were walking along the corridor.

"The wards seem in place which is worrying," he muttered. "If someone can skip straight in with those up then we're at risk all the time. The queen's arrival will strengthen it but still. Worrying."

Odella frowned. "It must be someone really high up to get past a court lady's protection though."

"It's not her protection they got through. It's mine."

Her feet stumbled to a dead halt and she stared at him in horror.

"What?! You're the one protecting the entire court?"

He grimaced. "Yeah, sorry. People aren't meant to know that. I do most stuff nowadays but calling in someone to do official protection magic would draw attention to why we need to ask them in the first place. I did my best with the training I've got and I've learned whatever I can, but it's exhausting."

Odella gawped, noting the tension in his shoulders and his overwhelming air of weariness. A seventeen-year-old boy had not only been running an entire court by himself, but also protecting it with what had to at least be some kind of advanced warding.

"Why is nobody helping you?" she asked.

"The ones who could take over are all too busy fighting amongst themselves to rule when the lady dies. The ones that could at least help me all want to avoid getting the work on their shoulders."

Odella clenched her fist at her side, a wash of unadulterated fury splashing through her. Sannar didn't glance her way so he didn't notice and she didn't want to interrupt.

"I was a fool thinking if I took on more work, I'd reap the rewards. The only reward you get is a reputation for being useful and a whole load more work. But when I do ask for help, they either look disappointed or say how they're sure I can manage if I try harder. Or 'work smarter', I hate that one."

This time he did look her way, a self-deprecating smile on his face. Then he noticed hers and grimaced.

"I can't believe you haven't... I don't know, quit yet or

something," she said.

"I'm sworn to the court, I can't quit."

"Well, thrown a tantrum then, or refused to let them use you like this!"

He blinked as if surprised by her vehemence. "If I don't do it, it won't get done."

Odella growled and stormed toward the door the man had been trying to open earlier. She slapped her hand on the wood, ignoring Sannar wincing.

"This one."

He frowned. "I don't understand why. The scrolls in that one are old history about the nether's appearance in the human world. Why would the Forgotten have any interest in the human world?"

"Maybe as a way to destroy it?" Odella asked, her mind still on the court's apparent injustices.

"Hmm. Maybe. Okay, I'm going to get the key. Are you alright here for a minute?"

She raised her eyebrows at that. "Don't trust me with your key stash? But yes, I think I can survive a minute without bringing the mountain down."

"Not *allowed* to trust you with the key stash. Wait here."

She nodded and watched him walk off down the hall. He had quite a nice walk, she decided. Hidden by the misshapen robe somewhat, but she could imagine it.

Not that I'm imagining any part of him. Not like that.

But it was nice to be friends with him again. She'd missed him a lot, or the memory of him at least from when he still lived in town with them. Mix and Sammy were always a duo, and Odella had known they were destined to be a couple long before they did. She didn't mind third-wheeling, but Sannar had always been the one she would laugh the most with and share her secrets with.

"You again."

A male voice made her jump. She cast a warding on instinct and turned to find the strange man from earlier standing behind her. His brown hair was short against his head like a slick of mud against his tanned skin, but his face was deceptively ageless. So many of the noble Fae she'd seen at the court in passing often glamoured away imperfections.

With a low growl echoing in her throat, she prepared to hold her ground. Sannar would return with the key and if he had any sense, he would retreat and put it back wherever it came from, or he'd hide it. Either way, she wouldn't be alone for long which gave her the upper hand.

She glared at him. "You're not part of the court so what are you doing here? Forgotten scum spying for your masters?"

The man laughed but she caught the narrowing of his eyes as he smoothed the collar of his cream shirt. Odella eyed the brown jeans and brown boots, but there weren't any telling signs of nobility in his clothing.

His arrogance though? That's entirely high Fae.

"What a rudimentary viewpoint," he said with an airy sigh. "'The Forgotten are entirely evil', what black and white thinking."

She shrugged. "Their actions spoke for them in the war. I'm nobody special and even I know that good people can be made to do bad things, but the ones pulling the strings are evil."

Come on, Sannar. She willed him to do whatever he was doing faster.

"You have a clear gift that could be very helpful to our cause. You also assume we're part of the Forgotten, but did you ever think-"

"Are you? Part of the Forgotten? You're Fae and can't lie, so answer me."

He looked so scandalised at being interrupted that she almost missed his mouth rolling for several moments over potential words.

But he was Fae and couldn't lie, so she had her answer.

"Nice try," she taunted. "I'm loyal to… well, I'm loyal to my people."

She wasn't exactly loyal to the Nether Court because she wasn't a part of it, although the town she lived in benefited from proximity to it. She couldn't exactly say she was loyal to Sannar, because that was ridiculous. She also had reservations about blind loyalty to the queen, inspiring though she seemed, which was why she wanted the chance to get a glimpse of her, feel her out. She wouldn't be in the town forever, not by choice, and joining a court might give her a chance at a more exciting life. The queen's court sounded as exciting as any.

She held her warding firm as the man stalked toward her and stumbled when he reached the edge of it.

"I would urge you to reconsider," he said. "We need someone like you, and if you're not going to come willingly…"

Odella clenched her fists around her connection, determined to hold her ground even though her heart was pounding.

"Why is it so important?" she demanded. "What is it you're looking for? I'm not going to be a mindless gift for people to use."

Sensing she might be weakening, his body language opened and he took a step back to take the intimidation factor down a notch.

"And you think this court wouldn't use you mindlessly? You assume that you're not going to end up being a pawn for the queen's side just as much? Except her side use morality and 'kindness' as an excuse to not give you any benefits for your efforts."

Odella's winced, her arms and shoulders shaking with the effort as she reinforced her warding. So many would take his words at face value, might even agree that the queen's court had said a lot about cultivating kindness recently and 'doing good' for others rather than blindly chasing benefit for the individual.

A trickle of sweat beaded her brow.

I can see why they keep coming back. But they'd picked the wrong person with her.

"I can see what you mean," she said. "But I still can't trust you, not after you tried to compel me. There's nothing of financial value in this room either, just some old scrolls about histories, so I'm not sure what you're after."

He eyed the door she stood beside, a slight moment of hesitation showing her suggestion had tripped him up.

"Only histories? Nothing about the flow of origins?"

"I don't even have any idea what that is."

"HEY!"

She'd forgotten about Sannar in the hope of getting the man to give her something they could use. She flinched against the door and almost dropped her warding as his yell filled the hall. As she tried to step forward to reach his side, a savage gust of wind sent her flying back against the door.

The whirlwind moved of its own accord toward the man, splitting into a lashing whip that swirled around him and trapped him inside.

"Don't go near her again," Sannar snarled.

Odella stared at him in awe, his robe fluttering around

his jeans as he held one hand out to wield the whirling air. His face twisted with rage, his eyes wide and his free hand clenched beside him.

The man laughed even as the whirlwind tightened around him.

"Mind your court and warn the queen then, brother. The Forgotten will never give up what's rightfully theirs, from Faerie to the nether and beyond."

Odella gasped as the man gave her a wink and vanished in a swirl of the nether.

Sannar kept the whirlwind swirling around empty air for several moments before letting it drop. He sagged, one hand against the wall and Odella rushed to his side.

"I'm fine," he mumbled. "Just been running on near empty for too long. Give me a minute. Are you okay?"

"Don't worry about that. Sit down."

Odella grimaced at the state of him and pressed a firm hand on his shoulder, but he gave her an uncompromising glare and refused to budge.

"'Della, are you okay?"

He used the same name her family did, dropping the O without thinking. She let that slide and caught his gaze with defiance. She pressed her back against the wall and slid to sit down against it on the floor, relieved when he joined her, his leg flopping against hers.

"Better now," she said. "I know you're used to running things but you need to learn when to do what you're told."

He huffed. "I do nothing but what I'm told. I'm so good at doing what I'm told, they don't even need to tell me anymore."

He sounded so weary and broken in that moment that she couldn't bear it. She slid her arm around his neck, ignoring him tensing under her touch.

"They suck. They should treat you much better. Are you allowed to take time off? You should come down to town, hang out with Mix and Sammy and me. They'd love to see you."

He snorted, his eyes half-shut already and his head dropping back against the wall.

"I doubt that."

"Nah, they understood that you had a big fancy future, way more than I did. They have each other though now."

He tried to lift his head but gave up. "They're *together* together?"

"Yep. And I never mentioned that fateful day we'll never mention again. They just assumed you're too busy, which I guess is kind of true."

"I was too ashamed to come down." He groaned. "Convinced myself I was busy doing great things. Then that it was you who didn't want to hang around with me. Then I left it too long and figured you'd all tell me to go away."

Odella grinned. "I might have. They wouldn't though. They're not as vengeful as me."

She froze as Sannar's arm wriggled between them and wrapped around her waist. It was too intimate a gesture, even though she'd essentially done it first. The times where they'd sit companionably arm in arm were long gone, but apparently he didn't care enough about awkwardness to be cautious.

"What did the enemy want?" he asked.

Relieved to focus on something that wasn't the unnervingly comforting feel of his arm around her and his fingers resting soft on her thigh, she turned her mind to the mysterious vanishing man.

"He said something about- oh orbs, I can't remember.

The origin? The flow of origins? I tried to tell him it was just old histories and he asked about the flow of origins."

Sannar grimaced. "That's odd. It's ancient news and not even necessarily real. I'll have to take all this to the lady, then to the queen tomorrow. Can I ask you to do something for me?"

"Sure. Might not do it but you can try."

He grinned. "Fair enough. If the lady for whatever reason says I can't tell the queen things, about what's happened, will you tell her? I can't promise I'll be able to get you in front of her, but if you have a chance."

Odella frowned. "Why would the-"

"I don't know. I've got a feeling certain things aren't right, and I'm not sure who I can trust."

"But you can trust me?"

He turned his head, catching her eye and smiling softly.

"You're the only one I've ever been able to trust."

Odella bit her lip, trying to summon some semblance of her usual chipper self.

I never get this awkward with anyone else. But I'm exhausted and we haven't spoken until today. It's bound to be weird.

"Alright." She nodded. "If I can, I will. Come on, you've got a lady to see and I should get some sleep if I've got a potential audience with the queen tomorrow. I might actually need to brush my hair."

He laughed as she clambered to her feet with a weary groan and put out a hand to help him up. He checked the hall both ways before conceding and taking her hand, using it as an anchor and the wall as well to get himself to his feet.

"Your hair is always perfect," he said.

Odella hoped he couldn't see the blush on her cheeks

and set off as fast as she could toward the trundles.

"I am intrigued though," he added, struggling to keep pace with her. "Why are you so interested in any of this? I gave you a chance to flee back to town earlier and you didn't take it."

She shrugged. She wasn't actually sure of the answer herself but she couldn't admit that to him.

"Something's going on and I want to find out what."

"But why?"

He opened the trundle gate for her, his brow creased in confusion.

Because someone has appeared to me twice outside this door and wants me to use my gift.

She hadn't told Sannar that bit, but given his sudden defensiveness of her, she wouldn't worry him any more by telling him that yet. He needed a sleep first and to get the Queen's visit over and done with.

"If something's going wrong, don't you want to find out what so we can make it right?"

As the trundle shot downwards, he started laughing.

"You always did have a very blunt outlook on right and wrong."

The man's comment about good and evil floated back into her head. Hadn't he said something almost exactly the same?

"Morals are rarely complicated," she muttered. "People just add layers to excuse their behaviour. You're either a good person, a misguided one who can fix their issues, or someone who tramples over everyone else to get what they want."

She expected him to continue laughing, but he sighed, his smile dissipating.

"I am sorry about what happened. I felt so bad

71

afterwards."

Unnerved, she frowned as the trundle came to a stop.

"What's that got to do with anything?"

"Well, I'm hoping I'm one of the misguided ones rather than the trampling ones."

Oh.

She hadn't really considered in the last four years how much his behaviour would have affected him. But she couldn't bring herself to admit that she'd forgiven him the minute he first apologised. Or at least she'd wanted to.

She shrugged as they walked through the tunnel toward the courtyard, then realised that she would need to go all the way down to town yet.

He looked a bit startled as she turned a sudden megawatt smile on him, but at least it would cover the uneasy nerves fluttering in her stomach.

"You could find me a fast way back to town for the night, if you're really desperate to make amends."

CHAPTER SIX
REYAN

The Nether Court looked beautiful in the balmy afternoon sunlight. Reyan soaked in the warmth of it with such delight that she almost felt bad after Kainen's suggestion that the Illusion Court with its underground shadows was her home. But he was smiling too, blinking against the light and glancing around them. He even looked rested for a change like he'd had a proper sleep, very unlike her night of getting up to check on the shadow-snake that had taken over dominion of her wardrobe.

All okay? Kainen's amused voice filled her mind. *Not panicking about a certain wisp of darkness eating our court while we're out socialising?*

She stuck her tongue out at him.

I'd hardly call being forced to play nice with the courts 'socialising'.

He snickered and she returned her attention to the courtyard. Banners in the Nether Court colours of deep purple and dusky brown decorated the low stone walls that surrounded the courtyard, with several matching ribbons fluttering in the breeze. Given how beautifully the place had been decorated, Reyan was relieved Meri had all but forced her to wear the dress for their arrival. As much as her ladyship was only pretence, she didn't want to risk letting their court down.

"Sannar, show our guests to their quarters."

A demanding voice filled the air and Reyan recognised it as belonging to the lady of the Nether Court. Tall and straight-backed, the woman had the haughtiest of airs as she cast a dismissive glance in their direction. No welcome or recognition, but Reyan had met the lady before and not exactly been impressed with the reception.

Sannar whispered something to the dark-haired girl beside him and hastened forward. He looked every inch a young man with a realm of stress on his shoulders, his red hair savagely raked through and his brown nether brother robe barely covering the cuffs of his jeans.

"No need to escort us, we know our way," Reyan offered with a knowing smile. "Same room as last time? We did request two this time."

Sannar nodded. "Yes, thank you, Lady."

Reyan wrinkled her nose at the title but other people were materialising out of thin air, realm-skipping in for the event, so Reyan marched Kainen away before Sannar could finish.

"Why did we ask for two rooms?" Kainen whispered. "Did you bring the snake after all? I'm not sharing with her."

Reyan gave him a look. "No, I didn't. She seems quite content inside my wardrobe. We asked for two because we aren't married and I imagine that some of the more traditional courts look down on all that."

Some courts not including theirs. The Illusion Court was no stranger to unsavoury behaviours and most of their courtiers thought they shared a bedroom already, but Reyan's separate room was only accessible from the multi-way door in Kainen's room.

"If you say so." He grinned. "Your reputation is safe with me. Although I'm a bit worried about these windows you mentioned. Anyone could sneak in and rob me of my virtue."

"You don't have any virtue left."

"Excuse me?! I- Okay, I can't argue with that."

Reyan grinned, nodding to people they passed. Some she recognised as part of the Nether Court, others she wondered about.

"Well now, last time I was properly here, I was half-dead," Kainen announced conversationally.

"You weren't half-dead," she snorted. "A little bit maimed maybe. You went home the next day."

He grinned, mischief swirling shadows through his eyes.

"You didn't think so at the time. You were so worried you shadowed half the way across Faerie to check on me."

Her cheeks burned but she couldn't deny it without lying and taking a penalty for it, and he knew it. He hadn't let go of her hand yet either, apparently content to stride along at her side swinging their arms gently between them.

"Behave yourself while you're here as well," she muttered instead. "No riling up the nether brothers."

As they reached the room Reyan usually used when she visited, the sound of feet tapping fast filled the air.

"Lady! Lord!"

A panicked voice echoed behind them. Reyan groaned under her breath, noting that whoever was calling them had mistakenly addressed her before Kainen, for he was Lord and she was technically yet to be Lady. They turned around to find one of the maids skidding to a halt in front of them. Alara bobbed a couple of hurried curtseys, her face a picture of panic. Reyan smiled as reassuringly as she could. To all eyes she was supposed to be a lady now, but she often forgot to act like it.

"Hiya. Something exploded?"

Alara's mouth twisted. "Not exactly. Um... There's

been an oversight. We tried to accommodate everyone, but there's minimal space."

"Meaning?"

"Um… you only have the one room. I can only apologise. Sannar's been working so hard trying to get everyone placed at such short notice, but the Flora court have taken the west wing and we've had to put the Fauna court right beside them even though they don't get on, and the Revels need to be near the-"

"It's fine." Kainen answered before Reyan could recover from the surprise. "We didn't bring an entourage anyway."

Which we should have done for appearances, Reyan reminded him sharply. *This isn't ideal.*

He grinned at her. *We've shared a room before, sweetheart. Even a bed once, right here. I promise to behave myself.*

And he would, she knew that. He wasn't going to lower himself to pushing where he wasn't wanted. But he would tease her mercilessly about it all the same.

Alara looked like she was about to cry. Although Sannar planned and coordinated everything for the Nether Court, Reyan realised the mistake might not have been his but hers.

"It's fine," she echoed. "Although he snores."

Kainen's face morphed into the perfect picture of outrage.

"I do not!"

"You do a bit."

"*If* I do, it's a manly kind of snoring."

She grinned. "It's not. It's like a cute little snuffling noise."

The moment the words left her lips, she knew she'd

walked right into a massive pit. His eyes sparked and he smiled wickedly.

"You think it's cute?"

"That's… irrelevant. You're not allowed to throw your socks all over the place here either. Bad enough our lot have to pick up after you at home."

Alara watched their double act with wide-eyed hope until Reyan gave her a weary smile.

"We'll be fine," she said. "Sannar might need some help though."

Alara took that for the dismissal it was and hurried back down the hall with flurries of gratitude bouncing behind her. Reyan ignored Kainen smirking at her and pushed the door to their room open. It still had a couple of her books on the nightstand from her last visit and her posh leather coat that Kainen had gifted her hanging on the wall-rail.

I'll need to make sure I grab those when we leave.

"Are you going to be warm enough?" he asked, eying her bare shoulders with a frown. "It's warm outside but if we're in their halls inside the mountain it might get chilly."

"If not, I can just wear that." She pointed to the coat.

He grinned. "You do realise this is the very same room that they gave me after I was injured in the tunnels here?"

Reyan had realised. The memory of her racing through the shadows to make sure he was okay had sat with her the whole time she'd slept in the bed over the past weeks during her visits, but she'd be damned if she was going to admit it to him.

"So it is." She shrugged.

He sat on the edge of the mattress and smoothed a hand over it, winking at her.

"Ah, memories."

She rolled her eyes. "You promised to behave."

"I did. Actually, did I? You told me to behave, which isn't the same as me agreeing to it. But even then, promising could mean any number of things and exclude a whole bunch of others. Are you going to give me ground rules like last time?"

She shook her head. She trusted him, more than she trusted anyone else which was worrying in itself. But the thought of playing lady to an entire horde of courts with leaders from great families trained for the sole purpose of ruling, it made her anxious.

"I want you to know you're free to say what you feel is right," he added. "You speak for our court as much as I do these days, so don't feel you can't join in the fun."

"Fun? Not likely."

He flopped back on the bed, his head turned so he could still see her. She wished she could do the same. Perhaps if she pretended to be asleep he'd do the gallant thing and refuse to wake her. Then she could miss the whole thing.

"What about support then?" he pressed. "We were the first court to openly support Demi's rule. We need to present a united front together, both as joint rulers of our court and as part of Faerie."

Reyan conceded and sank onto the bed beside him, fidgeting to ensure her skirts weren't too pinned down.

"We're not actually-" She switched quickly to mind-speak. *We're not actually joint rulers though, are we? It's all pretend.*

He shrugged, his gaze fixed on her.

It is what it is. What's pretence about it if everyone believes in it? To all the folk of Faerie, you're Lady of the Illusion Court, or close enough to being one. If I died right now the court would claim you.

She sighed. *I don't remember agreeing to that.*

"Ah, but you did, sweetheart. Until we decide to tell the truth, you're mine and I'm yours. You're secretly delighted, admit it."

Even when he was being a complete pain in the behind, she had the frustrating urge to smile.

"No."

"No you won't admit it, or no it's not true?"

She counted to three and let a mask of calm fall over her face. She relaxed her shoulders and pulled the shadows from the room around her body, letting them soothe her. She could hide in the shadows, become them and travel through them, but mostly she saw them as companions and silent comfort.

"You tell me," she shot back. "You've been trained for this your whole life. I've been used the whole of mine. Being tied to a court again is both comforting and frightening for me."

Footsteps echoed outside the door and she flinched as their bedroom door swung open, two people walking in without knocking. Even as her body instinctively fought to kneel, her mouth lifted in amusement as the Holly Queen of Faerie and her king consort marched in without knocking.

Kainen grumbled something under his breath and sat up, but Reyan was already on her feet as Demi approached, while Taz shut the door behind them. Decked in smart jeans and a jewel green cardigan, Demi looked nothing like a queen of Faerie. Taz was even less formal in a baggy *Demolition Ducks* t-shirt, and Reyan wished she had the energy to glamour herself into something more casual.

"Nice dress," Demi offered by way of greeting.

Reyan shrugged. "Wish I could have worn jeans like you have actually."

"Ah, joys of being a queen. Although Milo's been sulking all morning because I'm refusing to wear the dress he picked out until the actual meeting."

Kainen was on his feet too now, his jacketed arm brushing the bare skin of Reyan's. He bowed his head to Demi, Reyan instantly going red because she'd forgotten. Demi acknowledged the gesture with a wry grimace, then turned her attention back to Reyan.

"Any news?"

They hadn't had a chance to speak properly in a while, but Reyan had been keeping a short overview in her head of everything she'd found in the Nether Court tunnels.

"There are records of PR," she said, keeping to the shortened reference to the Prime Realm. "I've seen various mentions of keys, but not what they are or how it works. It keeps going on about access too, and the 'route', although it's spelled root, so not sure if there's a flora aspect to it?"

Demi nodded, her face descending into grim acceptance.

"It'll be something we can ask the Flora Court, definitely."

"Can we trust them?" Kainen asked. "We trade, but they keep to themselves."

"I trust them as much as I can risk. Their lady is cautious but she's talking of retiring rather than living out her entire rule. I've also heard good things about her daughter who'd take over as their lady."

"I've met Lady Leilania a couple of times," Taz added. "She's very opinionated about plants and not much bothered about anything else. If there's something flora-related though, they'll likely know it or have some record of it."

Reyan wondered if she could ask Kainen to ask Meri to

send over a cardigan for her after all. The coat would be too much, but without the warmth of the sun and after spending a restless night twitching nervously over a slumbering shadow-snake, she was feeling a shiver right through to her bones.

"We've also had rumours that the enemy are reforming themselves as the Blood and Bone Court," Kainen said.

Demi huffed, a loud noise hissing through her nose. Taz's hand settled on her back as though it was his natural instinct to calm her, and Reyan tried not to smile as she imagined Kainen doing the same for her.

"My sister has sided with the traitor, we know that already," Taz said.

Demi nodded. "Belladonna is out for revenge because she's been passed over twice for succession to the Oak crown. She and Emil are likely pissed that the nether named me queen as well. They'll attack, but I'm hoping by the time they can form a worthy fight we'll be ready. If they are after access to the Prime Realm, we need to find out why. And we need to find the way in before they do."

Three pairs of eyes turned as Reyan shivered. Kainen eyed her bare shoulders with a disapproving look, one she shot right back at him.

"Coat?" he asked.

She shook her head. "Be too much. I'm fine."

Embarrassed that the queen of Faerie was watching him fuss over her, even though Demi was kind of her friend as well, at least she insisted she was, Reyan sought for a way to keep the discussion focused.

"Do we have any plans beyond the meeting?" she asked.

Kainen clicked his fingers to summon the glittering black smoke of his gift, and Demi's flinch at the action was so slight it was barely noticeable.

Reyan knew the two of them had a less than cosy history left over from the recent war, but she trusted Kainen and hoped one day Demi might be able to forgive him enough to do the same.

A random wrap of dark purple silk appeared in Kainen's fingers a second later and Reyan stared as he held it out. All thoughts of the queen, friend or not, and the king consort fled from her mind.

"That's not mine."

Kainen frowned. "Oh. Does that matter?"

"Well, yeah. What if someone's looking for it?"

He seemed to be struggling with his thought process for a long moment. Then he held it out toward her a bit more.

"It's clean."

As if that made the whole 'stealing someone else's stuff from the laundry' okay. She could see Demi and Taz trying not to grin out of the corner of her eye, but she folded her arms and stared Kainen down.

"No, put it back. Can you not finger-snap your way into my wardrobe then?"

"Of course I can. But it doesn't feel right to go rummaging around in your unmentionables."

He made a soft hissing sound and she stifled a laugh at the thought of him reaching into her wardrobe and coming up with a startled shadow-snake instead of a cardigan. But she didn't want to explain that to anyone, not if they made her give the snake back.

"But stealing from the laundry is fine?" she asked.

He opened his mouth. Hesitated. A moment later the wrap vanished and a different one of charcoal grey wool finely woven appeared.

"I don't recognise that one either," she groaned. "I'm

fine, seriously."

"It's one Meri bought for you before you refused all of my wealth and riches," he protested.

When she narrowed her eyes at him, although well aware he couldn't lie, he pushed the wrap around her shoulders. It was the same charcoal grey as his suit and blissfully warm. Her arms slid into the delicate sweeping sleeves, the shape of it more like a hooded cloak than a wrap.

I will accept this one thing from him because I'm freezing, and that's it. That and the coat. And the books. But that's it!

"Thank you."

She ignored the pleased look that graced his face briefly, her cheeks burning as she focused back on Demi and Taz, both eying the room innocently.

"Well?" she asked, somewhat irritably considering she was addressing an actual queen. "Do we have any plan or aim?"

Demi nodded. "We get them all to agree to support us. We get them all to agree not to host the Forgotten, or Bone Court or whatever they're called. We enlist their help to lure out some of the well-known Forgotten sympathisers in the hope we can find out their plans. After that, we see where we are. For now I need to do more paper-type stuff, Faerie knows why."

Taz shot her a grin and opened the door with a flourish, bowing low as Demi walked past him. She flicked a weary look at him, the "idiot", trailing behind her as they left the room.

"She almost didn't flinch that time," Kainen said glumly.

Reyan smiled. He was a total pain sometimes, but she

didn't want to see him sad or feeling guilty over the past.

"Worth it though." She made a show of shrinking into the wrap-cloak. "This is so comfy."

He smiled, but the hint of regret still shone in his eyes.

"Right, tour?" she asked.

"We already know the place."

"Yeah, but if we go for a tour, we're not sitting in here brooding and waiting to get summoned. Unless there's some sketchy reason you're lingering in here?"

That perked him up, the chance to tease her never one he passed up.

"Do you really want me to answer that?" he asked hopefully.

She opened the door and pointed to the hall.

"Of course not, now *out*."

CHAPTER SEVEN
SANNAR

The first group of nobles to arrive was from the Illusion Court, Lord Kainen and Lady Reyan. Sannar forced his shoulders not to sag, aware and gratified by the quick glance of acknowledgement Lord Kainen shot his way before facing the lady of the Nether Court.

Lady Aereen stood to welcome the guests with a serious air of 'why am I tolerating this' wafting around her. They'd unearthed a muted purple gown decked with ribbons of brown for her and someone had tamed her wispy white hair. She'd also seemed to be in one of her more lucid moods that morning, so he could only hope she'd stay that way and not ask any of the others what moon cycle they were on.

Sannar frowned to see Arno rushing toward her and whispering. Lady Aereen pressed a gentle hand to Arno's cheek and patted it before shooing him away again.

He's always been her favourite.

Reyan shot Sannar a knowing smile as the lady hollered for him to guide them, and he pushed thoughts of Arno aside. Lady Aereen really did seem to be on imperious form that morning and he couldn't refuse a request.

At least I have Odella helping.

She stood close by, ready to remind him of all the things he needed and several he hadn't even considered yet.

He'd found her one of the bikes the brothers used to go back and forth between town and the court the night before and waved her off, watching long after she disappeared into the night with her brown hair waving out behind her. Only a few hours later, he got up from an unproductive night's sleep to find her already back and helping the others. Most of the brothers scurried straight past her, but the maids who were still up decorating the courtyard with the ribbons and floral arrangements seemed grateful for her help.

"Can you keep an eye on Lady Aereen for me?" he whispered. "No need to talk, just let me know if anything goes hideously wrong."

Odella's eyes widened but she nodded. The lady wouldn't listen to her, probably wouldn't acknowledge her either, but Odella would find some way of distracting everyone until he returned.

"No need, we know our way." Reyan took pity on him with a grin. "Same room as last time? We did request two."

Sannar nodded. "Yes, thank you, Lady."

Reyan wrinkled her nose at the honorific but glanced over her shoulder at the assembled crowd and said nothing. While lords and ladies could request familiarity and casual behaviour where they chose, Sannar couldn't.

Reyan and Kainen walked off toward the accommodation block. Sannar eyed the courtyard again with his nerves fluttering. The forecast was clear and dry for the day so tables had been set out in a horseshoe shape, the purple tablecloths rippling lazily in the breeze. The brown leaves of their local flowers had been tinged with gold, and clusters of purple heather picked up the sunlight.

"Who's next?" Odella asked.

She had a small pad and pen with what looked like a lifetime of scribbles on it. Sannar didn't dare ask if she was taking notes for him or for herself. Thoughts of her somehow being a Forgotten spy flitted into his head, then just as quickly out of it as she smiled at him.

"Whoever arrives," he admitted. "I've put the Flora Court in the back section because it's the closest to the views of the meadows. Fauna the same, although they don't get on. The Word Court won't care where they are, but we'll have to keep them from going to the upper levels and trying to 'liberate' our scrolls."

He pulled a face, unable to keep the wry grin away as Odella laughed loudly. A few people looked their way and she clapped a hand over her mouth.

"Sorry, practicing my propriety," she muttered, her cheeks dusting pink. "So that's the Flora and Fauna courts, Nether and Illusion, Words, and what about Revels?"

Sannar risked leaning closer, although he saw her tense and fall still as his head neared hers.

"I'm just hoping they all keep their pants on," he murmured.

The noise she made echoed across the whole courtyard. He knew it was bordering on cruel, but the delight he felt when he saw her blush made the risk worth it. She stared at him, aghast, and he thumped his fist on his chest to cover for her.

"Sorry everyone, wrong hole."

She folded her arms and gave him an acidic glare before turning away. Amused that he was getting to her, he waited a few moments for the low hum of conversations to resume.

"I didn't realise you were going to make such an unladylike noise," he murmured.

Odella gave him an unimpressed look, but he could see the corners of her mouth lifting.

"I didn't realise you still had a sense of humour," she shot back.

He might have continued goading her but the air in the middle of the courtyard wavered and the Flora Court appeared.

Where Kainen and Reyan had been clothed in darkness and swathes of grey, the Flora Court ladies were decked in exquisite finery of dark greens and pale pinks. Lady Flora's dress had a train and her wife wore a smart green suit with pink flowers stitched over it. Behind them was Lady Leilania, their daughter and the future of their court, her dress of pale pink contrasting theirs and highlighting her auburn hair. Sannar tried not to stare while wondering how she'd been blessed with more burnished, autumnal locks and his own messy mop of hair was more a fire shade.

As Lady Flora walked forward, Sannar risked another look at Odella. Her eyes were wide, her lips slightly parted. She'd pinned her dark hair but a few bits had escaped.

"She's beautiful," she said under her breath.

He nodded, his eyes fixed on her.

She really is.

He froze as she glanced and caught him staring. He absolutely had no idea who she was talking about.

"Sannar!"

The bark in his lady's voice wasn't one he heard often, mainly because he kept on top of things. Now here he was staring at a girl he'd known since childhood instead of attending to his duties. He grimaced and hurried to his lady's side.

"Apologies," he said, using his most soothing voice and bowing his head low. "You are most welcome to the Nether Court. Allow me to show you to your quarters. We've chosen a suite in the far wing as it has the best view of the meadows."

The ladies of the Flora Court were holding hands and regarding him with a knowing smile. They'd ruled their court a long time, almost as long as his lady had ruled the Nether Court, so they knew what he was having to deal with.

He also bestowed the same welcome to Lady Leilania next, bowing low. Rumour had it her parents were considering stepping down, an act unheard of in Fae court history. The only way out usually was death but by all accounts they wanted to try the natural, relaxed way of things. He wondered if it was a sign of the new queen's rule settling around Faerie, that those who didn't actually want to rule could step down rather than be tied to their duties forever.

A comforting thought, although I doubt I'd be allowed to leave the Nether Court as easily.

He straightened up, conscious this wasn't the day to let his mind wander.

Last time he'd seen Lady Leilania, she'd been a girl but now here she was dressed like a main character in a fanciful legend with what looked like half a flower shop on top of her head.

Her expression said it all: *this sucks and I'm about to riot.*

Sannar didn't have the same familiarity with them as he did with Reyan and Kainen so he was left to guide them to their rooms personally. Regretting putting anyone at the other end of the court, he led them through corridors while keeping up a steady stream of polite chatter.

"What grows here?" Lady Leilania asked.

Sannar smiled. "*Baida* root mainly. We have a lot of vegetation further down near to the town and the meadows beyond are full of flowers that sing at certain times of bloom, but up here in the mountain it's mostly root."

Lady Leilania frowned and asked no more. One track minded, Sannar realised. No plants equalled no attention. Luckily he found someone ready and waiting to show them the rest of the way to their rooms.

"Go." Lady Flora laughed. "And do not worry, word reaches even as far as the Flora Court about who really runs things here."

Sannar froze. "I'm sure I don't know what you mean."

She gave him a withering look and moved away to follow her family. Unnerved, Sannar strode back the way he'd come. He didn't want anyone thinking he was trying to take over the court, or that he had any aspirations of being lord of it. One whiff of that and all the would-be successors might suddenly find reasons to fault him and make his life even more difficult.

I joined this court hoping I'd be able to use connections and see more of Faerie, not be tied to one place forever.

The thought plagued him all the way to the courtyard, where he found a crowd full to bursting.

He scanned the crowd, suspiciously lacking any sign of brown robes. His brethren were happy to be part of a court and conduct their research, but expect them to pitch in as they were supposed to and suddenly they were all away or sick or mysteriously stuck in one of the tunnels.

If there is ever an option to quit, I'm taking it. I'll travel to the furthest end of the realm.

Then he saw Odella hurrying toward him.

Maybe she'd come with me.

She tumbled to a halt in front of him, cheeks pink and her eyes wide.

"They all turned up at once," she hissed. "Your lady has refused to house them until you get back."

Sannar groaned. "Oh orbs alive, can't she do anyth-" He inhaled a sharp breath. "Right. See that group over there, the one that looks like they're about to go to carnival?"

Odella nodded. "Revel Court. You wanted them housed near the kitchens because it keeps them out of trouble and it's close to the courtyard if they get restless."

"Exactly." He hesitated a moment, surprised she'd remembered his reasoning. "Could you show them? Would you mind?"

"Nope. Introduce me though first. I'm not in a robe or anything."

Relieved someone was helping him for once, Sannar grabbed her hand and ignored the indignant squawk. He towed her across to the Lord of Revels and bowed low.

"Welcome to the Nether Court," he began. "My companion will lead you to your quarters."

He dropped Odella's hand, the feel of her warm skin sliding away from his like a lifeline slipping through his fingers.

"I do hope it's somewhere fun." The Lord of Revels winked.

Odella smiled back at him, her natural instinct for mischief shining in her eyes.

"I doubt we can rival the revels for fun, but we do our best. Follow me please."

She gave Sannar a reassuring smile and he clung to it as he turned to find the next three courts essentially queuing up to speak to him.

This is a complete disaster.

He didn't dare look his lady's way, knowing he wouldn't be able to keep the irritation off his face if he did. Instead he threw himself into the task.

Lord Rydon of the Fauna Court and his entourage were

taken the same way as the Flora Court had been, and the Lady of Words was happy to be housed near the courtyard, although the she didn't hide her intentions when she enthused about the proximity to the mountain of scrolls.

Finally Sannar found himself facing Queen Demerara and her king consort. He dropped to his knees, waiting for her to summon him to his feet again. She flashed a hand in his eyeline and he stood to face her. She hadn't bothered to dress up as the rest of the courts had done, her hoodie and jeans at odds with the finery around them. She was wearing a silver circlet of holly woven into her black curls though, which was something. Sannar had met her a couple of times previously, but even now she radiated power and he was in complete awe of her. At her side the king consort, also the previous prince of Faerie, looked around with renewed intrigue.

"Thank you for agreeing to host," the queen said. "It's an absolute pain in the behind but we needed to get everyone in one place without risk of them being able to wander off."

Sannar managed a nervous smile.

"We're only too happy to host, my queen. We're here to-"

"Ah." She frowned. "I told you to call me Demi, remember?"

Sannar glanced around and noticed his lady watching them with renewed intrigue, as well as the rest of the court.

"Of course, forgive me. We have your quarters ready in our lady's block of rooms, and our meeting hall is ready whenever you choose."

He made a mental note to check the hall had been done to a proper standard as he hadn't had a chance yet, but Demi's eyes flickering sideways drew his attention to

Odella appearing beside him. She technically shouldn't have approached until either the queen summoned her or vacated the area, but she wouldn't have any idea about royal protocol and court visits. He saw the fresh curiosity on the queen's face and the wariness on the king consort's, and decided he would tow Odella along with them.

"This way, your- my qu- De-"

He couldn't say it. The withering look Odella gave him didn't help, but the queen started laughing.

"You'll get used to it," she said. "Honestly, if you feel safer calling me by title then fine, but you don't have to."

"Demi," he said, feeling three parts brave and ten parts foolish. "I can do that if you ask."

"Sannar!" Lady Aereen's voice rang across the square.

He tensed. She only ever summoned him by name in that barking tone when he was in trouble. He turned to go to her, but she was already on her way to join them.

Has she not even greeted them as guests yet? Odella's words floated back to him, that the lady was waiting for him to come back. *Surely she at least greeted the queen personally?*

"My lady," Sannar bowed his head, which was more than he usually bothered with lately. "I was about to show our queen her quarters."

Lady Aereen inclined her head to the queen, then the king consort and a large part of Sannar's constant ability to cope through anything dissipated into the nether. In not bowing her head or at least making some reference to kneeling or her inability to do so, she was essentially brushing off Demi as inconsequential.

"Lady Aereen." Demi's voice was cool, unemotional. "You have a very dedicated court."

No personal compliment as was the custom. Even if the

compliment was a faked bundle of word-tangling, it was expected. But then so was bowing to the queen.

Sannar stood with awkward anticipation between them, nowhere near bold enough to intervene as they locked eyes. The king consort gave him a weary look, as though this was something that happened to him daily.

"Sannar?" Odella's voice made him jump. "You wanted me to remind you the hall needs a final check. I assume you wanted to check it yourself even though we spent hours on it this morning and it looks fabulous."

He could have kissed her. In playing dumb and interrupting the stand-off, she had drawn the attention of both queen and lady because she wasn't supposed to be there.

"Forgive me." Sannar tried his hardest not to grin. "My duties beckon. Let me show you to your rooms first."

Demi waved an airy hand. "Oh no need. I can remember the way. Come on, Taz."

Sannar watched as she strode across the courtyard with the king consort at her side. He seemed to be whispering something frantic to her but she didn't slow her pace. Checking that nobody else was waiting to harass him, Sannar caught Odella's eye and started toward the mountain entrance.

"Wait."

He groaned under his breath as Lady Aereen called him back. Beside him, Odella sniggered.

"You can show me what efforts have been made on *my* behalf," Lady Aereen said. "You can meet with your girlfriend later."

Sannar blinked as his cheeks burned, the sudden fear that Odella would assume he'd been giving people the wrong idea making him panic.

"She's not my girlfriend," he mumbled.

But the lady was already moving past him with a surprisingly determined stride in accompaniment to her steely expression.

Odella gave him a dark look. "You don't need to sound too horrified at the idea."

Stuck for any words at all, Sannar watched as she turned away from him and stalked across the courtyard to a cluster of maids. He'd not noticed her making friends with anyone at court before, but then she helped her mother often so she probably had.

I just never really noticed her beyond thinking she used to be my friend.

"SANNAR!"

As he rushed after his lady, he wondered why exactly he was spending so much time and trouble noticing now.

CHAPTER EIGHT
ODELLA

"She's not my girlfriend," Odella mimicked under her breath.

Of course he had a point. She wasn't. But still, he didn't need to sound so mortified by the mere idea of it. She readjusted one of the banners in the court's main hall and glanced down at her outfit. Tugging at the hem of her plain blue t-shirt, she kicked one dirty boot against the other, unsure why her appearance or lack of it was bothering her so much. But at least the main hall looked fit to host a queen now.

Built under the mountain, the hall was a curving masterpiece of architecture, complete with rambling fire troughs that travelled overhead to provide light, and strategically placed mirrors to reflect it. The black marble floor shone enough to reflect the figures that walked on it, and now she could see a vague depiction of herself staring back at her from that floor.

All around the room maids and attendants were dashing to put the last touches to everything, straightening cutlery, tweaking teetering piles of fruit and pastries so they looked in line and fussing over specks of dust on chairs and pillars.

The fragrantly sweet scent from the table pulled at Odella's empty stomach and she risked a sniff, knowing she couldn't exactly rush across and grab any of the mouth-watering offerings for herself.

I bet the food is to hide the 'hardly ever used' smell that usually haunts this place.

She snickered to herself as the ladies from the Flora Court wafted in, their appearance dragging the smile off her face. Lady Leilania glanced around with a doubtful frown, but she looked as breathtaking as she had outside, her dress exquisite and her fiery hair now tumbling down over her shoulders. Regal and elegant, slender and willowy, she looked exactly like a lady should.

Odella glanced down again at her reflection in the dark marble floor and sighed. She wasn't in any way slender or willowy, and words like regal or elegant were realms away from any description of her. Her arms were strong from helping her dad on the harbour and her figure was curvy, although not always in the right places.

"Oh, hello."

She turned at the sound of a female voice beside her and flinched away from the person it belonged too.

"My queen!" She dropped to her knees, head down.

Sannar hadn't introduced her earlier and she hadn't expected him to, but nobody seemed to notice the ill-timed curtsey she'd bobbed as Demi passed her. Now having seen Sannar kneel before, she figured doing the same wouldn't get her exploded into bits or thrown in some royal court dungeon or anything.

"Up you get," the queen said cheerfully. "This floor doesn't look comfortable for the knees."

Odella scrambled up, ignoring her smarting kneecaps. She had no idea where to put her hands so settled for clasping them in front of her. The quickest of glances and she realised not only was the queen no longer wearing her crown, but they were both dressed in a similar pair of flared blue jeans. With the *Demolition Ducks* hoodie swamping her body, the queen looked more like someone Odella would find in the tavern down in town.

Do I have to say something, or should I wait for her to address me?

"I like your bracelet," the queen said.

It wasn't the first thing Odella had expected royalty to say to her, not that she'd ever expected to be this close to royalty let alone talking to it. She looked down at the silver wire with glass beads in rainbow colours that wrapped around her wrist and shrugged through a wave of shyness.

"Thanks- thank you, your majesty." She bobbed another curtsey to be safe. "I make them from whatever my dad brings back from the realms. He imports stuff on the boats."

Well aware the queen probably didn't need to know the ins and outs of her family, Odella toyed with the bracelet instead. She definitely didn't have to explain that the more exclusive pieces she made usually had semi-precious stones in, ones that she'd unearthed from walking around the mountain paths and guessing where to dig with her gift.

"It's really pretty. Do you sell them?"

Odella nodded. "Here and there. Makes me a few *percats* around yuletide. These are only glass and wire, but I make orb chains too."

"Can I buy one? How much are they?"

"I- really?"

"Yes, really." The queen chuckled. "I don't have anything on me. My aide, Milo, has been catching up on films from the human world and now he's running around quoting them. The latest was 'royalty isn't supposed to jingle', so now I'm not allowed to carry coins around."

"You wouldn't want them to call you the Jingling Queen. Although I guess it would fit with the whole holly season thing."

Each sentence sent a fresh slap of nerves through her

but it appeared to be putting the queen at ease.

"Very true," she agreed. "Maybe he has a point. So, how much are they?"

Odella hesitated.

Mum would never forgive me if I charged her.

She slid the bracelet off her wrist, a newer one thankfully.

"You can have this one if you like," she offered. "Or I guess I can run down and get the rest if you wanted to choose, but it might take me a while and you're really busy-"

The queen took the bracelet and slid it over her wrist.

"Thanks, I love it. Soo… how much?"

She's actually going to make me say it.

Odella cringed into her bones, scrunching herself small.

"It's a gift, no charge," she said.

A strain of discomfort passed over the queen's face.

"You don't have to do that. If you tell me how much I can get Taz to pay it. He's apparently allowed to jingle all he likes."

Odella almost snorted hysterically at the thought that conjured, but she took a deep breath and squashed the urge down deep.

"Honestly, it's fine. I can say my work is worn by royalty. If anyone believes me, I'll make a killing."

The queen laughed at that, her expression easing.

"Fair enough, I'll take that. So tell me, what's going on here that I don't already know?"

Odella frowned. "Well, what do you already know? More than me I bet if you're any kind of Fae noble."

The sound of it came out of her mouth then registered in her brain a moment later. She slapped a hand to her mouth.

I'm going to get pulverised. This is it. One piece of backchat because I can't keep my mouth shut and I'm done for.

The queen started laughing, her vivid blue eyes picking up a determined sparkle.

"Finally, someone who isn't placating me. I already know that the Lady Aereen isn't my biggest fan. I know Sannar does most of the actual work around here, bless him. I know the other courts are concerned that this might be a prelude to another war with the Forgotten."

Odella bit her lip. Sannar had asked her to tell the queen about the man she'd come up against in the upper levels, and she'd get no better chance than this.

"There was something," she admitted. "Sannar asked me to tell you in case… well, you know."

"I do know as it happens. He's on my trusted list, others aren't. What did he ask you to tell me?"

Odella took a deep breath. She explained in low tones about the strange man trying to access the archives, what Sannar had told her about the flow of origins being in there, and finally about the man's ability to vanish through wardings. She watched nervously as the queen's face changed from watchful to wary.

"Can you describe him?" she asked. "I know folk that aren't sworn to this court can't glamour inside it, but then I don't know how far the court trusts its brothers."

Odella frowned. Glamouring definitely wasn't one of her strong points, but she wondered then who might be willing to risk betraying their court for a group like the Forgotten if it was one of the brothers.

Either someone zealous about their cause, or someone with literally no other choice. Or someone being forced to betray their own through debt or blackmail.

"I can't see any reason the court wouldn't trust its own," she said hesitantly. "But I'm not actually part of it myself." She raced on as the Queen's eyebrows lifted. "My mother works here, and I help her sometimes. Sannar and I used to be friends- well, we still are, or rather we were, then we weren't, now we are again, kind of. Sorry, you don't need to know all that. It's not every day I get to talk to nobility, let alone royalty."

She could feel her cheeks aflame but the queen was smiling again now which had to be a good sign. Unless she was the kind of person who delighted in the torment of others, but from everything Odella had heard on *The Faerie Net*, not only was their new queen a fairy rather than full-blooded Fae, she also believed in progressive tolerance and kindness.

"Would it help if you called me Demi?" the queen asked, her amusement flitting over her face.

Odella let out a strangled laugh. "I don't think I could. I'm just a girl from town helping out here."

"And I was just a human who found out she had a speck of fairy blood. Now I'm a queen of Faerie. Crud happens."

Amused, Odella tried to hang onto at least the tiniest shred of propriety. Lady Aereen would banish her from court if she found out about any strain of insolence. Her mother would fuss about her being rude. Her dad would laugh for days.

Sannar would be mortified if I strolled in calling the queen by her name.

She grinned. "Demi. Orbs that feels strange. Sorry, not your name is strange. But you're like a literal *queen*."

"Don't remind me." Demi groaned. "At least you don't have to spend the next however many hours refereeing a bunch of courts who are all determined to disagree with whatever the others say, whether it makes sense or not, and convince them that your idea is the one they need to champion."

"You could bribe them," Odella suggested, keeping a straight face with difficulty. "Or threaten to remove them from the nobility."

Demi snorted. "Not likely. The amount of paperwork that would create. I'm not above bribing either but even bribes have to be done with the delicate sensibilities in mind. You can't make it obvious it's a bribe, even though you both know it is."

Odella couldn't be sure if Demi was teasing about the bribes, but she knew it was almost currency for Fae to bribe and barter, and a queen wouldn't survive long without at least acknowledging that.

Over Demi's shoulder she noticed the king consort approaching and tried to modify her open posture into something meeker, clasping her hands in front of her and trying to look small. Not because she was so much worried about the royalty thing anymore because Demi's rule trumped his, but mainly because she was so embarrassed to remember having a poster of him on her wall from an ancient issue of *Faeshonista* magazine's society page when she was younger. He was less groomed than the poster, his honey blond hair a total mess and his hands in the pockets of well-worn jeans.

"The courts are getting restless," he said, sparing a smile for Odella also. "They want to know when we'll begin because, as the Lord of Revels insisted, this isn't a place he'd have chosen for a holiday."

Odella bit down her smile as the king consort rolled his eyes and Demi huffed under her breath.

"It was nice to meet you…" Demi left the space open.

"Odella. Dewlark. From town."

Demi grinned. "Nice to meet you Odella Dewlark from town, friend of Sannar. Okay, let's get this farce over with."

Odella watched them cross the hall to the enormous marble table that filled the centre as the rest of the courts filed in. Realising it would look like she was spying if she lingered much longer, she shuffled toward the doors.

She dodged a couple of maids bringing in refreshments, mumbling apologies as she dodged left and right.

"Sorry," she muttered. "Excuse me. I just need to- Oh."

The doors leading out to the hall slammed shut. She twisted around in time to see the maids form a line to distribute drinks and then file out of a side door at the other end of the hall.

Crud crud crud.

Hidden by the shadows of a nearby pillar, she was invisible to those now sitting down at the table. She could make a run for it. She still had time before-

"Welcome and thank you for coming." Silence fell as Demi stood at the head of the table to speak. "I know this is unexpected, but I wouldn't have dragged you all you're your courts unless it was necessary."

Odella crowded into as small a space as she could manage behind the pillar, her heart hammering. If they found her they'd suspect her of being a Forgotten spy. But she couldn't interrupt the meeting either or they'd assume it anyway, or at the very least refuse to let her go anywhere near the court ever again.

She didn't want to admit to herself that in her heart of hearts she yearned to do something other than spend her life in town. Her friends and her parents were more than happy with their lives and that was great for them, but she wanted to see other realms, and the court was a potential way for her to do that. She didn't want to burn any bridges through a simple mistake.

Although given how Sannar is treated, I doubt they'd ever honour any promises to send me to other realms even if I did get far enough to earn them.

She nestled against the pillar. Perhaps if she could make it to one of the nearby doors in the other wall without being seen, she could lie down inside one of the side rooms and pretend she passed out.

"What exactly is this unexpected threat?" A female voice asked.

Odella peeked out enough to see the Lady of the Flora Court standing to speak. Her voice was soft and curious, but wary.

"Two of the courts, Words and Fauna, have been approached by emissaries of the Forgotten," Demi announced. "They're regrouping as we knew they eventually would. The traitor Emil is still leading them, and I'm worried that if they get enough strength, they'll find a way to challenge us."

The Lord of Revels stood. "To challenge you, you mean."

Odella scowled at him as if she could attack him with a look. She'd seen the tiny ripples that Queen Demerara's recent rule had brought to the town, nothing major but there were more opportunities being instigated for the future and more avenues of help for those who needed it during tough winters.

No doubt a fancy revel lord like him, sitting in his fancy palace or whatever, holding revels and pretending everything's a party, has no idea what the real realms are like.

Demi flicked a dismissive look in his direction, forcing him wordlessly back into his seat.

"Those who wish to align with the Forgotten are free to do so," she announced, her tone pure acid. "Those who don't appreciate the openness of the freedom my court and my rule offers can defect."

Lady Flora eyed her wife and her daughter. While her wife looked contemplative and calm, her daughter seemed to be giving her mother an 'are you serious' look.

"Nobody said anything about defecting, my queen," Lady Flora said. "But we are concerned about putting our courts in jeopardy. What about your FDPs, can they not hunt out the enemy where necessary?"

A smatter of approving murmurs filled the room, quietening as Demi shook her head.

"Arcanium are the eyes and ears of the realms. We take on charges, not wars. After the last battles where Arcanium shouldered the brunt of the fighting, I cannot and will not ask any more of them than I am already. If the courts aren't willing to fight for their queen and the realms, what is the use of them swearing fealty? Why have courts at all?"

Odella wanted to cheer. The sheer granite in Demi's voice charged her with some sense of hope, of wanting to be a part of whatever mayhem Demi was about to unleash and taking on anything that came her way.

A firm hand landing on her shoulder wasn't what she had in mind.

She flinched, fighting the other person's hold as an arm came around her waist to hold her still.

"Shhh, stop struggling!" Sannar hissed in her ear.

She froze, heat flooding every single cell of her skin as she realised his head was right beside hers, his arms now around her waist.

"What are you doing in here?" he whispered.

Uh-oh. He sounds mad.

She didn't dare look back at him, both because she was still trying to recover her pounding nerves and also because it would have put their faces ridiculously close together.

"I got caught in here, the doors were shut before I could leave, then the meeting started and I didn't want to interrupt!" She hesitated. "What are *you* doing in here?"

He said nothing for a long moment. Then he let go of her and grabbed her hand instead.

"Hey!" she hissed.

He dragged her toward the nearest door, easing it open and hustling her into a storage room full of chairs. She stared in alarm as he pushed a wardrobe aside with a hefty grunt to reveal a dark passage.

"Well?" He glowered at her. "Do you want to find out what's going on or what?"

She *did* want to find out what was going on but the passage looked incredibly narrow. Catching her hesitation, he rolled his eyes and held out a hand.

"Don't you trust me? Or are you afraid of the dark these days? The Odella I knew wasn't afraid of anything."

The taunt landed exactly where he intended it to and she knew it. She scrunched up her face as she stuck her tongue out at him and strode past the outstretched hand into the passage. Her elbows scraped the wall on either side as she ventured further down, her step slowing.

"Here," he whispered.

He reached up to a tiny brass hook hanging on the wall and used it to unlatch a strip of the wall which let light and sound filter in.

"It's a viewing hole in one of the paintings," he explained. "The light hits it in a way that doesn't show the gap, so we should be safe to observe. But not a word to anyone, I mean it."

Odella nodded. She could keep a secret.

There wasn't much room for them both to see by, but he had gotten them into this situation so he could be the one to step aside. Ignoring the fact it was his court not hers, and that she'd been caught snooping in it whereas he probably had full access, she jostled next to him and pressed her head to the gap.

Sannar inched closer, his cheek all but brushing her head.

Okay, this is ridiculous. She forced herself to focus on the courts gathered around the table and the argument brewing about the Forgotten. *He's my friend. Getting flustered about being this close to him is… it's… it's improper!*

Sannar didn't seem bothered about their closeness like she was, his gaze fixed on the scene outside. Knowing that he was essentially running the Nether Court and they were holding the meeting without him, she bit her lip and tried to keep her breathing as quiet as she could.

CHAPTER NINE
REYAN

Reyan froze as Demi issued her first challenge, the not-so-veiled threat stilling the entire group into silence.

Why have courts at all? She sent the panicked thought into Kainen's mind. *Surely she knows how much good they can do?*

Seated beside her, Kainen reached over and took her hand in his, placing them on the table for all to see.

She knows what she's doing. Remember what I said, you say whatever you think. You speak for our court as much as I do.

She let that slide, guessing that he was worried about her silence being construed as down to dominance on his part or something that might jeopardise their pretence.

When nobody replied and Demi's hands turned white on the edge of the table, Reyan realised she could take Kainen at his word, not as lady of his court necessarily but as Demi's friend.

"The courts do a lot of trade which helps Faerie prosper." She gulped and forced her wavering voice to reach louder. "Some courts help the folk of their realm too. But the Illusion Court vowed to support you and we stand by that. If the Forgotten are regrouping, we'll do whatever it takes to push them back."

Not a stretch to intend 'we' to include her as part of Demi's supporting group rather than the Illusion Court specifically. Even with Kainen's permission, she still had no right to speak for his court in reality.

Kainen sank back against his chair with a lazy grin, his fingers toying with her hand. She held herself stiff, ready for whatever insult inevitably came next.

"You have been lady for a mere few weeks." Lady Aereen sniffed. "What would you know about ruling a court?"

"You haven't even been titled officially yet either, have you?" the Lord of Revels added.

Reyan couldn't argue against any of that. They were right, and the realisation that she'd come in unprepared crept into her head. Her first taste of court politics and she was wordless.

Inadequacy burned hot across her face. She sat in a grand court hall with the highest nobles of the realm. Kainen of course, then there was Lady Flora of the Flora Court and her family. She glanced to the Lady of Words whose name she didn't even know sitting alone. Lord Rydon of the Fauna Court was also alone, but he had none of the graceful elegance the ladies did. Reyan tried not to stare at him, but she'd met so few trolls and somehow she hadn't expected it here. The Lord of Revels had two unknown men with him, one old and one young, but while they stood behind his chair, the lord himself lounged with one leg thrown over the arm.

In the face of them all staring at her, any remnant of bravery Reyan might have clung onto before leaked away.

A warm tingle crept over her hand and she looked down to see glittering black smoke curling from Kainen's fingers.

"Reyan speaks for our court as freely as I do," he said, his tone unnervingly calm. "To sleight her is to insult me, and I won't tolerate that. She is Lady of the Illusion Court and you will show her the same respect you show me."

"You've been a court lord for barely a year yourself," Lord Rydon of the Fauna Court countered.

Kainen shrugged. "And raised for it all my life. Can you say the same, my lord? You may have ruled for a handful of years, but would you like it if I called your legitimacy into question? Or challenged the lady you chose to rule beside you?"

Lord Rydon's burly shoulders hunched as he leaned forward, hands braced on the table to stand.

"Well, we've proven one thing," Demi said, her tone flat. "The courts are no better than squabbling children."

Lord Rydon sank back down, his irate expression narrowing.

You've got this, sweetheart.

Kainen brushed his thumb back and forth across her knuckles and Reyan let a few seconds of silence reign before speaking up, his support giving her strength.

"Lady officially or not, I've seen both sides. Nobility and normal life. I may not be born to rule, may not even be titled to it, but rulers are there to govern and protect their people. Anything else is sheer arrogance. If we can't look after our Fae, we're no better than the Forgotten."

"And our nature," Lady Leilania piped up. "We need to look after that too, perhaps even more than the Fae."

Lord Rydon nodded reluctantly. "And our wildlife, I'll agree there's something in that."

"And our ways of life too," the Lady of Words added. "While we need to honour our traditions, they're nothing without the people to follow them. As Lady Reyan says, people are under our care as part of our courts and our realms, and we are responsible for them and their safety."

Reyan noted the soft amusement in the lady's voice, and the subtle use of the title being given to her name.

Her chest squeezed with gratitude. Nether, Revels and Fauna might not want to recognise her as lady, but Words did which was a start.

"Lady Reyan is right," Lady Flora said. "We are here to help govern Faerie, and to ensure we look after not only our people but our land and its wildlife too."

Kainen squeezed Reyan's hand.

Two courts supporting your title, sweetheart. He grinned lazily at her. *Not bad for the start of your first battle.*

Subtle warmth kindled inside her chest at his playfulness, but she tried to keep the reality of the situation in front of her.

Lady Flora probably wants us to support her imminent retirement and Lady Leilania's succession, she countered. *I don't know what the Lady of the Word Court's angle is, but there'll be one.*

Kainen nodded, a slight dip of his chin in agreement.

True enough. But that's as good as it gets in terms of support for court Fae.

"So we're all agreed we should be looking after our people, our nature and our wildlife. Great start," Demi said. "Now, are there any Forgotten supporters here who want to declare it and leave early? Show of hands maybe?"

A collective look of suspicion ran around the table. Two men standing behind the Lord of Revels grimaced at each other before the older of the two bent down to whisper in the lord's ear. Demi ignored that, gazing at each of them in turn.

"No takers for the enemy then," she continued. "So the question now is whether any of you will answer their call when they inevitably attack."

"Why would they risk it now?" the Lord of Revels

demanded. "We've had a year of peace."

Lady Flora scoffed. "A year of fragile stability while they rebuild themselves is nothing."

He folded his arms across his chest, so slouched in his seat he was almost horizontal.

"My question still stands."

Demi nodded. "A fair enough question. We know the enemy are still out there. We've heard rumours they're reforming themselves as the Blood and Bone Court or some nonsense. Then we've had odd happenings. The *Maladorac* beneath this mountain was woken to cause chaos. Unknown Fae are being seen and found in courts where they shouldn't be."

"Even if nothing happens, we should be prepared all the same," Kainen said.

The Lord of Revels chuckled. "Surely after the last war you'd be the best person to start with then?"

The shadows in the vast room responded to Reyan's anger instantly, clustering to her and swathing her shoulders in roiling darkness.

"And where were you, my lord?" she asked, her tone soft with danger. "When the tricks of the last war were going on, where were you? Whose side were you hiding on?"

Kainen laughed before the Lord of Revels could gather himself. He lifted Reyan's hand to his lips and kissed it as he had done in the tunnels the day before, forcing a blush to her cheeks amid the fury.

"I have nothing to hide," he said. "If the queen wishes to interrogate my loyalty again she's more than welcome to, but looks like she'll have to go through my fiancée first."

Reyan rolled her eyes at him as Demi grinned.

"I wouldn't dare. The Illusion Court have my trust because of the past and in spite of it. The rest of you now have a chance to prove your loyalty to the crown. Information has already come to light that worries me. Proof that the Forgotten are massing again. I won't let them take Faerie and force its people into some pre-historic hierarchy of cruelty."

The ladies of Flora and Words nodded, and Lord Rydon gave a satisfied grunt.

Revels and Nether were silent. Taking that as assent, however unwilling, Demi sank into her seat.

"For the moment we don't have much," she admitted. "But if the Forgotten are approaching courts to suss out loyalties and also sneaking into courts for information then it means they're after something specific."

"Any idea what?" Kainen asked. "Should we be on the lookout for anything specific?"

Demi nodded. "If you have old histories, archives, libraries or anything informative, those might be targeted next. Or your allegiance might be sought, either openly or through trickery. Be on your guard."

The Lord of Revels glared at the man hissing in his ear and leaned forward, his arms braced on the table.

"You say information has come to light that worries you. What is that exactly?"

Demi hesitated. Taz straightened in his seat beside her, but she faced the Lord of Revels with a tight smile a moment later.

"Information that suggests the Forgotten are looking for something that would give them resources, possibly strength."

"Well of course that would worry you if you had to face them strong," he scoffed. "By all accounts you had help from Faerie itself last time. Has the favour dissipated so readily?"

Taz's wings flared out behind him, a look of pure acid on his face. Demi's hand settled on his thigh, her blue eyes turning icy as she fixed her gaze on the Lord of Revels.

"My link with Faerie is my business," she said. "I don't answer to you or to any of the courts. The nether crowned me and Faerie accepted me to rule. Are you saying you're looking to challenge not only a queen, but the very fabric of Faerie and beyond? If so, please speak up."

Power crackled around the room, electric blue light fizzling across the surface of her skin. The glow caught on the fiery orange flicker of Taz's wings as he kicked back his chair to stand behind her.

Kainen still had a hint of his black smoke curling on one hand, and Reyan kept the shadows cloaking her. She wondered if they should have a warding up but the Lord of Revels slouched back.

"No, of course not," he muttered.

Demi reined back her energy with a grim nod. Taz sat down.

"But we don't have any proof," the Lord of Revels added. "Can you give us some detail at least, something more than just hearsay?"

Reyan flinched as he turned a vindictive smile in her direction.

"It's as she says," he finished, nodding in her direction. "We need to think of our people before following into another of *your* wars."

CHAPTER TEN
SANNAR

Sannar held himself rigid with the unsettling warmth of Odella right next to him as the courts fought against each other in the main hall.

Don't look at her. Don't look. Just focus on the courts. Why did I think bringing her in here was a good idea?

He was sure she must have been able to hear his heart galloping but she was transfixed on the court meeting. Like he should have been. Pushing past the subtle scent of *brindleroot* that seemed to be coming from her hair, Sannar turned his attention to the meeting.

"I have it on trusted authority," Demi said, her voice tense.

"Whose?" the Lord of Revels demanded. "You can't tell us this without…"

"She is your queen, watch your tongue," Lady Leilania from the Flora Court growled.

Sannar raised his eyes skywards. "They're impossible."

"Yes, but what are they actually talking about?" Odella asked.

Demi banged her hand on the table moments later, silencing the entire hall and also the tiny passage Sannar and Odella stood in.

"I cannot lie to you," Demi thundered. "If I say it's trustworthy then I mean it. This court has been targeted by the Forgotten for information on the flow of origins, which we all know means the Forgotten hope to target the Prime Realm next. They've already tried to access information from this court, I'm assuming without the court's permission."

She eyed the assembled group but Sannar froze. When he turned his head to Odella, she shrugged.

"You asked me to tell her if you couldn't," she muttered, her cheeks pink. "So I did."

Sannar rubbed a hand over his face. "Yeah, but I meant if all else failed. Now I'm going to get slaughtered for not telling the lady before the queen."

Odella folded her arms, her elbow brushing his ribs and making him flinch.

"I'll tell them it was all me then," she insisted. "I'm not sworn to the court so I'll leave you out. Nobody need know you were ever involved at all."

Sannar sighed. "Don't do that. I'm just navigating how awful my job is going to be for the foreseeable future."

Ignoring his self-deprecation, she put her finger to her lips and gave him a prim look.

"Shhh."

He rolled his eyes and focused back onto the meeting.

"Why would the Forgotten want to go after the Prime Realm anyway?" Lady Leilania asked. "Nobody knows what's in there, or how to get to it. The mere existence of it has passed as nothing more than a myth."

Demi sighed. "It's true that nobody knows for sure but there are theories. Memories. Old tales told that have become legend. If the Forgotten are after information on the flow of origins, that'll likely be why. Perhaps they want a new realm to wreck without our interference, or maybe they hope it'll have lots of resources for them to ravage. Either way, we can't let them gain power again."

"What do you propose?" Kainen asked.

Demi shot him a grateful look.

"The Forgotten will attack," she said. "It'll probably be soon as well. We don't know which court they'll target, but if they can't get to you through coercion or persuasion, they may try other methods. I want to ensure we have a united front before that happens."

Reyan glanced at Kainen before standing.

"You have our loyalty and allegiance," she said, then hesitated. "The Illusion Court stands with you."

The room fell silent for several seconds. Then Lady of Words stood.

"The Court of Words stands with Queen Demerara and the royal family of Faerie," she said.

"She's a lot more formal than Lady Reyan," Odella muttered.

Sannar nodded. "Demi and Reyan are friends already."

"Oh *Demi* is it now, and so easily?" She grinned at him and he rolled his eyes. "It's okay, you're not special. She told me to call her Demi too."

Sannar muffled his urge to laugh. "So neither of us are special. Lovely."

They fell silent as Lord Rydon of the Fauna Court rose to his feet.

"The Court of Fauna stands with Queen Demerara and the royal family of Faerie," he said.

Sannar had no idea when, but as he lifted his hand to wipe his forehead, he found Odella's fingers tight around his. He glanced at her, noticing the wide-eyed horror on her face.

"She's going to make them show their truths now," she murmured. "She's got guts."

Not wide-eyed about the hand holding then.

He inhaled a shaky breath. "She always has been brave by all accounts, not that I know her well."

Odella squished his hand even tighter. He couldn't shake her off, but even though tiny fizzles were tingling up his arm from the contact, his fingers were losing all hope of feeling.

"That only leaves Flora, Revels and…" she turned to him, her mouth dropping open. "And Nether."

He nodded. "I reckon our lady will leave her answer until last. She doesn't like the fact Demi is so young and already a queen, or that Demi hasn't shown the usual arrogance of insisting on dealing with her instead of slumming it with me."

"She's an idiot then." Odella snorted. "No offense. What will the two other courts do?"

Sannar eyed them, the Lord of Revels whispering with the older man at his side and a younger man standing behind him leaning over his chair. The Flora Court were in heated, hissed conversation with each other.

Demi sat back in her chair, still as a statue. Beside her the king consort's wings continued to flicker with flames.

"Flora will side with her," Sannar whispered. "They're just cautious. They have no protection if a war does come for them, at least none that I've heard of. The Revel Court though, they will argue for the sheer fun of fighting and I reckon Demi knows it. She could have approached each court personally one by one, but then they would find ways to wheedle out of it. Excuses."

"Of course they would. No decency these highborns."

Sannar might have agreed with her, at least in his head, but the Lady Leilania of the Flora Court stood while her parents were still muttering to each other.

"I can't speak for my mothers," she said. "They do however want to retire which the whole of Faerie finds baffling. Should I take over and the Flora Court becomes

118

mine to lead, then the queen and her family will have our court's support. The new ways have already benefitted our people and we don't want to go back to the days of being paranoid because we don't have some grand fighting force. We don't want to rely on others to defend us either."

She gave her parent's the brattiest look Sannar had ever seen, and that was saying a lot because he'd grown up with Odella. The thought made him smile as the Lady of the Flora Court stood.

"Our daughter has a point," she said with a sigh. "We want to avoid a war, especially one that could spill onto our soil and harm our people. *But* we can't avoid the call if it's come for us either. The Flora Court stands with Queen Demerara and her family. All we ask is that thought is given to those who cannot defend themselves."

Demi nodded. "This is why I'm determined to catch the enemy early. My court has extra defences and my protection, but do you really think I want the Forgotten storming Arcanium again? With any luck, we'll be able to challenge them before any of your courts get involved. But as is tradition, the courts are requested to agree and we've still two to hear from."

"Bold," Sannar muttered. "She could have passed it off as a majority and let Nether and Revels slink away, but she's forcing them to be open."

Odella's fingers slackened around his hand and he wondered if she finally realised what she'd done.

Unless she thinks I held her hand first. He tensed. *I'd never live it down.*

He waited several agonising seconds but she didn't let go. Another bout of whispering in the main hall ended with the Lord of Revels huffing at his companions and standing.

"My court will stand with the queen on this matter," he

said grudgingly.

Demi smiled sweetly. "I am relieved to hear you say that. I was wondering over the allegiance of your court for a moment then, because the Court of Revels and whoever is *chosen* to lead it have always supported the royal family previously."

The warning rumbled around the room, echoed in the flare of firelight from the king consort's wings and the paling of Demi's skin as the air in the room turned cold. Then she tapped her hands on the table and the air seemed to right itself, as though the warning had been nothing more than a momentary hallucination.

"She's a bit scary," Sannar whispered.

Odella nodded. "Yeah, she's amazing."

"I have FDPs I can call on to monitor the Forgotten's search for the Prime Realm information," Demi added. "But short of sending FDPs into the hearts of your courts, I'd rather do this on trust. But be warned, you'd be advised not to mistake my trust for weakness."

"Excuse me, my queen." Lady Leilania stood again, her back stiff and her intention blazing. "We have links all over. Perhaps you'd permit us to keep an eye out also, ask a few questions of the right ears? One of our own joined the Arcanium ranks some years ago, so she should be able to vouch for our court's discretion and trustworthiness."

Demi smiled at that, her face lighting up instantly with undiluted warmth.

"She already has and I absolutely welcome your support. It will definitely be remembered."

Next to the Lord of Revels his two attendants were still whispering frantically in his ear. He stood, drawing Demi's attention and fading smile onto him next.

"We uh…" He sighed. "We are also well-linked to the

outer realms. We can assist the Flora Court where needed. Perhaps a party to draw out the nobles of both sides for scrutiny."

A look passed between him and the Lady of the Flora Court, both of them nodding a wordless agreement.

"Good, thank you." Demi leaned on the table. "Now then, the only thing we need to-"

Sannar closed his eyes in torment as he recognised the sound of a throat being cleared. He'd forgotten about his own lady seated right there on Demi's left side. But given the slow turning of the head and the absence of panic or embarrassment, Demi hadn't.

"Yes, Lady Aereen?"

Sannar couldn't help squeezing Odella's hand tight this time, but she didn't so much as flinch or squeak.

"You may have left one out, I fear," Lady Aereen said.

What a time for her to have one of her 'with it' days. Sannar couldn't think of a single thing to do.

"Maybe I can go in and ask if they need anything?" Odella whispered.

Horrified he hadn't thought of the idea himself and touched Odella had offered to do it for him, he tugged her toward the exit. They only made it two paces before Demi's voice filled their tunnel, strong and sure.

"Have I? I know certain theatrics are necessary for these things, but if the Nether Court wants to disagree or contest what the others have agreed to, please go ahead."

A Fae-like stab at the lady's lack of welcome earlier perhaps. Sannar didn't blame Demi for it either. He only wished he could have been there in his lady's place because the pride of the woman meant this would be moaned about for *weeks.*

Lady Aereen sniffed. "I simply believe the right

behaviours should be observed-"

"Like kneeling or at least bowing to your sovereign?" Demi asked.

Again the lady fell silent for several moments. This time, Odella squished past Sannar while still holding onto his hand and dragged him back into the storage room.

"We can't go back out there yet!" he hissed. "They'll know we've been listening. Also, I haven't closed the gap."

Odella rolled her eyes at him. "Well do that quick. Worst case we burst out and they'll assume we've been, you know."

"What?"

"You know. That."

Sannar frowned, searching the dusty recesses of his mind for some kind of reference that might-

"Orbs alive! We can't let them think that!"

Odella started giggling. "Wow, your face. I'm not *that* bad a prospect for a quick kiss in the cloakroom, am I?"

Sannar's cheeks burned, the heat spreading across his face even to the tips of his ears.

"You know that's not what I meant. But…"

He had no answer but she flicked her hand as if dismissing him so he rushed back into the safety of the tunnel to replace the shutters. Grabbing the little hook, he lifted his hand to cover the gap that looked out into the hall.

A resounding crash shook the entire mountain.

Sannar pressed a hand to the wall to steady himself and looked back down the passage to make sure Odella was okay.

The sounds of shouting echoed outside and he squinted through the viewing gap as every member in the main hall drew protection wardings and summoned gifts that sizzled through the air with the promise of a fight.

Letting the shutter slam down, Sannar shoved the hook back on its peg and rushed through the tunnel to Odella.

"Forgotten?" she asked.

He nodded. "Probably. I'll try and clear a path for you to get across the courtyard. Take one of the bikes and get yourself out of here."

She stared at him as moments passed, moments where he should have been charging out, issuing orders, making sure the lady was safe because she wouldn't be able to do much more than protect herself or dissipate into the nether and translocate to safety with so much chaos around. She had gifts, he knew that, but she wouldn't descend to using them unless she had to.

Not even to protect her own court.

Then Odella grinned spirited mayhem at him and the thoughts of his lady fled from his head.

He reeled behind her as she grabbed his hand and threw open the door to the hall.

"Where'd be the fun in that?"

CHAPTER ELEVEN
REYAN

Reyan darted after Demi as the rumble from the mountain died away and the shaking underfoot dissipated. Thoughts of the *Maladorac* slumbering deep in the tunnels filled her head and she jostled alongside the lords and ladies to exit the hall.

"Reyan, wait!"

Kainen grabbed her hand and held her back until she turned to face him, hair and skirts flying.

"I need to make sure it's still asleep," she insisted.

Comprehension dawned on his face and she took the moment of hesitation to tear her hand free. Before she could move more than a step, he grabbed her by the wrist.

"Stand still a second."

She obeyed, trusting he wouldn't be trying to trick her into behaving. He wouldn't dare.

He summoned the glittering black smoke to his fingers with a snap and in that moment she thought he was about to send her back to their court like a doll to be kept safe in a case. With a glance up and down, he flicked his hand at her and a tingle rippled over her skin.

The weight of the cloak disappeared along with the brush of air around her legs. She looked down with a gasp at the blue jeans now cladding her legs and her favourite black sweatshirt covering her body. Even the dainty slippers that went with her dress had vanished and in place was her favourite pair of boots.

Not a glamour, but an actual full reclothing.

"That's a court secret," he said. "Not a word about me being able to dress people by magic or everyone will be expecting favours."

She nodded. "Thank you!"

A brief smile flickered over his face, freezing as a loud scream echoed outside.

"I'm coming with you," he insisted.

"If it's awake, it's not safe for you. I can't sense it but just in case. I'm no fighter as it is."

"I'm coming with you."

"Kainen…"

"I'm coming with you, sweetheart, whether you protest or not. Last thing we need is you coming back with an army of snakes or something. You want to stand here arguing about it?"

"Stubborn arse," she muttered, turning on her now happily booted heel and dashing out of the door.

The sunlight streamed around them and she blinked against the glare as shouting and the sizzle of gifts exploded around them as the courtyard filled with fighting bodies. The crowd separated her from Kainen in one swift surge, so she stuck to the shadow of the mountain and gathered the darkness around her as best she could.

"Reyan!"

Kainen shoved someone she didn't recognise to the ground as he fought the sway of the chaos, his elbow slamming into the neck of someone else racing at him with metal pins dancing on the surface of their hand.

Reyan watched in horror. She had very little in the way of gifts beyond her shadow-merging ability. She'd taken defence training classes at court and she was handy with household tasks, but fighting wasn't her forte.

A woman darted toward her with a hand outstretched,

an eager snarl on her face.

Warding up!

Kainen's voice screamed inside her head and she unfroze from the jolt of fear holding her still. She ignored the demand and vanished into the shadows beside the door leading into the mountain. The woman came to a halt some paces away, looking around in confusion.

Kainen skidded to a halt beside them and the woman turned. She pulled some kind of air around her, the sensation of being sucked forward swelling as Kainen lashed out a hand to swipe the effect aside.

The woman produced a long thin sword next, from where Reyan had no idea, but Kainen was unarmed and for some inane reason, grinning widely.

"Thalia, it's been a while. Still fighting the bad fight?"

The woman, Thalia, swung the blade in a swift arc. Reyan gasped but it rebounded off of Kainen's warding as though his protection was made of granite.

"Traitor filth," Thalia spat. "By all accounts you've renounced the true ways."

Kainen clicked his fingers, summoning smoke that roiled around his hand. Reyan could almost feel the pull of it, as if the shadows wraithing her body were calling out to him.

"I've renounced the Forgotten, or whatever mad name they're taking on now. Stepping on other people instead of standing on my own merit lost its charm in the end."

He sent out the smoke but Thalia sliced through it with her sword and it domed around her warding. Reyan watched it scatter.

And sprinkle down behind her like dark snow before fading into nothing.

She's shielding. Not a full dome, just frontal protection.

"You'll be the first one she tortures personally traitor," Thalia added. "You and that bloodless whore you've taken alongside you. She'll scream for mercy long before the end, if she even has a mouth left to scream with."

Reyan didn't care about threats or what she got called, but Kainen apparently did. His eyes turned inky, the smoke curling up his arms and rippling from his face. She'd never seen him do that before, not from the eyes.

Worried he might end up killing someone given the pure fury slashing his mouth, Reyan dodged out from the shadows and shoved Thalia toward him from behind.

"Call me what you like, even I know you ward front and back," she shouted.

Thalia landed on her knees, twisting with the sword in hand and somehow managing to vault back to her feet in one fluid arc.

Uh-oh.

Reyan flinched backwards. Thalia had to keep both her and Kainen in sight, but Kainen's fury was still a serious threat. He had the ability to twist minds and cast visions, but the glittering smoke swirling around him had thickened enough to choke.

Thalia slashed her blade at Reyan's middle without warning. Reyan ignored Kainen's roar, dredging the shadows into the sunlight with great effort and using them to dodge the sword. She twisted behind Thalia again, slamming her elbow with her whole weight behind it into Thalia's back.

Before Thalia could ward herself, Kainen was on her, the black smoke wreathing over her head.

"Try to touch her again and I will kill you," he snarled.

Reyan stood panting with fear pounding through her chest. She could hide and defend but she was outclassed to fight anyone on her own.

Across the courtyard Sannar and Odella were sending balls of what looked like bare rock sailing into the crowd. Taz and Demi stood taking down multiple enemies at a time with deft coordination as a team. But Reyan had Kainen to worry about, and he seemed more likely to destroy than to disarm.

She sent her mind out to him, trying to stay calm when her skin was buzzing with adrenalin and her heart was racing too fast for her breathing to regulate.

Okay, calm it down. I don't need the vigilante dominance routine right now thank you very much. I need to get to the Maladorac.

The wretched darkness voiding his eyes turned to her, soulless to the depths. She held her shadows around her, the dark of her beseeching the darkness inside him.

Thalia's arms were still visible but she was struggling, her hands clawing through the smoke as her legs flailed. Reyan ignored the wholly natural echo of fear urging her to run and walked the few paces to Kainen's side.

"Let it go," she begged. "She's not worth it."

She threatened you.

His voice was deathly quiet, circling around her mind despite the crash of the battle.

Reyan reached out a hand. "I don't care. Let the darkness go right now, please. For me."

It was a mad idea to assume that he'd do anything for her, let alone push through whatever gift-mania he seemed to be suffering from. But the smoke receded from around his eyes, the normal brown colour reappearing.

"Tell me what the Forgotten are planning," he demanded.

While focused on Thalia he didn't glance Reyan's way

once, but she held firm when his fingers snaked around her hand. She'd deal with the freaky possessiveness and the fact he'd apparently lost himself in his gift later.

Thalia struggled, a worrying gurgle coming from inside the smoke.

Reyan grimaced. "We won't hear her if she can't breathe."

"Fine. Answer me."

The smoke receded and Thalia fell still, the only sign she was still alive the subtle gasping that huffed in through her slack lips.

"Go… die… both of you."

Kainen dropped his hand to his side. "Swear-block for protection. I can't compel it out of her. Come on."

Reyan gasped as Kainen pulled her around the edge of the courtyard and toward the entrance to the tunnels.

Floundering with the fast pace, she sought for something to say to calm him down as they sped into the mountain and down the tunnel toward the iron door.

"Okay, I'm not going to push this, but you freaked out back there, and I'm- *Hey!*"

She lost her breath as Kainen spun her around. His hands landed on her shoulders and her back hit the wall of the tunnel.

"What colour are my eyes?" he demanded.

She blinked. "What? Brown but they were pure dark while you were trying to- I don't know what you were trying to do to her."

"You can't protect yourself," he snarled.

She frowned. "I do okay. I can vanish anyway so I don't need to protect myself."

He shook his head, his gaze drifting back down the tunnel toward the dim glow of light.

"You barely have any gifts to trade on as it is and you're the lady of our court. Who ever heard of a lady with no gifts?"

Realisation dawned as his head turned and he glared down at her, his chest puffing up and down with fury.

He was mad at himself. For not thinking ahead to gifting her with protection or power. For not considering that his new enemies would take her as the first available target to get back at him.

"You're saying I'm an embarrassment?" she asked, hoping her indignation would unseat his anger.

He sagged, his shoulders rolling forward and his forehead almost bouncing off her chin. She had the idea she should be patting his back or saying something to reassure him, but there was a whole battle raging outside and she was supposed to be checking the *Maladorac* was still asleep.

"Of course you're not. Half of Faerie is probably wondering what you see in me other than my title. But you don't have the standard gifts most court Fae and those from noble families get, like speed or charm or enhanced sight."

"I don't need charm, and sure speed or sight would be handy." She put a hand on his shoulder to steady them both. "But most people don't get those chances. Most people aren't court Fae or from fancy families."

"Maybe, but for as long as you're lady of our court it's my job to protect you, or at least ensure you can protect yourself. I'll think of what best to gift you with, don't worry."

Unnerving as the declarations were, she knew he was acting out of guilt.

"Look, dramatic lord stuff aside, gifts or not, I need to keep going," she tried.

He chuckled, the sound grating out of him in waves of self-deprecation.

"I know. Give me a second. I'm sorry."

Reyan bit her lip. He sounded devastated now, and she couldn't feel any sense of the nether beast awake in the lower tunnels. The shadows were still, silent and heedless of the mayhem raging above ground.

"Is she an ex-girlfriend or something then? The one that attacked us?"

Another chuckle that sounded less tortured than the previous one.

"No. Member of the Revel Court who used to visit a lot. But I lost control. She threatened you and I lost it. I've only done that once before, and that was to protect my mother from my father. I failed back then. I was so determined not to fail this time too."

"Well, mission accomplished," she muttered.

"I think maybe because the court sees the whole thing between us as real my gifts do too, because they're tied up in the court, maybe, I don't know."

She'd never seen him babble before. Talk eloquently at length to confuse people, definitely, but never once had she seen him that out of control, that *vulnerable.*

Instinct put her hands on his forearms, fingertips rubbing back and forth over the soft fabric of his jacket in some vague hope of soothing him.

"It's okay though. You didn't do anything others haven't done in defence. She attacked you first."

He sighed. "No, that I can handle. People attack me more often than you'd think in one way or another and I'm fine defending myself without losing control. But I can't handle people attacking you."

"Okay, well practice it, I guess. You want me to step

131

down? We can tell people we broke up. Then the court won't see me as your lady and you won't be so driven to protect me. The other courts will be thrilled."

He lifted his head at that, panicked hurt shining in his eyes and her heart gave an almighty thud.

Oh boy, this is getting way too serious.

"There's no need to go that far," he insisted. "I'm fine. It won't happen again. I'll make sure of it. Come on, you need to check the beast."

She nodded. She could sense the *Maladorac* was still sleeping from where she was, but Kainen needed to walk off whatever internal stress he was suffering from. The last thing they needed was him going back up to the fight and accidentally killing someone. She reassured herself that Demi would have it covered and didn't argue about Kainen holding her hand tight as they started down the tunnel. She couldn't think of anything reassuring to say so she went for inane nonsense instead.

"That meeting was pointless, wasn't it?"

He nodded. "None of them are going to risk saying they support the Forgotten, even if they do. But it showed us which ones we need to be wary of at least. I also need to tell Demi about Thalia because she was best friends with Belladonna. She said, 'you'll be the first one she tortures personally'."

"Were you friends with her too? Belladonna?"

She risked a glance and saw shame light in his eyes.

"Both Belladonna and Thalia, yeah. I decided when I was sixteen that distancing myself from them was wise because they were known for being extreme and I wanted to get FDP experience before taking over from my father. Actually, I wanted to crush him, and contacts in the FDP world are worth a lot."

She shrugged. "I had a friend once. He wanted to be a goods transporter so he could see the whole of Faerie."

"Boyfriend?"

She snickered. "No, we were six."

"What happened to him?"

"He became a goods transporter and last I heard he was travelling the whole of Faerie." She caught his eye and smiled. "I didn't say it was a good anecdote, or even a relevant one."

Kainen rolled his eyes and stopped when she did. The sound of the battle was almost inaudible now and she shook her head.

"No sense of the beastie. We should be okay to go back up."

He nodded but didn't make any move to turn back. Instead he rotated her to face him.

Uh-oh. She gulped as her gaze met his. *Big flashing-light-style danger zone. People are fighting and we're here staring at each other.*

She flinched as his fingertips skimmed her jawline, his thumb stroking down her cheek.

He's an actual court lord and I'm just a fake lady.

"I don't care about that," he murmured.

Crud, he must have somehow picked up my thoughts. On purpose? This can't happen.

She forced her brain to stop thinking because she couldn't risk any more thoughts transmitting to him. Or maybe he was saying he didn't care about the sleeping nether beast and going back up to the battle. All she knew was that his face was blurringly close now.

"It has to be this way!"

A loud screech filled the tunnel. Reyan froze as Kainen twisted to face the origin of the noise with a feral grumble.

"Into the shadows quickly," he hissed.

She glanced around the tunnel and shook her head.

"No, in here."

He didn't resist as she grabbed his hand and pulled him through the nearest doorway, pushing the door mostly closed behind them. The room was cluttered with furniture, enough to hide behind if someone opened the door, but it rambled a fair way back.

Memories of the latest *Carrie's Castle* book she'd been reading where Carrie and Malachi had been stuck in a broom cupboard filled her head. She fought the ill-timed urge to giggle. Hysteria bubbled up but at least she had room in there to give Kainen space. She would deal with the whole 'he was about to kiss me' thing once her brain had time to unfreeze from the shock.

The moment she dropped hold of his hand, he reclaimed it with a stubborn frown on his face.

"The attack doesn't sound like it's still going." A female voice echoed close to the door. "Do we flee?"

"Flee? What do you think we are, cowards? We have what we came for. If the Prime Realm is based in the human world as we thought then we need to find where and how to get through."

Reyan winced. She recognised the first voice well enough having been on the receiving end of Blossom Elverhill's threats not that long ago. Despite being Taz's sister and a princess of Faerie, Blossom had apparently thrown in her chances with the enemy.

They've not found out about the keys by the sound of it, whatever the keys actually are, but at least this is confirmation that the Prime Realm is they're looking for.

Kainen caught her eye.

"*Belladonna*," he mouthed.

Reyan suppressed a shudder. She'd heard scary things about Taz and Blossom's older sister through rumours in the Illusion Court, including mentions of her enjoying tormenting people for the fun of it and 'dabbling' in torture.

"We incited an entire group to distract them and keep them out of the way so it'd be safe, and now it's gone," Belladonna seethed.

Reyan inched toward the gap between the door and the frame, dissipating her body into shadow as she peered out.

"The shell was still there so it must be down here somewhere," Blossom insisted. "We can find it."

"How? These tunnels span the entire mountain. Do you know the amount of favours and jewels we had to trade to get a shadow-snake egg? And it's gone, a total waste of time and resources."

Reyan flinched as Belladonna came into view. She almost dodged back but in her shadow form she was all but invisible to Fae eyes.

"We can ask someone to keep an eye out," Blossom suggested, her tone wavering. "They keep the iron door shut, but we can have someone sneak down and keep looking."

Belladonna scoffed. "You do that. You run around wasting your time. But we need to move onto the next part of the plan. We have the base for our court and Lorens is getting us the location. All we need to do now is find the key."

Reyan inched away from the door. The footsteps grew quieter as the danger walked away, but the furrow in Kainen's brow suggested he was as worried as she was. She let her body re-form and folded her arms across her middle, the information racing through her mind.

Belladonna had mentioned locations, a base for their court and finding keys.

Reyan stared up at Kainen, her heart pounding at the sheer focused dedication in his gaze. He was dangerously close to her once again.

"I think it's safe to go outside," she murmured.

He inhaled sharply and let a sigh tumble out, straightening up enough to lessen the tension. She didn't say anything about him keeping a hand around hers as he opened the door, but she managed to dredge up some previous irritation when he tried to walk off without closing it behind them.

"We need to-" She froze mid-sentence as his hand tightened around her fingers.

BANG.

Reyan flinched, instinct driving her body into the shadows as something searing hot flared toward them. As she dissipated, Kainen's touch never once wavered away from her. She sensed the warding he cast over them and reformed herself, relieved and petrified in one swoop as two women strode toward them.

She'd only seen Belladonna a handful of times at a distance but Blossom she recognised easily. Both women had the same honey-blonde hair as Taz, but the similarities ended there. Blossom's smart dress looked fit for a court appearance, but Belladonna wore a sharply cut white suit that screamed family money.

Reyan clenched her free hand into a fist as she realised Kainen had a point; she had no way of defending herself other than by warding or fading into shadow, not something that would help anyone except herself in a fight.

"A shadow-weaver." Belladonna tutted. "You've been hiding all sorts of secrets it seems, Kainen." She flicked an irritated glare at Blossom. "Although from what my sources tell me, you've claimed her in more ways than one. Bed-mate or toy? Or have you lost so many of your senses that you actually think you can claim her as your lady?"

Reyan sought through the mayhem of memories rolling around in her head. Blossom had seen her perform with the shadows a month ago, but perhaps she'd assumed it was an illusion rather than Reyan being an actual shadow-weaver. It didn't answer what they'd wanted with the shadow-snake though, or why Belladonna was now eying her like an interesting new specimen.

Kainen relaxed his body, a mask of sneering indifference falling over his face. It was the court lord most of Faerie knew and many feared.

"And that's your business how?" he asked, his entire essence screaming boredom. "Tell me, princess- no, not even princess anymore, is it? Tell me, outcast, what do you possibly think this little attack can achieve? Hoping to get to the queen?"

Belladonna stood with her hands in the pockets of her suit jacket, her white trousers pristine and perfectly straight.

A woman who probably doesn't descend to straight fighting unless she has to, not when she can no doubt flick a finger full of gifts as easy as breathing.

"Her time will come." Belladonna scoffed. "I could ask what you're doing down here, traitor. Hiding from the fight? That was always your style."

Kainen laughed, the sound of cruel amusement filling the tunnel. Reyan sensed the shadows pulling back from the malice inside him but she stayed at his side, standing as wordless as Blossom while their two counterparts fought out old scores.

"It's not only a woman's prerogative to change their mind, Belladonna," Kainen said. "I fought until I realised I was on the wrong side. Touching sentiments that I'm sure your stone heart can't fathom. You're unlikely to answer me and I'm not answering you, so we're at a stalemate."

Belladonna shrugged off her jacket and handed it to Blossom, rolling up the sleeves of her blood red shirt.

"How do you come to that conclusion?"

Reyan flinched as Kainen dropped her hand and his voice echoed in her mind.

If the warding falls, shadow to Demi. He gave her a fierce look. *I mean it.*

He couldn't command her now that she wasn't sworn to his court any longer, but he could still compel her. It had been a small mercy of his own personal growth that he wasn't already forcing her to obey, but she had no intention of listening. They could ward until they got out. If Belladonna wasn't attacking Demi, it was because she knew she wouldn't win, so she wouldn't risk going up to the courtyard.

Which means the whole fight is a distraction to keep watchful eyes seeing what they're doing down here. Reyan tensed. *They came back for the snake.*

"You want a fight?" Kainen shrugged. "Fair enough. I've been very good up until now, almost immaculate in my behaviour. Not sure Reyan would agree with that, but if you want to spar now I have nothing but time. I would suggest standard rules but you'd only break them."

Belladonna smiled wide, her face a portrait of spite and her piercing brown-eyed gaze dripping poison.

"You know me too well."

Kainen took a step back as Blossom handed her sister something, long, thin and smooth with a familiar metallic sheen that seemed to call through the shadows to the enormous iron door further along the tunnel.

She has metirin iron! Reyan threw the words into Kainen's mind as a warning. *Your warding won't be worth a percat if she aims right.*

He grimaced. *She never usually misses but I'll be fine. Go get Demi now.*

Reyan didn't hesitate as Belladonna lifted the arrow in hand, holding it like a throwing pole with the sharp end pointed directly at Kainen's chest.

Get Demi, a fabulous idea, but as Reyan tore through the shadows, the arrow left Belladonna's hand.

The zing of the metal wisped through the tunnel and panic tore at Reyan's mind, the emotions all-encompassing when she was nothing but sensation in her shadow form.

She lunged, reforming her arm in mid-air. Thoughts of wincing filled her as the flesh of her palm scraped the point of the arrow. A wave of fearful pain hit her from behind, the feeling of someone roaring in agony, but she closed her fingers tight over smooth coldness.

She reformed her body before Belladonna could recover from the frozen fury stamped over her face, darting back on stumbling legs until Kainen caught her.

"Get me another one!" Belladonna screamed.

Blossom dropped the jacket, her hands fumbling, but Kainen had one arm around Reyan's waist and his other in the air.

The arrow flew back the way it came, piercing through Belladonna's warding and sailing narrowly past Blossom's head.

Reyan dissipated and surged after the arrow, trusting Kainen to do whatever he intended to do. In that moment, for his redemption or their downfall, she didn't care how far he had to take it or who he had to hurt.

She reformed and grabbed the arrow, summoning her own warding and holding firm. She had the arrow inside her protection, but Belladonna and Blossom separated her and Kainen now.

She took a step forward, faltering when Belladonna dropped awkwardly to her knees, her body jerking as though she were fighting an almighty huge hand pushing her down.

"What are the Forgotten planning?" Kainen asked, his tone swirling with furious darkness.

Belladonna spat on the ground in front of her.

"Go choke on spikes," she snarled.

Kainen frowned. "Why attack the Nether Court? Rey, go and get Demi, now."

Reyan nodded and took a couple of steps back. She didn't want to leave him even though he seemed to have control of Belladonna, but that didn't account for Blossom still frantically muttering. If Blossom did somehow have access to another arrow, that would be Kainen done for.

"We needed what we hatched in the tunnels." She huffed over a choked breath. "Orbs alive, I'm going to kill you so slowly, make it hurt."

Reyan resisted the bubbling urge to hurl the arrow right into the back of Belladonna's head. Kainen flicked an irritated glance past them and Reyan stood firm, refusing to leave him.

"You'll regret this, traitor," Belladonna insisted.

She forced out a hand with great effort, Blossom reaching for her. Belladonna grabbed her jacket up from the ground as Blossom's hands touched her shoulders and both of them vanished.

Reyan sagged as Kainen stormed through the space

they'd left behind, his face pinched with fury.

"Keep your warding up," he demanded. "Let it merge with mine."

Reyan did exactly that. The moment he was beside her, he landed one hand on her shoulder and dragged her against his chest. She froze, rigid against him as he hugged her, then with a lot of effort she managed to get her arms around his waist.

"You're going to be the death of me," he said reproachfully. "I could have avoided that throw and you know I can skip back home at will. Of all the mad things to do."

"Oh." She didn't let go or look up, instantly feeling foolish. "I forgot you can skip, of course you can."

"Well, do as you're told next time. Did you hurt your hand?"

Reyan pulled back enough to bring up her hand between them. She hadn't felt a lick of pain while worried for him, but now she winced at the bloody mess of her palm.

"We'll get that seen to immediately," he insisted.

She shrugged, not wanting to think about it. It wasn't exactly a hardship to press her face against his chest and let him hold her, not when her head was swimming from the after-effects of adrenalin.

"I had to," she muttered. "All I could think was even if you dodged it, you said yourself she never misses and it sounded like Blossom had another one handy. I couldn't risk it."

He chuckled. "Worried about me? Be careful, people will start to assume you actually like me."

"You're lord of the court that's currently keeping me," she said with an undignified sniff. "Letting you die would be wholly unhelpful. What is it about this place? Every time you're here you get into trouble."

She let him turn her in the direction of the courtyard, his arm tight around her waist as they started walking.

"Tougher than I look, sweetheart, don't worry. But at least I managed to get out of her that it's definitely the snake she was after."

Reyan nodded. "It's something to do with shadows. She noticed me as well. If I weren't a shadow-weaver she probably wouldn't have bothered taking any interest in me at all. I guess at least she didn't call me a skinned rat like Blossom did once."

"Well she'll have to get in line if she's interested." He grinned. "Skinned rat or not, you're mine, sweetheart."

It precisely the taunt she needed and he knew it, something inappropriately harmless for her to fight against.

"That's hardly encouraging. Besides, you freed me so I belong to nobody but myself now."

He shrugged. "Well I tried complimenting you before but it didn't work. I can write you a poem if you like, but I'm awful at it."

She fought the urge to smile. "No thanks."

Fearful of someone overhearing them, she sent her mind out to him instead of her voice.

At least we don't have to worry about anyone claiming Betty back now. I'm not letting anyone give her to the Forgotten.

Kainen's lips twitched. *Betty?*

Yes, and? That's her name.

She'd decided as much the night before, not sure where she'd heard it or why it had popped into her head, but when she'd used the name out loud, the snake had given a satisfied little hiss, so that decided it.

Kainen came to a stop again near the exit to the courtyard. There were sounds outside, but none that suggested the fight was still raging. Reyan stood still when he reached out and entwined his fingers with hers, his other hand taking her wrist to avoid her bloodied palm.

"What made you call her Betty?" he asked quietly.

She hesitated in case anyone was outside about to burst in, but all was still.

"I was trying names to see if she reacted. When I said Betty, she hissed and blinked which seems to mean she approves. Or at least it's the same thing she does when I put her somewhere really dark. Why, do you have a problem with Betty? Not mysterious enough for the Illusion Court?"

She smiled at the thought, that Kainen might expect her to name the snake something cool and edgy like Viper or Venom. He shrugged, his gaze fixed on their hands.

"It was my mother's name. Bettina technically, but everyone who loved her called her Betty."

Reyan's insides crunched tight. She opened her mouth to backtrack, but Kainen lifted his head and caught her eye.

Don't start gabbling about changing it, he whispered into her mind, predicting her next move dead on. *Betty the shadow-snake, who is safest at our court. We should be fine to go back outside now.*

Reyan nodded. "We've still got no idea how they got in here if it's impossible to skip in without permission."

She was wasting time now but when they went back upstairs she would have to have her hand sorted out which would hurt. She'd have to resume the lady role which was tiresome and have Kainen at his social best, which was irritating, especially when she knew the real him lurked underneath the lordly mask.

"It's worrying," he agreed. "I'll keep a warding over us for now until we know we're safe. Then when we get home I'll have a think about what to gift you with. Something cool and fitting the lady of the Illusion Court."

She sighed. "We need to get to Demi and tell her what we've heard before we plan anything else."

"We'll do all that, but I don't want you fighting until we know you can protect yourself properly. The last thing I want is anything happening to you."

Thoughts of his previous possessive behaviour filled her head, and she was almost sure he nearly kissed her before Belladonna and Blossom interrupted them.

I need to stop any misunderstandings. We can't have any kind of real relationship while we're faking one.

"I can defend myself fine," she mumbled. "Also, I'm not sure I'm ready for any kind of relationship right now. Not a real one anyway. Not that I'm assuming you're assuming that, but the whole possessive thing, I'm not... you know."

The words burbled out but even though her cheeks were burning and she could barely meet his gaze, it had to be said. He might be thinking that kissing her was a random, passing impulse or he might have convinced himself that he fancied her. But after a whole life being tied to her father's whims and then those of the court, she wanted to cling to her newfound freedom a while longer.

The realisation that perhaps he wasn't going to kiss her at all filled her head and her pulse started to thunder again.

Kainen smiled, a small, soft curve at the corner of his mouth. She froze as he reached up and pushed a strand of hair behind her ear.

"Alright, sweetheart. Continuation of our fake engagement it is. Can I still hold your hand?"

She nodded. "Previous examples of pretence that are necessary are fine."

They started down the hall toward the eerie waft of quiet now coming from the courtyard. When she looked his way, she caught him smirking.

"What?"

He grinned wider. "So you go back to kicking and spitting and poking me, and nagging me about my socks. And I go back to calling you sweetheart and holding your hand and sleeping in your bed. I've had many worse relationships."

She rolled her eyes. "That's not what I meant. Wait, how many?"

"A gentleman never tells."

"A gentlem- You know what? We need to find Demi and tell her what we've heard, so you be quiet until we get there."

She was dying to push and insist he tell her what kind of relationships he'd had already, although she could well imagine given her time at the court and the kinds of people he used to hang around with before the recent war. She wouldn't descend to asking, but even so his smile could have lit the entire network of tunnels.

"Yes, dear."

CHAPTER TWELVE
ODELLA

Odella had no idea what she planned to do beyond dragging Sannar outside when the enemy struck. They caught the tail end of the lords and ladies rushing out to the courtyard, but nobody noticed them as they charged into the chaos hand in hand.

Without waiting to discuss a battle plan, Odella threw up a protection warding, but she flinched when it batted against Sannar's already firm one. His was invisible whereas hers tended to keep a pale blue hue to it, and she could see where hers was pulsing outward and being blocked.

"I'm better at wardings than you," she said, arrogance overtaking the realisation that he might be better than her at everything now given his court training. "I'll keep us safe while you attack."

He stared at her as gifts started to whizz around them.

"What do you mean? Get to the lane and down to town now!"

Irritation swelled and she glared back at him. "I'm not leaving. Come on, do your tornado thing."

He seemed to be considering several possible options, his eyes wide with disbelief aimed at her, but she held her ground. She wondered briefly if he was considering trying to bundle her over his shoulder, but she'd like to see him try given how sturdy she was.

Someone rushed them, pushing against Sannar's warding. Without looking he flicked a hand out toward them and a gust of air sent them flying across the courtyard. Surprised at the ease he'd managed to do it with, Odella gulped.

"Please, let me help."

"Orbs alive, 'Della, you're going to be the death of me," he grumbled. "Fine. But stay inside the warding, got it?"

Realising she'd essentially asked his permission rather than battered him into conceding, she wrinkled her nose and stooped down to press her fingers against the earth. With her gaze fixed on him as he created several mini whirlwinds to attack different people with, all the while holding the warding above them, she begged the courtyard stone beneath her fingertips to yield. The moment her gift zinged into it, she grabbed a handful and moulded it into a crude ball.

"Here, think fast!"

Sannar looked her way, registered what she held in her hand and opened his mouth to protest as she threw the ball toward him. He struck out his free hand and sent it flying through the warding, wincing as it hit a woman right on the behind.

"Your gift has come on a bit," he said through gritted teeth. "Okay, truce?"

She raised her eyebrows. "Were we fighting?"

"Not anymore. Pitching practice?"

She grinned and gouged another clump of rock from the ground, forming it into a rough sphere the size of a tennis ball.

"When you're ready." She didn't wait for him to be ready, throwing the rock-ball at his face.

He lifted his arm high and swiped it through the air, his gift catching the rock and sending it flinging into the crowd.

"Nice shot!" she shouted, already throwing him another one as his levitation gift turned them into a two-person batting team.

She started laughing, the sensation closer to hysteria as they worked together. Sannar grinned, his face alive and flushed with exertion as he sent her rocks out along with little gusts of his gift where needed.

Just once Odella caught sight of Demi, her frost and fire taming the edges of the battle even as Taz fought beside her with a blade in hand. They moved as one unit and Odella glanced at Sannar as he sent another of her rocks flying into the battle.

A whip came at them fast, a length of leather wound around some kind of bulging red-brown vine, the lash headed straight between them. Sannar was occupied with his flurries and she panicked. Darting sideways, she heaved through the line of his protection and separated herself from it. She couldn't see the lines of his warding but as the whip cracked into the ground right by her feet where the ground was still pliant from her gift, the force of the attack lifted her clean into the air.

Someone was yelling, but as Odella threw up her own warding and encased herself in pale blue, the whip lashed at her a second time and the force of it knocked her sideways. She crashed onto her shoulder, rolling onto her back and falling still.

Her breaths weren't reaching her insides, each huff pointless as her head swam. The sound of the battle was distorted and she tried to get her thoughts clear enough to regroup, to stand.

I can't leave him to fend for himself.

Even though he'd proven he was capable of fending for himself, clearly more so than she was, the thought forced her eyes open.

From her slumped position, she could see a tilted view of the courtyard. And Sannar gathering his gift as the man, a mere blur of brown and green, lashed his whip at her again even though she wasn't moving, wasn't a threat.

Sannar roared something she couldn't understand and formed a hand from of the wind, the air shivering in the faintest lines of a fist as the fingers closed around the whip. With an almighty pull, he yanked his gift back with all his might.

The man let go of the whip and stumbled forward, jolted off course by Sannar's fury. The face swam past her line of sight and she gasped, recognising the man who'd tried to get into the upper levels before. She watched spellbound as Sannar summoned many irate flurries of air, whirling them around the man's face until the man sagged and dropped to his knees. Moments later he keeled over, unconscious.

Stop now, Odella begged without opening her mouth. *I'm okay.*

As if he'd heard her, Sannar released his air and staggered to his knees beside her. She wanted to tell him to recast his warding over them, but he already had his hand out to hold one. His eyes were half-closed, his face flushed and sweaty. Even without touching him, Odella knew he'd be too hot, that he'd come close to exhausting his gift.

"Odella!" He shook her shoulder.

She blinked at him, noting that his breathing was off and his eyes seemed to be filmy with the threat of tears.

He's that upset about me being hurt? Is he going to yell at me for leaving his warding?

The mere thought of it tickled some instinctive part of

her, and when she laughed, Sannar's horrified face only made it worse.

Even when he pressed his fingertips to her cheek, possibly worried she might have been hit with some kind of madness or some invisible pain was making her delirious, she couldn't reassure him as laughter turned into hiccups.

With all the strength she could muster, she huffed in a few breaths and calmed the laughter.

"Don't be such a drama queen," she grumbled. "I'm fine."

She smiled wide to prove it, even though inside it felt like her bones would rattle if she so much as twitched, but he wasn't smiling back.

His gaze caught hers at the same moment she remembered that his hand was still pressed against her cheek.

"You left the warding," he mumbled. "Why in the name of Faerie did you do that?"

"It would have split us anyway. At least this way, he was focused on me and not you. Took your time hitting back at him though, didn't you."

It was ridiculously unfair and he scowled at her, his entire face shadowing with incredulous fury. Around them the battle seemed to be waning but Odella didn't want to look up and see what side was winning. She didn't think she could look up yet, with the odd sensation of the world still spinning around her.

"*Never* do that again," he said.

She pulled a face. "You can't tell me what to do. Why are you so bothered anyway?"

His face turned bewildered in an instant and his eyes caught hers again.

Why did I ask him that? Why? Now he's going to think I assume he fancies me or something, and then he'll try to let me down gently, even though I don't think he fancies me. He wants friends because this place sucks and he feels guilty for the reason we haven't been. That's all.

She shuffled her shoulders, then her hips. Convinced she hadn't broken anything, she rolled sideways to try getting to her feet, wincing when a slice of pain zigzagged through her shoulder.

"Here, stop trying to be a hero," he grumbled.

Before she could fend him off, at least verbally, Sannar had his arms around her waist.

"No, don't. Seriously stop. I'm too heav- Aah!"

She flailed her good arm and her legs as he sat back, heaving her body against his chest. With an incredibly un-Faelike grunt he staggered to his feet, her legs dangling. Out of all their friends, he had always been the tallest by a good few inches but he seemed to have grown taller since then, her toes not even scraping the floor as she dangled against him.

"Will you stop making things difficult?" he huffed. "First you leave the warding, which was an absolutely ridiculous idea. Then you play dead, and now you won't even let me help-"

"I wasn't *playing dead*!"

He let her feet settle against the ground before turning her so she could see his irritated face in all its scrunchy glory. Perhaps she should have been nervous, or at the very least worried he'd have her banned from the court. If he was anyone else he could have had her mum dismissed from her job or something just as bad.

But all she had was the irrepressible urge to prod the frown lines in his forehead. Preferably with the most annoying 'boop' noise she could conjure up.

"You're impossible," he told her.

She shrugged, then yelped when her shoulder pinged with searing agony. Sannar gave her a doubtful look before his fingertips landed on the collar of her t-shirt. She held her breath as he inched it sideways slightly, nowhere near enough to be accused of exposure but enough that he could see the top and back of her arm.

"That's going to need healing. We'll have Lindy take a look, come on. Can you walk okay?"

He twisted around to stand on her good side, his arm sliding around her waist. All around them the battle seemed to be over, people checking on each other and Demi issuing some kind of order about cells. Odella guessed they must have taken some of the attackers captive but it wasn't her job to ask, even though she really wanted to know.

She frowned instead at the familiarity of Sannar's hold on her, but the first step she took wobbled her shoulder and she seethed through her teeth.

He huffed. "I can-"

"Don't you *dare* mention carrying me. I can walk."

He might have smiled just a little. She risked a glance up at him as they walked, his attention solely on dodging people around them. His cheeks were still flushed and he looked exhausted.

He used his gift way more than I've ever seen him do before. Splitting air like that and forming it into shapes must take such a huge effort, and now he's all but hoisting me to the healer.

A plan came into her mind and she looked ahead to where Lindy was hovering. She noted the way Lindy's eyes flickered over both of them, settled on Sannar with a worried quirk of the mouth, then grudgingly returned to Odella.

"He used his gift too far because he's an idiot." Odella spoke up before either of the other two could. "Have you got anything to fix it?"

Lindy raised her eyebrows but Sannar only sighed loudly.

"I used it saving you."

"Yeah, which makes you an idiot."

"I'm an idiot for saving you?" He rolled his eyes. "Can you maybe tell me these things beforehand next time then? I'm fine, Lindy, but she needs her shoulder seeing to."

Lindy gave him a weary look and pointed to a high bench against the nearest wall.

"No fix for gift exhaustion except rest, none that I have access to anyway. But bones and breaks I can mend. Let me have a look."

Odella sank onto the bench and pointed to her bad shoulder. She flinched as Lindy pulled the neck of her t-shirt aside, but it was the tutting that unnerved her. As she bit her lip, Sannar sat on her good side and slid his fingers through hers without a word.

Why am I blushing? This is ridiculous. She refused to look at him, closing her eyes instead and pretending the pain was the reason. *I can't develop some kind of crush on him now, not simply because he's being nice to me. I'll fall head over heels for him and it'll happen again. I'll start liking him and he'll eventually remind me that he's part of a court now and I'm just a girl from town going nowhere.*

She gritted her teeth through the hot, needling pain that permeated her shoulder moments later. She didn't want to know if Lindy was using a gift of her own or some kind of healing balm. None of it would work on her mind.

Sannar's words from that day long ago, the ones that led to them not talking for four years, filled her head. They danced as clear as they had that day, as clear as they had every time she'd seen him or thought of him since.

'You can't come up and speak to me like this now, 'Della. You just can't. I'm part of a court and I'm going to need to make friends here. Important connections. I can't do that if they see some girl from town hanging around me. The others have already said things.'

She didn't wait around to ask what those 'things' might be; the tone he'd said it in told her enough. He never called after her either, that was what had hurt the most. Never came down to town to apologise, or to ask her to forgive him. Never bothered to send a note down even to explain.

Now here she was sitting with tingles all over her hand simply because he was holding it. Wondering what he'd do if she just up and kissed him. Wondering if that moment before where he'd stared into her eyes close to crying because he thought she was hurt was guilt or panic, or something more.

"There you are," Lindy's voice broke through her melancholy. "No heavy lifting for a while. Rest it tonight, then tomorrow move it gently to ease the stiffness. As for you young man, a day's rest. Even the rest of today knowing how indispensable you are. I'd have a word with *her ladyship* if you'd only let me."

Odella's eyes snapped open. Given the derision in Lindy's tone when she mentioned the lady of the court, and the subtle 'if only you'd let me', and Odella wondered if Lindy hadn't spent a lot of time trying to defend Sannar against his will. Lindy blinked in surprise when Odella smiled brightly at her, but Sannar was already groaning his way off the bench.

"Nice try, but I'm fine. Ah, here comes the queen."

Lindy disappeared like lightning but when Odella tried to take a step away, Sannar clung onto her hand. She let him, knowing she owed him for saving her.

"Well, that was eventful," the king consort said with a grin. "I've missed the fighting. Especially now I don't have to worry so much about Demi given she's one of the most powerful Fae in existence."

Odella smiled but a quick glance at Sannar and he was already marking out the damage to the court, assessing their numbers and the state of their guests.

Always working. She rolled her eyes.

"First proper battle I've been in," she admitted into the waning silence.

Demi smiled. "You did well."

"Not really, but I'd happily learn." She ignored the scrunch of Sannar's face that suggested she was testing his last nerve by suggesting it. "Luckily Sannar has all the answers."

He gave her his most unimpressed look but she simply blinked back at him, daring him to disagree with her.

"We have no idea how they managed to get in," he admitted. "The court perhaps could be warded better but it should be enough to keep uninvited people out at least. We need to find some way of identifying everyone."

"I suppose anyone can put on a nether brother robe." Demi sighed.

Sannar nodded. "They can but I would notice anyone I didn't recognise. I didn't see anyone unexpected wearing a robe."

Demi rubbed her chin and Odella almost beamed with pride at seeing her rainbow bracelet sparkling right there on the royal wrist.

I really have to find some way of asking her to endorse my flyers. Maybe not right now though.

Demi might have been thinking the same as she frowned at it.

"During the last war we had certain wristbands so we'd know our own even if people were glamoured," she said.

Odella flinched as the royal gaze swung to face her, determination firing in the bright blue eyes.

"How many of these could you make do you think?" Demi asked.

Odella stared at her. Sannar went one better and let his mouth drop open, which she thought was a bit overly dramatic.

"Um… Maybe seven a day? I have about twenty left from the last time I had a stall in town as well."

Demi nodded. "Right, make me as many as you can. Send the invoice to Milo care of Arcanium and I'll let him know to expect it and have it paid straight away."

Odella knew she should be weeping with delight or dropping to her knees in gratitude, but her brain was too busy calculating how much that would be and whether she had enough beads left to work through the night with.

"What do you need to shore up your court?" Demi asked Sannar next.

He rubbed a hand over his face and immediately Odella felt awful for adding to his stress. Even though he was still holding her hand, he'd probably forgotten about it and she was simply a burden hovering on the edge of his 'to sort' list while she was the one profiting from the whole thing.

If I get paid, I'll do something nice for him. Drag him down to town to see Mix and Sammy maybe. She bit down the urge to grin. *Not as a date or anything, but he needs a break.*

"The damage is minimal," he said. "Although to be fair, half of the actual carnage was Odella's handiwork."

"Hey!"

She stared around at the courtyard, heat creeping over her cheeks. There were small pits and furrows in the stone, but only in the one spot where they'd been fighting. A few smoking windowpanes, the odd bit of masonry missing in the surrounding walls that definitely wasn't her handiwork. Nothing that couldn't be fixed.

"Lord Bryson!" Sannar hollered, making her jump.

The lord in question hurried over, bowing low to Demi then to Taz. Now that she scanned the courtyard again, Odella realised that most of the other brothers and nobles of the Nether Court had fled inside, including the Lady Aereen, which left Sannar to mop up the aftermath.

"Are we all accounted for?" Sannar asked. "No damning injuries?"

Lord Bryson nodded. "Nothing that won't heal, and a few of the orb-munchers are in the Deep Keep."

Odella tried not to smile at that, knowing that 'orb-muncher' wasn't the kind of thing one said in the presence of royalty. But Demi didn't so much as blink at it, her expression never faltering.

"Tell me, Lord Bryson." She eyed him with that piercing gaze. "Who would you choose to succeed your lady when the time comes?"

Lord Bryson's face froze. His entire body went rigid, his brain no doubt ferreting fast through the possible comebacks that might work in his favour.

"Other than myself, you mean, my queen?" He smiled frantically. "I find Sannar does the multitude of court business these days, but I doubt many of the lords and ladies would accept an elevation to the position rather than a natural progression of rank. The Nether Court has always prided itself on clinging to tradition."

Odella slid her free hand behind her back even though her shoulder ached. She clenched her fist tight, willing her irritation not to show on her face. Sannar might have noticed as he squeezed her other hand in his when Demi faced him.

"And would you want the job if it were offered?"

No! Odella wanted to scream at him. *You'd be even worse off than you are now.*

She refused to let a single shadow of it cross her face, clenching her fist so tight she was sure her palm would begin to bleed or her bones would splinter from the force.

Sannar shook his head. "I lead from the shadows. But I suppose if I *were* to put a name in based on my experiences at court so far… well, you only have to look around to see who stays past the drama and who doesn't."

Demi did as he suggested, casting a look around the deserted courtyard before settling on a rather startled Lord Bryson.

"Noted," she said. "I'm going to go and crash for a while until the next grand hurrah, whatever that is. Might I give you one instruction though? Consider it a command if you like. Oh, that'll be all Lord Bryson, thank you."

Lord Bryson didn't look at all miffed to be dismissed, bowing four times as he hurried off. When Demi focused on Sannar once more, Odella couldn't stop the nervousness covering her face.

"One instruction," Demi insisted. "Take today off. Hell, take tomorrow off as well. Go have some fun. If your lady asks, tell her I've pulled rank."

Odella half-expected Sannar to protest. She waited for the inevitable resistance to spew forth, that he had too much to do, that he was grateful but he was fine.

Orbs alive, how I hate the word 'fine' out of his mouth.

"Okay." He nodded. "I'll obey that one. If someone can maybe make sure the injured are being looked after though, and someone will need to do a double sweep of the-"

Odella clapped a hand across his mouth, giving Demi a firm nod.

"He'll do as he's told," she insisted. "Or else."

Demi laughed and Taz gave them a wink before hustling her off toward the lady's quarters. The moment Odella dropped her hand, Sannar huffed at her.

"That was so rude!" he said.

"Well, so was you saying you'd do what she said then insinuating a hundred 'little jobs' that no doubt you would have ended up doing yourself." She tried to fold her arms but it hurt so she settled for folding one to make a point and looking ridiculous. "Am I wrong?"

He opened his mouth. Inhaled sharply. Froze.

Odella grinned. "Go and sleep. Or rest or, I don't know, whatever you lot do. Read something, or catch up with *Siren-Sing-Along.*"

"I have never in my life watched *Siren-Sing-Along.*"

She laughed. "That is very sad."

He let go of her hand but finally he was smiling and that was enough for her. She watched him carefully as he wrapped both hands around the back of his neck and groaned.

"Maybe you're right. Will you be okay heading down on your own? Do you want me to walk with you?"

She made a show of eying him up and down. "Would you make it back up the hill again if you did?"

"Probably not, but I'd try."

And he would. If I asked him to, he would without

159

hesitation.

The scary part of her chest, the one that seemed to have tightened feelings at the worst possible times, gave a petrifyingly sharp twist.

"Right, well. I'll come up tomorrow anyway, in case you need any help."

He nodded as she turned away. "'Della?"

"Yeah?" She glanced over her shoulder at him. "What?"

He smiled that smile, the lopsided one with the twinkly eyes that had started to make her insides go *'flgurp'*.

"Try not to tear up any more stonework on your way down," he said.

She stuck her tongue out at him and started walking without looking back until she was on the lane leading down to town and out of sight. She had a disconcerting feeling that what he'd actually said wasn't what he had intended to say at all.

CHAPTER THIRTEEN
SANNAR

Sannar walked through the deserted courtyard bathed in the late afternoon glow, through the empty halls of the brothers' quarters and into his room. Before he could even collapse on the bed, let alone kick his shoes off or wriggle out of his robe, the knocking started.

He stayed silent. The queen had told him to rest. He could pretend to be so exhausted he'd passed out.

But I didn't lock the door...

The handle turned and he knew he wouldn't make it to the bed on time to feign sleep.

"There you are." One of the brothers hurried through the doorway. "The whole place is in uproar. They didn't get anywhere near the research thank the nether, but a couple of walls will need resurfacing, the guests need hosting because they're threatening to leave again, and the lady is throwing a tantrum because you haven't reported to her yet."

Sannar groaned. "You saw the tantrum? What scale?"

"She was talking to the queen just now and she had her hair down. Like properly down, wisps everywhere."

Torn, Sannar nodded and let the brother escape. He shuffled back to the doorway and closed the door with a sigh. He could obey his queen for the sake of a day's peace, or save himself a lifetime of stress by going to placate his lady.

Demi asking about a potential successor for the court worried him too. He had no say in who was chosen but

Demi had asked him if he wanted the job. No false modesty there because he couldn't think of anything worse.

Maybe if 'Della was up here it'd be worth the prestige. Doubt she'd be impressed by a title though.

He shook his head but the sudden smile wouldn't dislodge itself. She'd let him hold her hand the whole time, even when Lindy was tending her shoulder. He'd seen the clench of her fist too when Demi had asked about who might take over the court, and Odella didn't want him to be the person chosen, that much was clear.

Despite his exhaustion, he started shuffling back and forth across the tiny square of floor in his room. Unlike the other brothers who shared rooms and dorms, he had at least managed to earn himself his own living space, the only perk of all the extra hard work he'd put in.

Even smooshed up in the small confine of the viewing tunnel earlier with Odella's scent surrounding him, he'd recognised what he was too young to realise before.

He was infatuated with Odella Dewlark. Had possibly been since before his mistake four years ago that was drenched in ridiculous arrogance.

Too soon to say anything though. She might not even see me like that.

He couldn't risk scaring her off. Emotion to 'Della was like water on a match. She had to come to conclusions by herself or she went on and on about being influenced. As much as he loved the idea of having another thing for her to rag him about, he didn't want her feelings or confusion over them to be one.

Another knock echoed on the door and because he was pacing toward it, he swung it open wide with all but a snarl on his lips. He froze with the expression stuck on his face.

"Demi sent me." The king consort marched into

Sannar's room and flopped onto his bed. "She says she has your lady well in hand, please don't panic. She will be returned safely to you in the morning."

Sannar stared back until Taz grimaced.

"Yeah she's not exactly smooth with the humour, but I love her anyway." He shrugged. "She said that she's brought in a couple of healers to assist yours, and Lord Bryson has been told to double the patrols on your levels inside the mountain. Oh, and one of our librarians has been brought in to discuss something really boring he read in some old manual about the nether. Your lot got *really* excited about that, so I'm guessing they're placated. The other courts have been released to go home, queen's orders, so you will have your peace back at least."

Sannar did the only thing he could do in light of being effectively rendered redundant. He sat down on the bed with a disbelieving sigh.

"You could go and spend the evening with your girlfriend?" Taz suggested.

"Ah, she's not my girlfriend. We were barely even friends a few days ago. Well, we were, but not for a while."

"You were, then one of you screwed up. You I'm guessing, no offense."

Sannar nodded. "The lofty assumptions of joining a court and thinking you're better than your friends. How much I regret that now."

"But never found the courage to tell her. Maybe even wrote it down on the odd occasion, binned it, burnt it, told yourself she'd probably have moved on anyway?"

"I... how did you know that?"

Taz grinned. "Experience. But she's forgiven you."

Sannar shook his head, then dropped it into his hands.

"I'm not sure. I mean, she said we could be friends. So

I'm being her friend. Then all this court stuff explodes and suddenly I'm dying inside because she's basically throwing herself at the Forgotten wanting to be a hero."

Taz's laughter all but rolled down the mountainside. Sannar winced as Taz clapped a hand to his shoulder and stood up.

"Yeah, they'll get you in an early grave. Almost literally in my case. But I wouldn't swap Demi for all the grey hairs and stress in all of Faerie."

Sannar rubbed his lip. "Funny, Kainen said similar about Reyan a while back. Shook his head and said he must be crazy because half the time he wants to strangle her, but only he's allowed to annoy her."

"Yeah, that's the one. Look, it's up to you what you do. But the Queen herself has given you a pass to escape the court for a day. Do you want to do the rounds other people are already doing, or do you want to wander down to town and see if… well, I don't know. What do people do for fun around here?"

Sannar didn't much enjoy the idea of going to town and doing what everyone else did. Not on his own anyway.

"I could go to the tavern, but my parents own it so it's not exactly my favourite place. Game hall would be open. The meadows are likely singing at this time of year, where the water in the river hits a certain note and the flowers pick it up and make it a rhythm as they move in the breeze."

That was what he'd do if he had his way. He'd take Odella out to the meadows with a picnic. She'd mock him mercilessly, probably insist she wasn't accepting him no matter how many *oia* berry-filled pastries he fattened her up with. Then, because it was her, she'd moan that she was already too stocky to be eating pastries and sit there waiting for him to give her a compliment.

Even the thought of it made him smile, so much that he jumped when Taz headed to the door.

"That's the one," he said. "Do whatever put that dopey smirk on your face. And do it now before you convince yourself otherwise. Oh, if you do go see her, can you let her know Demi wants a word with her as well? Nothing damning, maybe an opportunity to be had which she could use her gift for."

Sannar frowned. "Not sure she'd want to leave her family but I can ask."

"Also, we went to check on the Forgotten captives," Taz added, his face turning grave. "One of them is refusing to talk to anyone but 'the fetching girl he met in the mountain'. He described Odella pretty well, so Demi thinks the Forgotten might be after her gift too."

He left that lingering and left the room, Sannar struggling over a sudden surge of worry.

Sannar waited until Taz was definitely gone before heaving himself up and hurrying across to shut the door. He hauled off his brother robes and eyed the jeans and t-shirt. He wanted to go and speak to Odella right away, but that didn't mean he needed to stick out in his robe.

Should I put on a shirt? Would that look too obvious?

He sorted through his scant wardrobe, choosing a white t-shirt that fit nicely enough and throwing a black shirt over the top. Stopping short of shining his boots, he spent a few minutes despairing in the mirror at the state of his hair which needed a wash, but he didn't want to waste time when he had so little of it normally.

He crept out of his room and down the hall. He would be going to see Odella, but first he wanted to see the Forgotten captives for himself. Maybe ask them a question or two, issue the odd warning.

He strode across the courtyard and passed the two guards at the mountain entrance with a nod. Neither of them batted an eyelid as he walked to the nearest trundle and sent it rushing downwards.

With the soft breeze ruffling his hair, he closed his eyes and focused on pushing thoughts of Odella aside. This wasn't about warning the enemy away from her. Never mind that the thought of them trying to get her on side made his limbs jittery with anger; he was going down to see they were being treated and guarded properly, which was something he would have done in any other circumstance anyway as Chief Assistant.

The trundle jolted to a halt and he stepped out, his gaze catching on the collection of guards outside the Deep Keep. Not only nether brother guards but what looked like some of the queen's too. Dressed in casual clothing, the unfamiliar faces didn't look remotely dangerous, but Sannar had heard many a tale of what people from Arcanium were capable of.

They eyed him as he walked up to them, no sign of suspicion despite the fact they weren't looking away. Madeleine at least gave him a smile, someone he'd trained and done induction with during his earlier years.

"Doing the rounds," he said.

She nodded. "Don't be too kind. They've got mighty attitudes on them. Be careful with the one in the far cell too. He's feisty."

Sannar inhaled deeply as she unlocked and opened the door to the keep.

Odella's previous taunt that he slouched filled his head as he walked through the doorway, so he dragged his shoulders up and straightened his back.

"Ooh look, a new morsel. I recognise this one. Where's your pretty friend?"

The amused voice came from the cell in the far corner. Sannar made a show of eying the cells and the rest of the keep before settling on the face he already knew the voice belonged to. The man who had been stealing around the upper levels the day before stood in the furthest cell from the door, his back pressed against the wall and his entire aura lounging indolently around him as he ruffled a hand through his short brown hair.

Above all things, he was not only the man from the upper levels, but also the one who'd attacked her with the length of whip during the fight in the courtyard earlier.

"She's busy," Sannar said, keeping his tone even with great difficulty. "I'm here as part of the court to make sure everything's as it should be."

The man scoffed. "I'm sure your queen would see our incarceration as correct procedure. We however have places to be."

Sannar shrugged, keeping his stance relaxed even though his pulse had picked up to an alarming level since walking through the door.

"I can send apologies for the delay to anyone you like," he suggested. "Then again, I'm sure whoever you'd contact wouldn't want to be linked to the Forgotten."

The man clapped his hands once. "Very clever. No, we won't be giving you any names. Perhaps if your young friend were to ask however-"

"No." The word shot out before he could stop himself. "She's not available for people like you. Leave her out of this."

The man's face brightened even more, amusement turning to delight.

"She has a protector, how sweet. You think a mere servant to a court would be enough for a girl like that?"

Even though the taunt landed where it was meant to, Sannar kept his expression calm. The man had a point. Odella had always talked of jumping on her father's boat and seeing the world, or apprenticing to some far-flung court. Sannar had once dreamed of going with her, until real life intervened and a place at court became a possibility.

Joining a court for opportunities was a gilded lie if ever there was one.

"It's not about me," he said. "She has morals that you'll never be able to shake, and you won't be able to trick her. And you won't ever get close enough to take her. Whatever you want her to open, she won't do it for you."

The air seemed to freeze around them, a moment of still silence taut and ready to snap. Several pairs of eyes widened in other cells, and although the man held his expression well, his smile dimmed.

"Who says we want to open anything?" he asked.

Without any idea of how much the queen knew about whatever the Forgotten were after, Sannar didn't want to risk saying too much. Nobody knew he'd overheard the meeting of the courts, or that Odella had too. Whatever was going on with the Prime Realm and the flow of origins was far above his level.

"You saw her gift in the courtyard," he said, keeping to facts. "Your kind are always trying to get into places you haven't earned, like the upper levels here, so it's simple deduction."

He turned on his heel and strode to the door far too fast to play it cool. He looked back over his shoulder to find the man grinning wolfishly at him.

"Guard her well then," he taunted. "We tend to get what we want in the end. Tell the queen that too. Her borrowed time is already running low."

Anger rumbled through him mixed with irrational fear. Odella was safe in town and the man was behind *metirin* iron bars. No gifts could permeate *metirin* iron and no strength could break it. Yet something about the man's unerring confidence had wriggled into his nerves and sent them scattering all around his body.

"Tell her yourself," he bit back.

Throwing the door open, he strode out and managed a grimace to Madeleine before grabbing the waiting trundle up to the courtyard. The glow of the fires and the soft evening light did nothing to calm him down. He only had one thought thundering through his mind: go to town, find Odella and make sure she was okay.

"Sannar!" A voice echoed behind him.

Crud. He panicked and dodged into the kitchen. *I need to get out of here.*

Lindy looked up but he pressed his finger to his lips. She pointed to the back door that led to the storage bay and the steep steps winding down to a lower part of the lane. Pressing his hands together in gratitude, he fled across the kitchen with the sound of his name echoing behind him. He burst outside and clung to the rickety metal railing with tight fingers as he dashed down the cracked stone steps.

The sun was already fading on the horizon and his mind began to race alongside his steps. Odella would be exhausted and her shoulder would still be hurting. She might have gone home to bed. Him turning up randomly at their house would cause uproar, although he missed her dad's lively sense of humour.

Or she'd be in the tavern he guessed, complaining about

169

him to the people he used to call friends. He'd have to spend time with his parents if he went in there, or pretend to at least while they asked why he never visited. Then they'd speak about themselves the whole time until closing and he'd have to admit defeat and walk back up to the court.

He shook off the bitterness as he left the steps and continued down the lane, the lights of the town dancing up to guide him.

He wanted to see Odella. Everything else was just another hurdle. Another task he had to do.

I'm good at that, and usually the reward isn't as worthwhile as seeing her is.

He let that thought sustain him even as his muscles screamed from the walk. He knew he should be resting, recovering his connection levels in case the Forgotten struck again. The lady would be going mad, Demi or no Demi, and he'd have to deal with her once the other courts were gone.

He nodded to a couple of people he vaguely recognised as he walked through town, choosing not to dwell on them staring back at him. He guessed they recognised him but had no clue what he was suddenly doing there.

They must have heard the commotion floating down and felt the vibrations from the fighting.

The main street was cobbled and led past the two-storey shopfronts selling all sorts of wonders to those who drifted up from the harbour. It took a good twenty minutes to get to the actual harbour from town but the silver water glistened over the rooftops as the ground sloped down toward it. The shops were in darkness already as he passed them, but raucous noises of merriment rippled out from the large building at the end of the street.

He took a deep breath as he strode toward the noise and pushed the tavern door open. The noise inside wafted out, hearty chatter and laughter swarming over him. The tavern was the same as he remembered, the length of it rambling backward with sturdy tables and benches of dark wood slung any which way. The bar running along the wall on the right-hand side had a woman he didn't recognise serving behind it, and he wondered if for once someone had given him a small dose of good luck as he couldn't see his parents anywhere.

The familiar scent from his childhood hit him square in the nose, earthy, wiped down wood with a fruity tang of spilled drink. He shuddered and let the door drop closed behind him, aware that any longer lingering meant people would start watching him. He scanned the heads, wondering if he should have gone straight to her house first.

His pulse echoed an excitable thud.

Odella sat at a corner table made of an old beer barrel. He'd missed her on his first glance but now he could see her, along with two young women sitting opposite.

One woman said something and both laughed while Odella gave them both a weary look and an embarrassed smile. She had her jewellery-making supplies on the barrel in front of her and he wondered if he should tiptoe back out and leave her to it.

He had no right to hope she was talking about him to her friends either, although he guessed she would tell them about the day's events.

Mix and Sammy hadn't changed at all, aside from growing taller. Mix had cut her brown hair very short and Sammy had hers in long blonde braids. Both wore black jeans and t-shirts, but he noticed how Mix's little finger was curled in Sammy's hand. Then Sammy lifted her head and looked directly at him.

He froze. He hadn't seen either of them in four years, not since that day he'd behaved so badly. Sammy muttered something to the others without taking her eyes off him, but as the three of them looked over, none of them were smiling.

Odella murmured something to them before she lifted a hand and beckoned him over. Squeezing through the crowd, Sannar made his way to the table. He had a pouch of percats in case he needed to buy drinks, and he had every intention of going to the grocer next door if his entire plan, which was absolute madness, became an actual reality. But before he could convince Odella to take a walk with him, he needed to brazen out this moment he'd been dreading for the last four years.

"Hello."

He could barely hear himself over the hubbub. Sammy and Mix exchanged a look, then Mix held out a hand to Odella who delved into her pocket and pulled out a couple of percats.

"Hi Sannar." Mix nodded to the bar. "Been a while. Do you want a drink?"

Sannar hurriedly pulled out his pouch and jostled a handful of percats out. Mix took a couple from his outstretched palm and she and Sammy set off to the bar without another word.

"What are you doing here?" Odella asked.

She had a drink already in front of her, most likely *Beast Lite* given the dark red colour, and she sipped it as she looked at him over the rim. He stood beside her, reluctant to assume he could automatically join them.

What am I doing here? I can't tell her how I feel, not

172

here, not like this. Possibly not ever.

"I thought it was time," he said lamely.

She eyed him for a long moment then nodded. Setting her cup down, she patted the bench beside her.

"Past time, but what's done is done. Stop hovering."

Relief fluttered in his chest and he did as he was told far too quickly, sitting down and trying not to budge up against her too suggestively as Mix and Sammy returned with four mugs.

"So, you finally have some time off and you decided you'd come slumming it down here with us?" Sammy asked. "We're honoured."

Sannar hesitated. He guessed Odella had told them long ago about his behaviour and they would be rightly angry with him, but he wasn't sure if he should apologise and make a thing of it, or brush it aside and risk upsetting them even more.

"Shove over, Sammy," Odella said. "The poor boy's had a tough day."

Mix nodded, grabbing two of the mugs and pushing them across the table.

"So we hear. Ignore Sammy, she still thinks she's funny. Tell us all the gossip then." Her face softened when she caught Sannar's bewildered eye. "Any attractive boys?"

Sammy snorted. "What do you need to know about fit boys for? Am I not enough for you?"

Odella gave Sannar a 'see what I have to manage' look, and he couldn't help but smile. He hid it in his mug, taking a long sip and almost spluttering over it. He'd had *Beast Lite* before, a weakened version of the original drink which didn't give the same effects and left no lingering queasiness the next morning after too many, but he wasn't used to drinking any of it at all now.

"I wouldn't know," he admitted. "The court keeps me very busy."

Mix nodded. "So we hear. You should pop down more often though. Poor 'Della's been stuck with us and our double act for too long. Told her she needs a nice harbour man in her life but she seems more interested in- *OWW!* Why are you kicking me?"

Odella's cheeks were bright pink, visible even in the dim amber lighting of the tavern. She gave Mix a murderous look and Sammy started sniggering.

"Well, anyway, we should get going," Sammy said.

Mix frowned. "But I haven't finished my- hey! Stop drinking my drink!"

Sammy downed both of their *Beast Lites* and definitely had a jaunty sort of sway about her when she stood up. Mix rolled her eyes and hustled Sammy off the bench.

"Come back when you get a chance," she said. "We've missed you."

Sannar nodded but the two girls were already shoving their way through the tavern to the exit. He wanted to ask what the whole kicking under the table thing was about but knew he shouldn't.

He definitely shouldn't ask her.

"Dare I ask-"

"No." She flicked an embarrassed glare at him. "What are you really doing down here?"

He hesitated. "I wanted to see you."

Odella tensed, her gaze fixed on her cup.

"Why?"

Think, idiot, think! He wracked his brain, then Taz's parting words came back like Fae song.

"Taz- um, the king consort stopped by my room the

moment I got back to it. He said many a thing, but one was that-" he hesitated, glancing around them and leaning closer against his better judgement. "Demi wants to speak to you. Nothing damning, his words not mine. Something about an opportunity."

He sat straight again to give her space. He considered offering to move to the other side of the table, but if she wanted him to move she'd tell him.

"He didn't say what about?" she asked, gnawing on her top lip.

"No, but he was adamant it wasn't anything bad. She's also made me redundant in a few simple instructions."

Odella snorted at that. "Good. They don't deserve you."

Praise from her. The glee swelled inside his chest, puffing him up a few inches, enough to embolden him to push her that tiny bit further.

"So you're willing to help if it's something not bad?" he asked. "You could come up to court tomorrow as planned and give your answer then."

"Help with what?" she asked, her tone instantly indignant. "How can I give an answer when I doesn't know what I'm answering?"

She flicked a disapproving look at him and he downed his *Beast Lite* for extra courage.

"It's so loud in here," he said. "Can we go somewhere quieter and talk about it there?"

He waited with his heart in his mouth as she eyed him. He felt stripped bare in those agonising moments.

"Alright." She started piling her jewellery supplies into a cloth bag. "The meadows aren't far and the flowers will be singing. I'm starving though so dinner's on you."

CHAPTER FOURTEEN
REYAN

"This is nice."

Kainen's voice almost woke Reyan from her slumped position against the side of their bedroom window at the Nether Court. She'd flopped on the bench seat the moment they had spoken to Demi and told her about seeing Belladonna in the tunnels, then they'd helped wherever they could to secure the Nether Court. Kainen had disappeared to check in with Meri briefly but Reyan hadn't been snoozing for long given the waning sun still visible through the window.

She smiled as he sat beside her on the padded bench chair. With her cheek resting on the warm stone around the window, she barely had the energy to open her eyes, let alone entertain conversation with him.

I still have to work out how to handle what almost happened between us in the tunnels. But maybe not yet.

"Here, I brought you this," he added.

She turned her head and smiled wider to see him with a small bag hanging off his shoulder and cupped Betty in his hands, his fingers curled cautiously around her shadowy body.

"Is it safe to bring her back here?" she asked.

He nodded. "I reckon she'll be okay. Some of the Forgotten are in the Nether Court's keeping and the rest of them will have fled. This little one must have escaped the wardrobe and gone roaming though, because she found me in my study."

Reyan held out a hand but retracted it when Betty shrank from the light near the window.

"She can curl up in the bedsheets for now," she said.

She watched as Kainen groaned to his feet and ambled to the bed. Betty slithered into one of the dark creases, and Reyan turned back to the scene outside, the sun setting fast now and lengthening the shadows over the now quiet courtyard.

"I can't remember the last time I sat in the sunshine for so long," she murmured.

Kainen sank back down beside her with a weary sigh.

"Doesn't help the court has minimal viewing decks I suppose."

She shrugged. "They're there for the nobles that want them, but those in service don't always get access to be fair. I bet loads of people would love to sit out with a drink after work and watch the sun go down over the mountains with the river rushing beneath us."

"Consider it done, sweetheart. I'll arrange one of the decks to be for staff only."

Forcing her head away from the cosy warmth of the window-side again, she blinked sleepily at him.

"You'd do that?"

He opened his mouth but for a long moment no words came out.

"Yeah. I don't always think of these things. One of the downfalls of being entitled is that I don't always think outside of myself or those I care about."

Reyan smiled at the flat note in his voice.

"You just have to practice. See everyone as people rather than certain types of people. Value behaviour over heritage."

He leaned back against the bench with a sigh, clasping

his hands behind his head and arching his back with a groan.

"The lady is wise," he quipped. "I've decided what gift I want to give you, but want to offer it rather than give it without asking you first. Shows a lot of personal growth for me I reckon."

She chuckled. "What is it then?"

"Can't tell you."

"I- what? Then how do I know if I want it or not?"

He grinned. "You have to trust me."

"Ah, more games."

"Okay, I will tell you, but you have to guess first."

At least he was amending the game for her. Amused, she pursed her lips, pretending to think hard. She could throw out random guesses, but she wanted to figure out what kind of gift he might choose for her based on him and what he thought of her.

It would be defensive. Perhaps the ability to summon a weapon to protect herself with, or maybe a gift that pushed some kind of force outward. She'd seen Demi fight with her energy gift before and always wished for something cool like that. She'd also considered the benefits and pitfalls of an intellect gift. Being able to read the truth of people or hear their thoughts sounded good in theory, but she wasn't sure she wanted to know what they really thought of her word for word while they were openly smiling to her face.

"Can I ask questions?"

He nodded. "Yes, but go and lie down before you do. You look exhausted."

"Seriously? This is how you get girls into bed?"

His eyes lit up, the brown depths dancing with delight.

"Not usually. You're a special case. We can argue about

it for a while first if you like, or do you want me to carry you over?"

That was enough to coerce her to her feet, adamant that she wasn't letting him manhandle her. The bed was comfortable and wide, and she'd already built a barrier of sorts down the middle out of rucked-up blankets.

After checking for signs of Betty lurking inside the barrier, Reyan clambered onto the side nearest the window still in her clothes and wriggled underneath the covers, tensing with nerves as Kainen got in beside her.

"I'm going to push the Vast Wall down a bit, okay?" he asked, his hand on the top of the blanket barrier.

She nodded. "Fine. So, my gift. You know you don't have to, right?"

"Of course I do." His face appeared as the barrier slid down to beneath her chin. "Even with everything else removed, the engagement and the titles, I hope we're friends too. I care about you. If I have the power to make sure you're okay, I'll take it. You did the same for me after all."

She frowned. The mention of friends and the fact she'd once come for him when he was injured jarred in her head.

That should be reassuring.

She swept aside the sudden uneasiness and focused on the gift thing instead. She had his word that she could call their court home for as long as she chose, and she'd wanted nothing except her freedom which she now had. Which he'd given her.

"Speed gift?" She threw out the first thing she could think of.

He shook his head, his grin widening. "Nope."

"Charm?"

"Nope."

"Hmm. Sight?"

"Nope."

"Weapon summoning?"

"Nope."

"Anything summoning?"

"Nope."

She huffed, irritated. "Well I can't think. Superior sock-picking-up skills?"

"Oh orbs, I should have thought of that one. We could have all socks in a certain radius attracted to you like a magnet. But no. Want a clue?"

"No." … "Yes."

He grinned. "It'll help you use your shadows for attack."

That could have meant anything, barely even a clue.

Is there some way he can make my shadows poisonous? I don't want to risk losing control of that.

"Is it the ability to get rid of light?" she asked. "Like removing candles or fire without having to physically snuff them out?"

He frowned. "Another one I should have thought of, but no. If you trust me, I'll gift it to you now."

She hesitated. She did trust him, which most people would probably advise her against, but receiving a new gift without knowing what it might be was both an honour and a risk.

"Okay." She closed her eyes then opened them again. "Wait!"

He ignored the protest, his face blurrily close as he dropped a featherlight kiss against her parted lips, the touch lingering before he settled back on his own pillow.

A prickling warmth tingled through her body, permeating the skin right down through her bones to the very core of her being. She couldn't tell in that moment what was the sensation of the gift passing into her and the subtle flutters of shock from the kiss.

"What is it?" she asked. "How does it work?"

He smiled, his face full of warmth and affection, so much so that she almost couldn't bring herself to look at him.

"Transmutation. You can turn your shadows into solids or liquids, your water into air, your bedroom furniture into a river. I've asked Taz if he could maybe give you a cheat sheet on how it works because he has the same gift. He agreed once I insisted it was for you and not for me."

Reyan stared back at him.

"I- you- it's- *really?!*"

Even more startling than the realisation that she had such a cool gift now was the knowledge that he'd gone to the person who really didn't like him for advice about it. For her.

He chuckled as she sat up in a flurry of blankets, both of them ignoring the softly indignant hiss from somewhere near the pillows.

"Really. Eventually you'll be able to form shadows into shields or walls around you then pull them down again. You'll be able to turn people's swords into liquid steel before they can strike."

"Can I try it now?"

He groaned as she scrambled off the bed and grabbed the decanter on the table, pouring a cup of water.

"How does it work?" she demanded. "Do I just visualise it and wave my hand or something?"

"I'm not sure, sweetheart. Try it now once but then you need to rest. It'll take a while and a lot of practice before you can wield it at whim without getting tired."

Reyan sank onto the bench with the cup in hand and focused on the water in the cup. She visualised it becoming solid, freezing over, dissipating into air. Nothing she tried worked.

"It won't happen instantly," Kainen said, his voice soft.

Maybe he saw her anxious expression, or more likely he knew that she'd want to transmutate the realm before she could so much as turn ice into water, but she placed the cup back on the table and returned to the bed.

"Thank you. It's a rare gift too. I don't know anyone who has it, other than Taz but I don't really know him. What made you think of it?"

"Honestly?" He pulled a face. "I was petrified when we were attacked and I realised you couldn't defend yourself, but it was Belladonna with that iron arrow. Metirin iron might not melt or dissipate from use of a gift, it's too impervious, but you could use everything else to cage it or trap it if someone had an arrow pointed at you. Or you could turn the entire realm into a shield against them to keep yourself safe."

Reyan sat with that admission for several long seconds. He'd not only reacted to keep her safe in the moment of the fight before, but he was now calculating ways to keep her safe in the future too. It wasn't a standard gift given either; often gifts would be speed or charm or special sight, something 'cool'. But he'd spent time thinking it through for her safety above all else.

"Oh." She gulped. "That's a… it's a very valuable gift."

He patted the bed and she had to slide closer, to inch herself into place beside him despite the huge mountain of pillows and blankets between them.

"I can't think of anyone better to have such a far-reaching and potentially lethal gift, sweetheart. You're too virtuous for your own good."

She had to laugh at that. "That almost sounds like an insult coming from you. Well, thank you. I'll be really careful with it."

Kainen grinned, his spirited gaze capturing hers. She refused to make a fuss when he pulled the covers over her shoulders and tucked her in, even though her nerves were leaping like jitter-kneed toads. She wanted to talk and stay awake but the sheer exhaustion of the day and the transference of her new gift had her eyelids closing.

"I know you will," he said. "I think if anyone's going to worry about us, it's me they're going to be watching carefully."

She frowned without opening her eyes.

"You're not a bad person. I don't know all of what you've done in the past, but you're making good choices now and that's what matters. You could have gone the same way as the Forgotten did but you chose not to."

"You have more faith in me than I do."

"Because I can see you without the hideous waft of self-pity and drama."

"Ouch, sweetheart."

She twisted onto her back, her hand skimming up over the pillow.

"Kind of true, but you've always been nice enough to me. You didn't have to make any effort to get me free of my father but you did it anyway. You didn't have to change all your father's horrid customs but you still made a huge effort with that. You took on all that stuff during the war even though it put you in a really cruddy position on both sides."

He sighed but she didn't dare open her eyes. It was easier somehow to talk frankly to him without seeing him.

I did that last bit because of Demi though back then, he spoke into her mind.

She nodded. *I guessed as much. But assuming you're not into her now-*

-I'm really, really not. I hope she'll be a friend one day but I think I fancied the idea of her rather than her as a person. I can imagine being her boyfriend in any normal situation is exhausting, let alone with the crown and extra court trappings added on top.

Reyan snickered, the breath almost choking her halfway out as Kainen's warm fingers slid around her hand. She'd told him before that handholding was fine but there was no need for it now. Nobody was watching.

She said nothing as he twisted their hands toward him, but she twisted them back because she needed some pretence at control.

Then a savage yawn almost cracked her jaw.

"Goodnight, sweetheart. Dream sweetly, my lady."

"I'm not a real lady," she grumbled under her breath.

She was so exhausted that his reply was lost into the bittersweet nothing of her tumbling unconsciousness.

You are to me.

CHAPTER FIFTEEN
ODELLA

I basically asked him on a date. What in the name of Faerie is wrong with me!?

Odella walked alongside Sannar as they left the lights of the town behind and set off over the bridge fording the river. Soon even the rushing of the water had quietened to a burble rather than a gush and Odella was left with her frantic mind.

Sannar coming down to the tavern was unexpected. She could have guessed Mix and Sammy would flee, especially after they'd spent the first part of the evening teasing her about rushing up to help him out.

But she couldn't let Sannar know any of that.

"Did they say anything specific?" she asked. "About what the queen wants with me?"

Sannar blinked like she'd roused him from a very faraway thought.

"Not really. Taz arrived to reassure me that I wasn't to worry about anything-"

"Which only made you worry more," she interrupted.

"Exactly. But I can't exactly disobey a royal order, and I'd never get any peace if I stayed up there." He gave her a weary smile. "Not that I'm likely to get any around you either."

She pulled a face. "Did they say when they're expecting me, or if I need to prepare anything?"

"No, sorry. He literally said that she wants to talk to you about an opportunity, and that it's nothing bad."

Odella brushed her hands over the bottom of her t-shirt, making up her mind to dress a bit smarter in the morning. She'd assumed that helping out would mean getting dirty, but perhaps a skirt or a slightly smarter pair of jeans wouldn't make her feel so grotty next to Sannar, who'd apparently decided to dress up for the evening. Even when they were younger, she couldn't remember ever seeing him wear an actual shirt and yet there he was all smart.

They reached the meadow, the subtle lull of flowers making soft *whumming* noises as the air danced off the surface of the petals. High above the luminous moon gave them enough light to see the outlines of the world around them, and the broad stars twinkled and danced colourful points of light across the sky.

Odella risked a quick glance at him, relieved he was too busy staring at the scenery to notice. The subtle floral scent was fresh and the evening air warm which didn't help with the whole 'this really isn't a date' theme she was clinging onto. But she couldn't tell him that either.

"I haven't been out here for ages," she admitted. "If we go to the base of the cliffs though, nobody from the court can see us."

Sannar's eyes widened. "I hadn't even thought of that. The last thing I need is the Flora Court hollering down that they need an extra pillow."

Odella snickered and led the way along one of the well-trodden paths in the grass. She wanted to reach her favourite spot, wondering if Sannar would remember it. Wedged between a crop of the cliff and the water's edge of the vast lake, they would have a couple of large, flat rocks to sit on. Not that she was planning to spend ages with him or anything.

"I remember we used to come down here all the time

before," he added.

Odella nodded. "I still do sometimes. Sit on our- *the* rocks and throw stones."

She was walking slightly ahead now and hoped he wouldn't see the stiffness of her body. The rocks weren't theirs anymore, and they hadn't been since that day four years ago, although she'd told herself she would forgive and forget now.

She reached the rocks a few paces ahead of him and flopped to sit down on one, dropping her jewellery bag on the floor at her feet. Sannar settled beside her, the cloth bag in his hand clinking as he set it on his lap. He'd spent barely any time in the market getting supplies for their dinner, insisting she waited at the edge for him.

"Right, I'm hoping you haven't developed any allergies," he said, his tone tinged with nerves. "I got a couple of meat pockets with everything in, some more *Beast Lite*, and a handful of berry pops."

Odella grinned at that, the scent of the still-hot food wafting out of the bag. She grabbed the meat pocket he handed her, the strips and salad wrapped in thick honeyed bread and almost spilling over.

"Thanks, and no allergies. When was the last time you had one of these?"

He took his first bite and closed his eyes with a groan.

"Can't remember. Definitely before I joined the court."

"Four years without a meat pocket?!"

She pretended to gasp with her mouth half-full and he laughed.

"At least you haven't gone all ladylike on me. The court kitchens do amazing food, but sometimes you need something solid and dependable."

Odella finished her food with a sinking sensation in her

stomach, and not because of the stodge. She was definitely the walking advert for solid and dependable. Glancing down at herself again, she slouched to make herself smaller.

Why am I so bothered? I don't care what people think of me, and I've never worried about not being delicate and ladylike before.

Sannar opened a bottle of *Beast Lite* and handed it to her, apparently not as self-conscious about his gorging as she was about hers. When he held out a berry pop next, she hesitated then shook her head. He frowned but retracted the pop and slid the packet back into the bag.

"So, you really don't know what she wants me for?" she asked.

It was literally the only conversation starter she could grab at, and he laughed as he set the bag aside.

"No, 'Della, I don't. It's not like I can lie to you, come on."

She shrugged. "You could word-tangle."

"No, I can't, I go bright red every time I try."

She remembered that and a smile crept across her lips. "Still?"

"Yep. But if you want my *opinion* for what little it's worth, your gift of moulding rock might come in handy for opening and finding things, or rather others would do the finding and you would do the opening. It's a request from the queen, but I reckon you could refuse without penalty."

Odella gave him a disbelieving look. "Whoever refused a queen and lived to tell about it? Don't be dim."

He was still chuckling under his breath, the gentle movement of his shoulders forcing his arm to brush against hers.

Unnerved by close he was sitting, Odella pushed herself

off the rock and strode across to the shoreline. The water lapped gently at her fingertips as she located a suitable stone and skimmed it across the surface.

She tensed as he appeared beside her again, ducking to pick up a couple of stones.

"Not bad," he said. "But I could always get them further than you could."

He couldn't have said a more blessed sentence as all her awkwardness dribbled away in a mist of indignation.

"You couldn't!"

He grinned and skimmed his first stone. It bounced over the water, venturing further than hers by several skips.

"I definitely can now though."

She scowled. "Nuh-uh. Best of three."

"You're on."

She found a second stone and tried again. Then a third. He beat her each time, all the while with that self-satisfied smirk on his face.

"Okay fine, you might be slightly stronger at chucking a bunch of stones-" She stared in horror as one of the stones at their feet lifted of its own accord and skimmed itself across the water. "Cheat! You dirty, lying, rotten-"

She couldn't finish the words and keep herself from laughing at the same time.

He took a step closer, his eyes catching the twinkling light from above and dancing along with them.

"You were always better at skimming," he said. "So you can't blame me for using gifts to impress you."

She gulped, her pulse beginning to skitter. She wanted to ask why impressing her was even in question, but she wasn't sure she could cope with what the answer might be.

Not yet. I've only just become friends with him again. He's being nice because he wants his friends back.

She took a hesitant step back and a flicker of something frowny and dark crossed his face. It was gone in an instant but she'd seen it all the same.

"Are... you going to swing by and see your parents?" she asked, her voice shaky.

Sannar shook his head, although he didn't make any move to step away or remove his unwavering gaze from her face.

"No point. They know where I am, and I've come down to see them at home more than they've ever come up to see me."

Odella folded her arms with a frown. "How many times have they come up to see you?"

"None."

That has got to hurt.

She could barely get rid of her parents when they were home, always asking her questions and wanting to know about her life. The pity twisted in her chest as he braved a wry smile.

"Doesn't matter. I am sorry about what I said back then, when I first started up at the court."

"Doesn't matter," she echoed.

Sannar turned to face the water and she sneaked a glance at him, the pensive profile of his face and the slump of his shoulders.

"It does, it really does. I wanted to fit in and be wanted by the court, to be valuable. Why else would I have taken on all the drudge work and made myself invaluable? I was too young and naive to understand that everyone will use a willing person and it had nothing to do with kindness."

She shrugged. "Okay, I'll admit it hurt me at the time, but it's fine. I got over it. You're the one who keeps bringing it up."

"Because I keep being sorry. I wanted to apologise after, even wrote you this ridiculous letter, but you made it more than clear you didn't think I was worth much after that so I got my punishment."

"I always knew you had worth," she mumbled. "You just didn't treat me very nicely that day, and you made no attempt to fix it after that."

He lifted his head and looked her directly in the eye before she could turn away. She caught the slightest hint of amusement on his lips before the words came out.

"I know, I'm-"

"Don't you say sorry again!"

He laughed and she relaxed. Her previous paranoia about feeling awkward around him still echoed in her head, but the worry that he was worried eclipsed all else.

"Well, I'm glad we're friends again," she admitted. "But that doesn't get me any closer to what the queen wants with me, or what the Forgotten are up to."

Sannar rubbed a hand over his chin and glanced up at the cliff even though the court wasn't visible. Odella recognised that look, the recollection that he had the weight of a whole court hanging around his neck like a dead weight.

"I have no idea, but they're always going to be pushing the boundaries aren't they, chasing power and the old ways. I imagine the queen will interrogate the ones we took captive. I popped in on my way down to check on them and the one you saw on the upper levels was there thankfully."

Odella gasped loud enough to startle him.

"Why didn't I think of that?" she said. "We can go and speak to them now and ask them what the Forgotten are looking for."

Sannar blinked enough times that she wondered if he was doing it on purpose to make a point.

"I- what?" he asked.

"We go up and speak to the captives! I mean, you basically run the court so nobody would question you being there. Say you're going to see if they're secure or something, then we can ask them what they're after. I bet that one I saw in the upper levels would risk talking to me. Even if he doesn't intend to let anything slip, he might. I can be quite convincing when I need to be."

Sannar folded his arms, his face immediately set in disbelief. She couldn't fathom how he could go from jolly to irritated in one quick twist of his facial muscles, but he managed it spectacularly.

"You can't be serious."

She nodded. "Totally serious. Come on, if he's targeting me and he's all chained up, there'll be no better chance than this. I want to know what they're after."

She heard her words dropping into the tense silence and wished she could claw them back. She hadn't exactly told him everything about what the Forgotten spy had said to her.

"What do you mean 'targeting' you?"

She flushed and pressed a hand to the back of her neck, taking a step back.

"I… it wasn't…"

"*Odella.*"

She huffed. "Fine! I wasn't going to tell you because you had more than enough to worry about, but when I first saw him in the upper levels, he saw my gift. The second time, when you went off to get the keys, he tried to convince me to join them. I bet I could get him to let something slip, and it'd probably earn us brownie points."

Sannar pressed his forefinger and thumb to the bridge of his nose and closed his eyes.

Odella grimaced. In that moment he looked very much like a man instead of the boy she'd been seeing him as still, a man who was very unimpressed indeed. She bit down on the urge to grin.

Uh-oh.

CHAPTER SIXTEEN
SANNAR

Sannar kept his eyes closed, mainly because it was the best way of handling what apparently was a complete breakdown in his common sense. He knew sneaking up to the court dungeons with a non-sworn person from town was a ridiculous idea, but Odella looked at him all excited and hopeful and he actually found himself considering it.

But he'd assumed earlier in the keep that the man with the whip was using Odella to taunt him. He'd hated him then but the fact that the traitor had actually tried to recruit her separately, it made him indescribably angry.

"It's a ridiculous idea," he began. "Even if it wasn't, they're not going to tell us anything. Even if they were going to, I can't simply stroll down to the dungeons with you. I do have to justify where I go some of the time."

Silence. He held firm for a couple of agonising moments, then risked opening his eyes.

She had her arms folded and the cutest little scowl on her face, staring up at him with haughty irritation.

"I bet we could sneak past," she muttered.

Even the thought of those Forgotten scumbags being anywhere near her made his insides flutter with panic, let alone the trouble she'd get into for sneaking about the court in places she shouldn't.

"Why didn't you tell me he'd targeted you?" he asked, even though she'd told him already. "You don't trust me?"

She glared back at him. "I knew you'd get all fussing and overbearing, like you're being now."

"I am not."

"Yes, you are." She sucked in a sharp breath. "That man said my gift could help them, so I could use myself-"

"Absolutely not."

"Will you stop interrupting me?"

Her voice fired through the air at him, killing any hope he had of holding his own stone dead. When he didn't say anything, her expression settled back into a frown.

"I only want to speak to him. Two minutes even to ask why they want me. I'd turn over anything I heard to the queen immediately, but he might consider talking to me if he thinks it'd get me on side. You said he's definitely one of the captives up there?"

Sannar froze. He would never forget that man's face, the taunting voice or the infuriating way he'd winked at Odella on the upper levels before vanishing. Or the amused look on his face as he sent that awful whip flying her way during the courtyard battle, even though she was already down and not moving.

Or the way he tried to trick me into telling him more about her earlier.

"Is he one of them?" she repeated. "You said he's one of the captives, so he must be."

"He's definitely one of the Forgotten, I know that much." Sannar tried to word-tangle without the thought that it was still kind of like lying dancing in his head.

Odella's eyes picked up a determined gleam and he groaned.

"He is!" She grinned. "You're going red, I knew it! Two minutes to speak to him, that's all I'm asking, please. Do you want me to beg?"

He shook his head. "Don't be dim, even when you try to beg it's still like you're demanding stuff. But no chance, it's too dangerous."

"They're contained."

"*You're* contained," he grumbled.

"Oh very mature. Look, they wouldn't be able to get at us. Is it because you don't trust me in your court still?"

He froze. As the hurt scraped his insides raw, realisation dawned on her face.

"I didn't mean it like that," she said. "I know I'm not a part of it and you lot have your secrets which is fine. But I won't be a liability or anything, I promise."

He couldn't dredge up an answer. One stupid mistake four years ago and she'd marked him with it for life. She would always assume he didn't trust her with the court, that he'd think she wasn't worthy of it all.

She sighed. "I'm sorry."

He tried to smile but couldn't quite pull the muscles into place. Muscles that dribbled to nothing as she appeared in front of him and wrapped her arms around his neck.

Baffled by the contact and petrified that he might either wake up or be suffering from some kind of hallucination, he lifted his arms to hug back but left them hovering shy of touching her waist.

"It's okay." His voice came out all husky. "Um, it's still too dangerous though, if that's what this- if you were- if-yeah."

"It's just a hug." She laughed but he caught the thin waver of her voice underneath.

So he hugged her back. Wound his arms around her waist and hugged her tight. Clung on like it was the last time he might ever touch a person again. She fit against him, warm and firm and smelling sweet.

Orbs alive, I'm screwed.

"I can't risk it," he said onto the top of her head. "If

anything happened to you it would be my fault. If they escaped, it would be my fault. I'm sorry."

She sighed. "Don't apologise, I get it. It's fine, I know you can't risk your place up there."

He gave her a doubtful look and realised that she was still hanging onto him, as if being in his arms felt so right that she'd forgotten.

Wishful thinking. Stop it.

"You were assuming I could get you into the dungeons without questions." He probably could, but she didn't need to know that. "Our guards might let me through, maybe even you if you're with me, but the queen has her lot there too."

Odella smiled and unwound her arms from around him. He let go, the subtle chill of the night flickering over his skin as if to mock the loss of her warmth.

"It was just an idea. I should be getting back though." She smiled a second later as though she could see his face fall through the gloom. "Grab your bag."

He grabbed the food bag, her jewellery one along with it, and set off along the path back to town. Odella fell into step with him, her movements jittery. He wondered if it was awkwardness because of the hug or because she thought he didn't trust her with his court. That still hurt but his mind was too awash with scarier possibilities to focus.

What would she do if I tried to hold her hand right now? Probably go all formal and awkward.

As they walked through the town, he couldn't stop the flare of nervous excitement. When they reached the base of the hill up to the court, he faced her.

"What are you going to do with the rest of your evening then?" she asked, the gentle smile still on her face.

"I'll go up to check the wards on the upper levels. Can't

be too careful. Then sleep. Guess that makes me boring."

She chuckled. "Not at all. We all need some proper rest after the last couple of days. You're not thinking of going to the dungeons without me, are you?"

"No." The thought hadn't even occurred to him. "Of course not. I imagine if anyone can get them to talk, it's the queen, so I'm going to make myself useful in other ways."

Now the thought *had* occurred to him, it began to wind itself around his mind. He could go in and do one more check before the queen got involved and whisked them all off. If he knew why they were targeting Odella, he could try to arrange some kind of protection for her.

Odella rolled her eyes. "Fine, I guess that's good thinking."

"Wow, an almost compliment. Are you okay?"

"Idiot. I can be nice."

He let her suffer in silence for a few moments, laughing when she prodded his ribs with a determined finger.

"I can!" she protested. "I'm nice to everyone."

She looked so beautiful with her grey-blue eyes shining and her face alive with amusement. Sannar did the boldest thing he could remember since... well, since randomly striding up to have the world's most awkward conversation with her after four years of nothing.

He lifted a hand and pushed her glasses gently up her nose, then slid his hands around hers, lacing their fingers together and hoping that she wouldn't start shouting at him. When she didn't pull away, he managed a weak, nervous smile.

"Uh-oh, trouble," she said softly, her head tilting up.

He nodded, almost breathless with anxiety.

"You *always* cause trouble."

"I do not. What trouble have I ever caused?"

"That time we lost your dad's boat," he murmured.

"Yes but that wasn't technically my fault."

"The time you got me caught stealing the apples."

"You shouldn't have been stealing them." She smiled. "Okay, it was technically for me, but still…"

He risked soft brush of his thumb over the back of her hand as she stared up at him.

"The time you convinced me to eavesdrop on a royal council meeting in my own court."

"Hey!" She stepped closer until they were almost nose to nose, her lips twitching with amusement. "You were just as up for that as I was."

He smiled; he couldn't help it.

"The time you forced me to involve you in a court fight."

"You didn't 'involve me', I got myself involved thank you *very* much."

Is she looking at me like that all sparkly-eyed because she wants me to kiss her?

He couldn't tell, although her face was tilted up at just the right angle. Her gaze flickered to his lips, so fast he was almost convinced he'd imagined it. When he risked taking her other hand so he was holding both, her eyelids lowered the tiniest amount.

"The time you tried to convince me to smuggle you into the court in middle of the night and down to the dungeon."

He could barely find breath, his heart was beating so fast.

Her nose wrinkled as she laughed. "That sounds so dodgy. Besides, it's your court's dungeon so you have every right to be in there. But I understand why you can't."

Every atom of his being wanted to kiss her.

I'm going for it.

He leaned forward.

"'Della! There you are."

The voice punctured the tense air between them before he could touch his lips to hers. Odella flinched, jogging them against each other so his mouth brushed over her cheek instead. He almost inhaled a mouthful of her hair and dropped her hands to swipe at his face as he stepped back.

Odella's cheeks were bright pink and she bit her lip while eying the hill leading up to the court. Her arms went around her middle, her eyes sharp and focused on anything but him.

"Hi, mum. Just finishing up work?"

Sannar hated people who threw tantrums or moaned about not getting what they wanted, but right then all he wanted to do was scream at the lost opportunity.

"Oh, hi Sannar." Odella's mum beamed at him. "Bit weird seeing you this far from court. Do you want to come back for dinner? I doubt it's equal to Lindy's calibre, but Sim will be happy to see you."

Sannar managed a weak smile. "Um, sorry, I already ate. That's not a reflection on the food or anything, I promise, just… I should get back to court. Things to do and, yeah. See you."

Drowning in awkward embarrassment, because where they were standing was extremely visible from the hill and Odella's mum was beaming at him with far too much fake innocence, he managed another excruciating grimace and fled up the hill.

She'll understand. He wasn't sure if he was thinking of Odella or her mum, or both. *But one thing I am sure of, she was leaning in.*

His insides exploded with excitable flutters at the thought. Odella might be argumentative and irritable. She might be trouble to the bare bone with her mad ideas, but she'd been waiting for him to kiss her.

With a jaunty swagger in his weary limbs, he almost felt strong enough to take on the court, its lady and all its enemies.

CHAPTER SEVENTEEN
REYAN

They're coming. The soft voice chased Reyan through her dreams. *Wake, they're here.*

She shifted through the hazy sensation of slumber, ignoring the dream until a sharp pinch pierced through. She flinched in bed as her mind woke, the subtle sting on her wrist the only thing still tying her to her dreams.

Kainen was fast asleep beside her, his brow creased slightly and his body draped more over the barrier of blankets than beside it. As her eyes adjusted to the darkness, Reyan noted the tiny streams of light coming from the window and the stars dancing outside. They hit a small patch on top of Kainen's head where the light seemed to get swallowed whole, a patch the shape of a curled-up serpent who'd apparently seen fit to use the Lord of the Illusion Court as a pillow.

Did you bite me? Reyan sent her voice through the shadow.

"Mmph, no," Kainen muttered under his breath. "Don't bite."

Reyan smothered a giggle but the soft words from her dreams hissed into her head.

They're here. Voices from the egg.

Reyan had no time to work out how Betty was apparently speaking to her through the same sort of mind-speak that she shared with Kainen, or how the snake seemed to understand any kind of mutual language.

Voices from the egg could only mean one thing.

What do you mean, they're here? How do you know?

Betty flicked the tip of her slender, shadowy tail against Kainen's ear and he shivered.

Shakes in pattern. Egg low in narrow tunnels.

"You can tell from the vibrations, and the narrow tunnels, like pipes?"

Realisation dawned as Kainen mumbled something else in his sleep, but Betty raised her head and swayed from side to side in agreement.

"Kainen, wake up." Reyan gave his shoulder a rough shake.

He sat up before fully waking, his limbs flailing as he tried to open his eyes.

"What? Where? Who?" He looked around and saw her. "What's wrong?"

"Betty says the Forgotten are here, or whoever brought her in the egg. Something to do with vibrations and I think pipes?"

Kainen's face went from sleepy confusion to alert in seconds. He threw the bed covers back, almost squishing Betty underneath them as he leapt to his feet.

"Might be nothing but we'll take no chances."

Reyan gathered Betty in one hand and shovelled her feet into her boots, touched that he trusted her word so easily.

"What are we going to do?" she asked.

"We get Demi, explain and see what she wants to do."

He grabbed her free hand and towed her out of the room. She had nowhere to put Betty so she cradled that arm to her chest, hoping Demi wouldn't ask questions about her.

The courtyard was deserted, the firelight flickering low and casting long shadows. Kainen hurried along to the long building that housed the Lady Aereen's apartments along with those of her guests and pushed open the door.

Reyan had no idea how he knew which way to go but she followed him through the opulent entrance hall, the floor a stretch of pale marble with the same brown and purple furnishings that had adorned the court's main hall. She broke into a jog to keep up as he swept them along a side corridor toward a set of double doors at the far end.

He knocked and glanced at her, a soft flicker of amusement crossing his face when he saw her trying to hide Betty with her hand. She tensed as he slid his arm around her waist.

"Slip her into my shirt pocket," he whispered. "It should be baggy enough."

Reyan held her hand up to his chest and Betty happily tumbled into the pocket with the tiniest echo of a hiss. Reyan froze with her hand hovering against him as one of the doors swung open to reveal a blinking and very startled Demi with an irate Taz shirtless behind her.

Reyan flushed and fixed her gaze on Demi's face, aware of Kainen snickering at her reaction.

"What's up?" Demi asked.

Reyan hesitated. She didn't want to explain about Betty in case Demi insisted she give her up, but leaving out that detail would make her sound crazy.

"Reyan sensed something in the shadows," Kainen said. "Something to do with the pipes and the Forgotten. We're not sure if it's a dream but there must be hundreds of hidden ways into this mountain. Figured we'd raise it."

Demi eyed them both for a long moment while Taz pulled on a t-shirt. When he pressed his hand to her shoulder, Demi folded her arms.

"You sensed it in the shadows? Like the nether beastie?" she asked.

Reyan nodded. "I- kind of. Not the beast exactly, that's still fast asleep."

"It all sounds calm to me," Taz grumbled.

Demi smirked. "It does. But you said you sensed it in the shadows. Would it by any chance have something to do with that subtle hissing noise coming from Kainen's shirt pocket?"

Reyan flinched in front of him before anyone else could react. She had no idea how Demi could hear the tiny noises Betty was making, indignation mostly it sounded like, but perhaps the whole queen thing gave her super hearing powers.

"She's safe, I promise," she insisted. "At least she's not done anything yet. She's literally just made of shadow."

Wild thoughts of the stinging pinch that had woken her drew her mind to the subtle tingle still lingering on her wrist.

I really need to do some proper research on shadow-snakes.

Taz sighed. "And you're hiding it because it came from something unsavoury? Actually, we're probably better off not knowing."

"She," Reyan corrected. "Her name is Betty. I maybe should have mentioned it but the evening before we arrived for the meeting I came to check some final things and we found the iron door open. Someone had been going through some of the rooms and left an awful mess, but then we were walking back and found an egg. It hatched when I went up to it and she came out."

Demi frowned. "So she belongs to the Nether Court?"

"She technically belongs to Belladonna." Kainen added, his tone withering with disgust. "We overheard her during the fight earlier saying they'd lost the egg and needed it as a way in. For some reason they snuck behind the iron door, left a shadow-snake egg to hatch there and came back to get it, although you might have more of an idea why they'd want to do that. Luckily for Betty, she'd already been found."

"You should have told me that."

Kainen nodded. "Agreed, but in all honesty I forgot about it. When we overheard them in the tunnels during the battle I was more concerned with what I told you about them looking for locations and keys."

Demi's mouth twisted doubtfully. Wild thoughts of grabbing Betty and insisting she flee into the tunnels filled Reyan's head.

"I should technically tell you to return her..." Demi said.

Taz grinned. "*Cough* Leo *cough.*"

He looked toward the ceiling straight after, his face a picture of unnerving innocence.

Demi pulled a face at him.

"I won't on this occasion," she said. "But only because she'll be better off with a shadow-weaver and definitely better off away from Belladonna. She told you about the Forgotten? How?"

Elated, Reyan reached into Kainen's pocket and lifted Betty out, holding her in both hands.

"She woke me and said they're here, and that she can feel the vibrations and something to do with narrow tunnels while she was in the egg, close to the ground. I need to do more research on shadow-snakes but haven't exactly had time. I can hear her though, I'm not hallucinating or anything, I don't think. It's a bit like the mind-speak Kainen and I have, except it's with her and I can understand the hissing. I thought by tunnels maybe she meant pipes of some kind?"

Demi disappeared behind the door and reappeared with a couple of hoodies.

"Taz, go and get Sannar," she said, handing him a hoodie. "If he's not here then come straight down to the dungeons. They've been in and out of this court for weeks at will, so there's only one thing they'd stage a sneak approach for."

"To free the prisoners?" Taz asked with a grimace.

Demi nodded. "Which means at least one of them is of importance to them somehow, and therefore to us."

Reyan shifted to the side as Demi strode past them with Taz hurrying in her wake. She closed their bedroom door behind them and hurried at Kainen's side after the others.

"Take Betty home, Kainen," Demi called over her shoulder. "Until we know exactly what they want with her, she's to stay safe at your court and in Reyan's keeping. Then come straight back and down to the Keep. There might be some of them willing to talk and you can try to help with those who are less willing."

Kainen nodded, taking Betty and giving Reyan's waist a quick squeeze before clicking his fingers. In a puff of glittering black smoke he disappeared and Reyan trotted after Demi.

"I know it might be nothing," Reyan said.

Demi shook her head as they strode across the empty courtyard and Taz went the other way to the main block.

"I thought they gave up surprisingly easy. Kainen mentioned Belladonna saying the fight was a ruse to get into the tunnels, but he neglected to mention they were there for something specific."

Reyan sighed at the disapproving look Demi sent her as they ventured into the firelit depths of the main mountain tunnel and toward the nearest trundle cart.

None of the guards at the mountain entrance had dared stop them, but given the no-nonsense expression on Demi's face, she wouldn't have dared stop her either, queen or not.

"Kainen didn't mean anything dodgy by it," she said. "Maybe he was protecting Betty because of me a bit."

Demi laughed as Reyan shut the cart's gate and she sent the trundle rumbling downwards.

"That boy would do anything for you. Luckily for him, it comes from a good place and I'll let it slide. If the enemy wants a shadow-snake though, we need to find out why. Why all this trouble for one animal?"

Reyan nodded. "I'll do some research as soon as I get home. I'll reach out to Milo as well, with your permission."

"Of course. We need to-" Demi froze as a loud rumbling noise shook the walls around them.

Reyan grabbed onto the side of the trundle as the quaking shook the cart until it bounced on the ropes moving it. She could meld into the shadows so that falling wouldn't hold any danger for her, but she couldn't leave Demi to fall if the ropes snapped.

The shaking increased and the cart bashed against the wall, jolting one of the rope's hooks free of the cart.

"Hold on tight to me." Demi reached up to grab a rope.

Reyan inched her arms around Demi's waist in the absence of any other hold she could find. Anchored together, she squeaked and wrapped her legs around Demi's calves as the queen of Faerie lit her fingertips on fire and burned through one of the remaining ropes.

A savage jolt made Reyan close her eyes and the air whistled past them. Self-preservation had her reaching into the shadows, tipping on the edge of merging with them. Another jerk almost tore her arms free of Demi's waist but the downward pull lessened.

Thoughts of dissipating into shadow filled her head, self-preservation roaring at her to vanish. She couldn't even summon her transmutation gift, more likely to turn Demi's blood solid and her bones liquid than anything else, and that was if she managed anything at all.

Kainen's face filled her mind and thoughts of what might happen to Betty if she didn't survive the fall swelled. She gritted her teeth, her limbs screaming from clinging on so tight to Demi.

"Brace for a bump," Demi shouted, seconds before Reyan crashed onto her behind.

Blinking in relief, she looked around. The walls were still shaking from some kind of impact and the guards at the far end of the hall were shouting inaudible words and banging on a large wooden door.

Hovering above them was a lopsided trundle cart and realisation of the physics hit as Demi hauled Reyan to her feet and pulled her out of the way.

Both of them scrunched their shoulders around their ears seconds before the almighty crash that sent splinters of cart and lashes of rope through the air. Even as Reyan regained her senses, Demi was already off again, striding toward the guards at the end of the hall.

Reyan took a deep breath to calm her nerves and almost choked on the air as Kainen appeared beside her. He took one look at her, another at the mangled trundle cart and his face twisted with dark fury.

"Dare I ask?" he said, his tone silky with warning.

Reyan let out the breath and managed a weak smile.

"Best you don't. Regicide wouldn't do our court any good, and I'm fine. Come on or we'll miss all the fun."

She grabbed his hand before he could protest and

dragged him toward the commotion with Demi's words dancing unnervingly in her ears.

"That boy would do anything for you."

As he glowered back at her, his irritation on hold only and worry swimming in his eyes, she realised the queen might be right about that.

CHAPTER EIGHTEEN
ODELLA

"I am *not* going after him."

Odella backed away from her mum, heading in the direction of the hill that led up to court with a barely baked plan forming in her head. Her mum glanced past her and up the mountain with a wide smile.

"If you say so, dear. I don't know what you're so flappy about. Sannar's a lovely boy. We'd be delighted if you and he were to-"

"*Bye mum*, I'll be back late."

Odella set off at a powering stride up the mountain path. Sannar, lovely boy or not, would kill her if he knew what she was planning to do. She'd tried to explain to her mother that she was only going up after him to get her jewellery supplies which he still had, so it wasn't a lie exactly, not if she did what she intended to do first then went and knocked on his bedroom door after.

But of course her mum didn't believe her.

It would have been quicker to go after Sannar up the steep steps that led to the kitchens, but being so late she couldn't be sure he wouldn't lock them behind him. She also needed to be on the mountain path to veer around the side of the court boundary so she could climb into the relevant air pipes that ventilated the inner parts of the court.

I won't get in the way or anything. I'll just ask that man what exactly he wants with me, then I can go and tell the queen. Or tell Sannar and he can tell the queen. Once he's finished shouting at me.

She grinned at the thought of that. He was usually so mild-mannered, or at least he always had been before, but he seemed to have developed some kind of protective bone. And when she'd hugged him, she couldn't tell if it was her heart pounding a race or his.

I hate it when Mix and Sammy are right.

She couldn't do anything about her friends guessing that she might have the teeniest tiny *hint* of a crush brewing, but she could still creep into the court and get herself some answers.

Nobody knew that she'd used the whole 'helping her mum' thing to veer off and explore the mountain, including several of the tunnels and pipes that intersected the court itself.

Her cheeks burned as she puffed up the mountain, but she kept pushing on even when doubt about what she was about to do flickered in her mind. After several minutes, she stopped at the side of rock she needed to climb.

I won't get caught, she reassured herself, taking off her shoes and tying them around her neck by the laces. *I'll just have a look. Maybe a quick visit.*

She'd only lost one pair of glasses while climbing before and now she either tied them around her head or slipped them in her pocket. It was also why she sewed zips or buttons on all of her clothing, to keep whatever was on her person from falling off again. Sliding her glasses into her pocket, she adjusted to the blurred world around her and pushed her gift into her fingertips.

Warming the rock, she set to climbing, knowing from experience where to be patient and where she could risk a little more hastiness. The open circle of pipe that led to one of the lower mountain tunnels appeared in front of her and she hauled herself in, legs flailing to propel her the last bit.

She rested a second, her heart pounding from the exercise, and wriggled forward on her forearms and knees. The tunnel would open out soon but she hadn't climbed these vents in a long while.

Several shuffles later, an echo caught her ears. She froze.

Just someone walking by in one of the halls, or one of the guards.

She moved one arm forward and hesitated again.

"…this way. Trust me, I know where I'm going."

That echo was from one of the tunnel openings to her right, which as far as she could remember led to nowhere, an unfinished vent-line.

I can't let anyone find me here.

She twisted her head to look back but in the darkness she couldn't see how far back the opening to the mountain was. Her muscles were searing still, a sign she probably shouldn't make the climb back down without a rest first.

Scuffling noises of people unused to moving on all fours filled the vent-line, growing ever closer. She could shuffle back quietly, stay at the edge of the tunnel until they'd gone past.

Wishing she had the ability to fade into shadow like the Lady Reyan was rumoured to have, she started reversing, her knees scuffing against errant screws of the pipe.

A flash of light both dazzled her and filled her with a frightening realisation that she was well and truly trapped.

No choice, they'll see me as soon as they reach me. I'll have to go through the Deep Keep. Orbs, this is going to get me in so much trouble.

She shot forward past the vent-line opening as fast as sound would allow, desperate not to be heard.

"What was that?" someone called out.

She winced and kept going.

"Don't know." The female voice sounded irritable. "Probably some kind of rat. Keep going."

"How much more of this do we have to crawl through?" someone else whined.

"As far as it takes. Once we've sprung the captives we need, we get Emil to contact his Prime Realm connections."

Odella scrambled the last part of the tunnel as the opening pipe to the deep keep loomed in front of her.

She pushed the grill aside and peered through to see the Deep Keep in all its gloomy glory. The vast room was surrounded by bare rock walls with a multitude of iron cells lining them. She almost expected a dank scent and something dripping nearby, but for a dungeon it was surprisingly clean and well organised, if a bit sparse.

Bursting through, she ignored the startled gasps echoing around her and tumbled out of the hole onto a waiting table below.

Seething through her teeth as the drop rattled her bones, she used the wall as support to get to her feet and stood on the table to push the grill back over the opening.

But it wasn't enough. She could see the echo of light flickering through the wires. If she'd popped through that easily, whoever was sneaking in behind her would have no trouble. They were here to spring the Forgotten prisoners, and she couldn't do a single thing to stop it.

"Ah, changed your mind did you, lovely?"

She recognised that voice, the smug, smooth tones of the man who'd accosted her twice in the upper levels and tried to attack her in the courtyard.

She ignored him, pulling her gift back into her tired

fingertips. It might not do much good, but she would protect Sannar's court as best she could and slow the enemy down before going straight to the guards outside.

Pulling parts of the rock from either side of the opening, she inched parts over the pipe's grill. It would probably decrease the ventilation, but she could fix it once the intruders were dealt with. If she could slow them down, she might have some chance of mending her mistake of sneaking through in the first place.

"Are our friends here then?" the man asked.

She heard his loud inhale and panicked as he prepared to shout for them.

"Who's Emil?" she blurted out.

It was the first thing she could think of. The only thing she could think of as she frantically forced her gift into the sluggish, unyielding rock.

A couple of quiet gasps and mutterings suggested she'd stumbled on something useful at least, but she didn't dare turn around and waste time looking.

They're in iron cells, they can't get out without help. I'm okay.

Her hands shook, both from fear and from the excess use of her gift, but she pushed on.

"Ah. Emil is as much a myth as I am," the man said. "The stuff of legends, some might say."

Odella snorted. "You seem to know enough about him to suggest you might know him personally. Or know about him at least. Why is he so important then?"

A moment of silence swelled and she had half of the pipe covered already. It would take the rock a few moments to harden again, but she could hear the voices on the other side, dipping about as though they'd taken a wrong turn. She couldn't think of any possible wrong turns, unless they'd gone the way she'd come in, but with their light it should have been obvious as an exit.

Unless they were always trying to get out and I'm wasting my time here.

"Why don't you let me out and I can tell you all about Emil," the man suggested.

"Why don't you tell me and I'll see if it's worth letting you out for?" she countered.

Feeling the fraying of her gift, the sensation that it was reaching its limit, she had to give up with the pipe almost covered.

"I thought Emil was the one with contacts in the Prime Realm," she said, risking everything as she struggled down from the table. "Maybe not then."

The man's eyes widened. He stood in his cell with his back against the far wall, his arms folded. But she'd seen his reaction even though he rushed to hide it with another smile.

"What does a girl like you know about the Prime Realm?"

She shrugged. "A girl like me knows many things. Hears many things. Too beneath notice to be noticed but always around to be seeing and hearing things. Hoity toity nobles often forget that."

"How true," he said, his smile not giving anything away.

"Perhaps if you promised, vowed even, to leave this court and the town below, and never return, and cause no hurt or harm to any of the people at court, we could consider things," she suggested.

All the while she held herself tense, inching toward the door. There would be guards outside and the trundles to take her up to the courtyard. She hadn't ever learned to glamour properly so she couldn't even sneak out incognito. She would have to own up and accept her punishment, but getting information as a trade of penance was her only option now.

"I could promise it," the man said. "The Nether Court has served its purpose. I'll even entreat my friends to do the same."

She reached the door, one hand hovering toward the handle. It would be locked so she'd have to knock, but even reaching for it made her feel bolder.

Unless the guards think it's a trick and refuse to open the door.

"What would you want for that then?" she asked. "If everyone's bothered about this Prime Realm and you don't need the Nether Court, you'll be gone to the forever mountains at the queen's command anyway."

"A predicament indeed. Then again, if you were to agree to join us-"

"No."

He chuckled. "Perhaps a one-time use of your fabulous gift then, to help me open rock whenever I call for it? For that I could share with you all manner of secrets."

One of the others in the neighbouring cell cleared their throat, but the man ignored it.

"What's your name?" Odella asked. "I should at least know that."

The man flourished a bow, one arm across his middle and the other out wide.

"I am Lorens, of no known family. Do we have a deal?"

He sounded far too eager despite the casual tone.

"So, it's only the one use, a one-time service, and when you call for me I have to open rock?"

He nodded. "For me, yes. No trickery about splitting a

random stone on the ground or any nonsense. You will open what I ask, when I ask."

"And for that you and yours will leave the Nether Court, the town and all their people alone. And you'll tell me what the Forgotten are after?"

He seethed through his teeth with a dangerous laugh.

"I never agreed to that. But as you know the Forgotten are after the Prime Realm and that they already have dealings with the folk there, I will-"

The door swung open and bounced into Odella's hand. She shrieked and pulled back, staring at the figure storming in.

"I'm just here to che-" Sannar noticed her and his eyes turned to orbs. "Ode- Wha- How- What in the name of Faerie are you doing?!

She managed to scowl at him even though her blood was thundering at a lethal pace and she knew she was in dire trouble already.

"I was doing what I thought I had to," she muttered.

He reached out, grabbed her hand and hauled her against him. Before she could even squeak a note of surprise, he had a warding domed over both of them.

"I am going to… you are so…" he huffed, unable to finish any of his threats. "Out now."

She resisted when he started to drag her, noting that the door to the hall was already shut. The guards might not have any idea she was in here. Perhaps it was sound protected enough that she could either finish her deal to keep the court and her friends and family safe, or at least get the queen a bit more information.

"There are people in the tunnels," she whispered. "I used the rock to block the pipe in but they're still there. They talked about getting people out."

She noted Sannar's stiff shoulders and a wave of guilt hit her, curling her insides into frantic knots. Whatever happened now, everyone knew they were friends and would probably assume he'd let her in after all.

The air around him was glacial, his two-toned eyes whirling with fury. Odella couldn't stop herself as she slid her hand over his arm like she had before. He tensed at the touch, but other than a momentary clench of his jaw, he kept his eyes on the captives.

"Oh we're cosy as critters in here, if you were wondering," Lorens said with a grin. "Your lady friend and I were just in the midst of arranging a little trade."

Sannar gawped at her. "Say you didn't."

"Not yet."

He huffed and faced the cells.

"No doubt the queen will have questions for you," he said. "But since you've already shown yourself twice in my court, and a third time to attack, I'd like to know why. Aside from trying to recruit unwilling participants to your cause, what is it you're looking for?"

Loren flicked his gaze to Odella. She squeezed Sannar's elbow as his body went rigid and he took a short step forward as if to put her behind him. Whether he was being protective out of duty or because of something more, she couldn't tell yet. But she'd seen Clara Honeyfeather eying him up like a prize from the other side of the tavern earlier, and she knew now that it was pointless resisting or lying to herself. She liked him, and if he liked her too then he was hers. Which meant she had to find them some way out of trouble that didn't jeopardise his place at court, his reputation or his future, even if she ruined hers.

Lorens hadn't answered but the mocking look in her direction was answer enough. Ignoring the knowledge that

Sannar would likely carry out his threat of bodily removing her from the room, she pulled her glasses out of her pocket and shoved them up her nose so she could see Lorens properly while glaring at him.

One of the women in the cells smacked her hand on the bars before any of them could say anything further.

"Enough," she said. "Stop playing with them. Offer and trade nothing. We have the plan to stick to."

The woman stood ready, her shoulders stiff and fingers flexing against the restriction the cells put on her gifts. One of the men started pacing in the next section. Only Lorens looked unbothered by the situation.

"Nothing further from you?" he asked, angling his head in Sannar's direction. "I am surprised. You were ready to choke me it felt like earlier in the name of her honour."

The wide smile was mocking, and Odella wanted to ask what that was about, but Sannar smirked, his gaze nothing short of acidic as he shrugged.

"You're wasting your time with me. I'm just the Chief Aide here and not a very popular one by many accounts. If it's something from the court you want, at least have the courtesy of telling me why. Otherwise there really isn't much point in us staying. The queen will be far keener to deal with you than either of us are."

Halfway across the room, a flicker of curiosity lit in Lorens' eyes. Odella watched the two of them stare each other out, confusion stunting her previous confidence. After trying to recruit her before, Lorens only had eyes for Sannar now.

"The same thing your queen wants, I reckon," Lorens said eventually. "Access. I'd bet you've learned a lot about our realm and the inner workings, what with you holding such a vital position here."

One of the women clicked her tongue sharply, a reprimand, and the other man halted his pacing.

"Access to what?" Odella asked, trying to keep the urgency out of her tone. "That room upstairs? He's already told you there's nothing useful in there."

Lorens rolled his eyes. "Nothing useful? There's *information* in there, enough to-"

"No more," the woman snapped. "Hold your tongue you worthless thief."

Thief. Odella frowned. *Has he been hired? Everything he said about picking sides last time, was that some kind of hint that he's only out for the highest bidder?*

"That's not very nice," she countered. "He didn't actually steal anything. Not that I know of anyway."

The woman gave her a withering look, her hands almost meeting the cell bars before she thought better of it. She tapped her foot, caged like her companions while Lorens looked completely relaxed.

"So he's an awful thief on top of being a loudmouth," she muttered.

Lorens gasped dramatically, grinning all the while.

"I shan't say another word. Not one murmur shall pass my lips. Even if pleaded or compelled, I would not dare to divulge that we're trying to find-"

"*Shut up!*"

Half the occupants of the cells had shouted it in unison and Odella choked back the ill-timed urge to laugh. Sannar might have joined in on any other occasion but his face was still twisted with irritation.

"I'd give anything to be one of the court lords right now," he muttered. "Some of them can mind-speak or cast compulsions."

Odella shrugged. He might not be a court lord, but she

wasn't even a court member. She didn't have a fancy family either, no recognition in Fae nobility circles.

Yet here I am demanding he get me involved in all of this, then sneaking in when he refuses. She lifted her head. *No more, I've asked enough.*

"Whatever you're planning, leave me out of it." She eyed Lorens as firmly as she could. "No clue who you are or what you're after and I don't want to know."

One of the men lifted his head, a similar look of curiosity passing over his face.

"What on earth would make you think we have any need of you?" he asked.

Odella took a step forward and smacked straight into an invisible wall of protection.

Of course he still has a protection up. She gave Sannar a weary look. *I should have thought of that.*

Stuck in the boundary with him, she folded her arms and faced the captives.

"Ask him." She nodded to Lorens. "He seemed quite happy to recruit me when he was poking around here earlier. Although, if he's hitting me up, maybe you're just desperate for new members. "

Sannar snared her hand in his and she flinched as he drew her back beside him. She couldn't help shrinking against him. He wound an arm around her waist and she risked a glance up at him, but his attention was on the others.

"We're done here," he said.

Odella nodded. She couldn't even work out exactly what possessed her to go through with approaching the enemy, and they'd learned nothing useful by it. She'd risked Sannar getting in trouble for nothing.

Not nothing. Her self-preservation fought with her

anxiety. *We know that Lorens is one to watch and that they're definitely fixated on access to something. The queen may even know what that is. Then there's the mysterious Emil who has access to whatever this Prime Realm is, they seemed really twitchy about that bit.*

With Sannar's arm still around her waist, she let herself be led back to the door.

She would apologise to him, not something she did easily, lightly or often. Not only about sneaking in either, but about taunting him earlier and stressing him out on the one night off he'd had in ages.

She almost missed the subtle rumbling sound, so trapped in her own thoughts. But Sannar stopped dead, his arm tightening around her. They rotated back around to see the captives on their feet and staring around expectantly.

The rumbling grew and the rock underfoot started shaking. A pile of plates on a table at the far end of the room bounced with the vibrations until they toppled over the edge and shattered.

"What the-"

Sannar's words were lost as the pipe grill and her hastily formed rock barrier burst away from the wall, shards ricocheting across the room followed by a forceful jet of water.

Lorens started laughing. "Our deal stands, lovely. I'll be coming to you when I'm ready to collect my end. You've heard most of the truth you asked for already, and the Nether Court is of no interest to me now anyway."

Odella spun to face him as a gaggle of legs and arms began to push through the pipe opening.

"Go!" Sannar yelled. "I'll hold them off."

She shook her head, refusing to leave him. The grimace of realisation twisted on his face and he pushed her toward the door. She lifted her arms, hands out to use the door as a brace point so she could turn to fight with him, but the door flew open.

She screamed in outrage as a purposeful gust of air caught around her and pummelled her right through the doorway. The door slammed behind her, leaving her in the corridor facing several astonished guards as the sounds of crashing came from the dungeon.

"He's in there alone!" she shouted.

Turning on her heel, she grabbed the metal latch and rattled it but the door was stuck. It jolted as if someone was struggling to keep a pressure against it.

"Get the queen!" she yelled. "Get the king consort, the lady, anyone!"

The guards manhandled her to the side and she grabbed handfuls of her hair in anguish as they began to fight against the door.

Her head swam, the flicker of the lamps making her vision sway. Panic tore at her insides as her nails bit into her scalp.

"What's going on?"

The voice echoed through the corridor like a blessing.

Odella looked toward the trundle shaft to see the queen striding toward them with a chaotic cloud of dust puffing behind her, the lord and lady of the Illusion Court also appearing moments later. Odella had no idea how or why they were there so quickly, but she'd never been more grateful to see nobility in her life.

"Sannar's in there," she gasped. "The Forgotten were… we were… he's in there on his own! I think he's trying to hold the door shut to keep them trapped."

She choked over the frantic catch in her throat as Demi eyed her up and down. She didn't have time to flinch as

Demi's hand latched onto her wrist.

The world swirled around her in a flash of purple and grey, the dungeon appearing the moment everything stopped spinning. The floor was puddled with water and people were still crawling out of the hatch in the wall, dropping right into a fight that Demi launched herself straight into. Lord Kainen and Lady Reyan appeared beside her, both swathed in smoke and shadow.

Before Odella could throw up a protection, Demi shoved her aside as a glitter of angry red sparks exploded right where she'd been standing. Sannar was almost on his knees, but she could feel his gusts of air buffeting the door to keep it closed.

"Talk him down," Demi shouted. "He's blocked everyone out but you might reach him."

Odella bit her lip. She had no idea Sannar could even do that, block people out. Perhaps it was the air whistling in his ears or his sheer stubborn refusal to let anyone get past. But she firmed her warding around herself even though she still felt sick from her first experience of realm-skipping.

"Sannar," she called out to him. "You have to stop, okay?"

Nothing happened. She pushed toward him despite the fight pinging around her, trusting the queen to hold the enemy back. She had to stop when her protection brushed Sannar's, but she could have sworn she felt a shiver.

"Can you hear me in there?"

No answer. She tried pushing her hand out but his protection fought her, the combination of the warding and the swirling wind of his gift forming an impenetrable barrier. She jumped and waved her hands trying to get him to look at her, but his eyes were rigid and unfocused.

Looking around in a panic, her gaze stuck on Lorens who seemed to be hanging back in the fight, sending out defensive lashes from a familiar looking length of leather and vine.

He was the one fighting us in the courtyard. He was the one who attacked me. His eyes met hers. *He was also the one who told me it was about access, which is something I can control.*

Odella turned away from Sannar's maelstrom of wind and inched along the edge of his protection. The door was rattling against him but he was still holding it firm.

With panic flaring through her insides, she pressed her hands against the rock. It softened under her fingertips, yielding to her. She pushed, widening the gap and beginning to dig with her clawed hands to create a hole. Hands arrived to help her but she shouted through not to interfere.

Beside her, the whirling of wind was a constant reminder that she had to keep pushing. Had to get a big enough hole to make him holding the door shut irrelevant.

"We'll fit, love," someone shouted. "Back up now."

Exhausted to the point of blacking out, she did as she was told. She moved away from the hole she'd created and staggered to rest against Sannar's warding. Even though it was rejecting her, keeping her out, she took comfort from its solidness.

Her mum would have insisted that she keep talking to him. Talking fixed most things, her mum always said.

"The queen's here," she told him. "So are her court. You need to relax now. Come back to me, please, before you drain your gift and screw yourself completely. I only just got you back in my life and I'll be damned if I'm going to let you ruin it!"

She was shouting by the end, and no doubt people fighting around her could hear. She had no idea who nearby was on the queen's side and who was the Forgotten, but Sannar blinked and none of it mattered anymore.

"Can you hear me?" she called out. "You can let the door go now. They're getting in through the hole in the wall anyway."

His head turned slowly. He blinked his eyes tightly and she choked over a whimper as he opened them again and saw her.

"Odella?" His voice sounded far away with the wind still whipping around him, but she heard it.

"Stop," she mouthed.

Then she held her hand out, palm up, begging him to join her. The wind dissipated, falling away in an instant. As did his protection, so suddenly she almost fell over because she was still resting against it. Sannar lifted a hand but she glared at him as she launched forward to grab it.

"You are an absolute insufferable arse," she growled. "What in the name of Faerie were you thinking? You think you can take the Forgotten on single-handed? What would I have done if you'd been pulverised or taken or Faerie knows what?!"

The residual panic splurged out, tears burning her eyes as he stood blinking at her like she was some kind of very startling insect.

"'Della?" he said her name almost disbelievingly, and she nodded. "We're in a battle right now, so can you maybe yell at me later? Also, I don't think I can ward right now so you'll have to do it."

She wanted to smack him. Throttle him. Boil him alive in the middle of his wretched court. Maybe even kiss him a little bit.

Lifting her hand, she summoned every last residue of strength she had and firmed a protection around them. The moment she wobbled from the effort, Sannar seemed to inhale some kind of residual strength. He stood straighter, his gaze sharpening as he hauled her against his side.

"Do we leave?" she asked, uncertain.

He frowned. "We should…"

Before she could admit she wouldn't be good for much except weak protection for a while, she noticed Lorens flying toward them. Sannar snarled and flicked out a hand, the instinct driving him as he whirled up some debris from Odella's wall-opening and sent it flying into Lorens' chest, felling him to the floor.

"You hit him!" she gasped.

"Good."

She decided not to plague him about his morality because the queen's side seemed to be winning, with a wave of struggling bodies being herded backward into the cells. Sannar grabbed a set of keys from his pocket with shaking hands and ducked away from her.

"Where are you going?" she shouted as he wove through the chaos. "*COME BACK HERE!*"

He ignored her and she realised why as the queen's massing forces drove the Forgotten toward the cells. The first one filled until it was ready to burst and Sannar locked the gate the moment someone slammed it shut. Odella eyed the rigid press of his shoulders and the way his hands shook as he tried to get the key in the lock.

Screw this for a pouch of percats.

She squeaked in horror as a sort of ridiculous battle-cry and set off toward him, holding her warding and wincing as those still fighting battered against it. The moment she was at his side, she spread her warding over him. The

228

second cell filled fast and she helped his fumbling fingers turn the key.

Frost burst out from the queen's outstretched hands, flakes weaving around those on her side and freezing those in the cells. Odella gawped as the noise began to fade and the final few of the Forgotten were rounded up and trapped.

"I am beyond furious with you," Sannar muttered as he locked the final cell.

Odella glared back at him. "Oh, I am ridiculously pissed off with you too, don't you worry."

She would have carried on berating him but the sound of an even more unimpressed throat echoed behind them.

Odella turned around to find the queen standing there with her arms folded and a decidedly unimpressed expression on her face.

CHAPTER NINETEEN
SANNAR

She may be a queen, but she has the worst timing.

Sannar had every intention of checking Odella was okay, maybe even apologising for losing control of himself. But instead the anger surfaced the moment he opened his mouth. Even as she snapped back at him, all he wanted to do was grab hold of her and never let her go.

But of course the queen trumped both of them and she was giving them a 'you will give me answers right now' look.

Sannar wanted to take Odella's hand as Demi unceremoniously threw everyone out of the Keep, but Odella had her arms folded tight across her chest, her gaze flicking worriedly to Demi and Taz. Sannar couldn't read their faces other than the grave looks, but he knew Odella well enough to recognise she was worried.

When he started toward the door, Demi shook her head.

"Not you two. Shut the door behind the others."

Sannar did as he was told.

Is she going to make some kind of example of us?

He eyed the frozen bodies inside the cells, all in various states of confusion or distress. If the queen wanted to give them the same punishment after questioning them, would he at least have time to get Odella out of it somehow?

"Explain." Demi frowned at them both.

Sannar eyed Odella and recognised the wide eyes and subtle shake of her shoulders. With a gulp, he garbled out as much of the situation as he could.

"We went to town, then I came up to check my wards were holding firm on the upper levels, then I went to bed, but I couldn't sleep. I came down here to check on things."

His cheeks burned at the information he conveniently left out, that he'd been all too ready to issue some warnings.

"I see." Demi's expression didn't soften.

"That man mentioned they might have an interest in Odella," Sannar hurried on. "I think because of her gift, and he said that all of this was about access. I can only assume that them looking for information on the flow of origins means they're trying to access, well… I'm sure you know enough about that anyway. Then the mountain began to shake, the cover exploded off the pipe over there and they were swarming in."

"None of that explains why you shoved me out though," Odella muttered.

"That's what you're worried about right now?" He gave her an incredulous glance, but she pulled a bratty face back at him.

"You were completely on your own!" she hissed. "Anything could have happened. Then you went all vacant trying to play the hero, like an idiot."

Sannar kept his gaze on her but he noticed the look Taz and Demi swapped out of the corner of his eye. Amusement maybe? Resignation? He couldn't tell. His limbs were like jelly and his insides felt scraped raw, but Odella glaring at him like she cared gave him an essence of residual strength.

"I kept them out of my court," he replied testily. "That's what any nether brother would have…"

He couldn't finish the lie because he knew all too well most of them would flee at the first sign of a fight. Odella's eyes sparked with something else, but Demi was clearing her throat again, although Taz was now grinning beside her.

"You kept them contained for a time which is everything we needed," Demi said. "I'll trust you both with whatever you're about to hear, but you're not to repeat it to anyone else outside of this room unless we agree otherwise. Got it?"

Sannar nodded, Odella doing the same. He shuffled closer to her until his arm was brushing her shoulder. She shot him a worried look.

"Do you recognise any of these people?" Demi asked.

Sannar opened his mouth to explain, but Odella's quiet voice echoed beside him.

"That one there." She pointed. "He said his name is Lorens. Okay, so I kind of asked Sannar to let me come up here and speak to him, because that man tried to recruit me before on the upper levels. But Sannar said no, so I climbed the mountain and came in through the vent-pipes."

Demi's eyes widened. "You cli- okay, carry on."

"Lorens was the one who tried to hurt me in the courtyard when we were fighting, and he was the one I saw twice in the upper levels, the one who mentioned the flow of origins. He tried to recruit me because of my gift. But while I was climbing the pipes, they were trying to get in. They said about releasing the captives here, and someone called Emil having connections in the Prime Realm. Then Lorens said to me about making a deal, a one-time use of my gift in exchange for information, not that he gave me much in the end. I think that's going to stand as well, because he said it would."

She sagged, out of breath after babbling so quickly. Demi strode to the cell containing the frozen Lorens.

"I'll need this open." She tapped the gate. "My gifts should work with a connection but not if the iron circuit is unbroken."

Sannar hurried forward and unlocked the cell, hovering beside the gate to relock it when needed. He didn't have to look to know Odella was right beside him.

Demi raised one hand and a moment later the tips of her fingertips glowed orange. She pushed her hand in a sharp outward motion, the jagged flash of amber light searing into the cell. Sannar sucked in a quiet breath and Odella's jaw dropped, her lips parting in awe.

Lorens was frozen with his arm outstretched upward, his legs bent forward as though he'd been trying to run backward. As Demi's gift sizzled toward him, the pale frost covering his body darkened. Smoke filled the cell until skin and the colour of his hair and clothing began to show through. His face contorted, his eyes blinking in surprise. Then he saw Demi and tried to draw himself up tall, a furious look in his eyes as he fought against the ice still thawing around his hips and legs.

"Let's do this the honourable way," Demi said, her voice like rolling thunder in the distance. "Who are you and why are you attacking this court?"

Lorens' gaze darted back and forth, taking in his still frozen companions and the lack of guards. His eyes raked over Odella briefly and Sannar forced himself to stay beside her instead of moving in front. Not only because it would give the others the wrong idea, but he knew Odella would readily grumble about him blocking her view and he was too exhausted to handle squabbling with her.

"I'm waiting for an answer and I'm not as chill as everyone makes out," Demi added.

She eyed her fingernails, her foot tapping while Taz

toyed idly with a small orb on a keychain.

Lorens grimaced. "I appear to have found myself in a situation, your majesty."

"Your majesty? Not 'my queen'? Interesting. And yes, you do, but it's the specifics of your situation that I'm waiting for. Are you part of the Forgotten?"

Lorens didn't answer. Perhaps he knew as well as Sannar did that the cells were made of *metirin* iron, unchanging. Sannar doubted even the queen would be able to overcome that element despite her bountiful power.

"Would you like us to remove him, my queen?" he asked, erring on the side of caution and using her title. "Although he seems to have a habit of being able to translocate even inside warded places. The wards could be stronger admittedly but they should keep most people out."

Demi raised her eyebrows. "And I assume he can't inside the iron or he would have done so by now."

She flicked a look at Taz, and his eyes shone with devilish malice.

"We could bring someone in to torture him," he suggested. "You know, the human way. Nails to scrape and blades to slice."

Lorens gulped, his legs wriggling against the last of the ice still holding his feet and ankles. Sannar bit his lip. The court had their own ways of dealing with people and torture wasn't one of them. He couldn't bring himself to disagree with the queen, but even the thought of Lorens attacking Odella couldn't quiet the discomfort.

It's not right, even if he is part of the Forgotten.

"We could send him into that pit, the one under the mountain," Demi added, her tone entirely conversational. "Sannar, is the beastie still sleeping?"

He nodded. "Sweetly, and I really don't think we want

to be waking it up right now, unless you can bring *someone* here to lull it again." He resisted using Reyan's name in front of Lorens. "Also, the lady might be a bit iffy about bloodletting captives under her watch."

"Noted." Demi snorted. "Which leaves us with questioning first. However, he doesn't seem to want to answer."

"He's not shy of wanting things though," Odella said. "He seems insistent that he wants me to join them. Or him, I'm not sure."

Sannar tensed beside her.

If Demi tries to use her, even as the queen…

"Did he now? Interesting. I know what your gift is so I can guess why he wants you. Unless there's some undying secret romance or illicit bond between you?"

Odella flinched. "Eww, no. I've met him four times now, two of which he tried to bribe me, or coerce me, I'm not sure which. The last two he tried to trick me into deals and attack me."

Demi's grin was nothing short of terrifying as she nodded and faced Lorens once more. Her skin paled, sparkles gracing the surface while hints of orange flame flickered underneath. The effect was somewhat ruined by Taz beaming lovingly at her as she advanced on the cell, but Lorens veered back as best he could while still tethered to the floor by the ice around his feet.

"The Forever mountains it is then," she said wickedly, her tone rolling dark and low. "I do wish your mother had let me overhaul it, Taz, but still. I'm sure this one has plenty of old friends there to meet and greet."

Lorens' eyes widened further. "You can't send me there. There's no way out, even for me."

"Answer her questions then," Taz said. "All we need is

to know why the Forgotten are targeting this court and what the flow of origins has to do with their plans. Also, the location of their base would be handy. Some names. Maybe even-" he hesitated as Demi shot him an impatient look. "Right, sorry."

Lorens mumbled something under his breath, his lips moving silently. Then he stood taller and stared Demi in the face.

"A lot has probably been kept from me but the Blood and Bone Court uses me to find out as much as I can about the flow of origins. They don't trust after the last war and would rather act in secret. I have tasks to do and there's some money, then I do the job."

He's a hired hand. Sannar stared at him with sinking realisation. *There's nothing much he can tell us about the enemy after all. And he seemed so confident.*

"Why do they want it?" Demi asked.

"Only they can say. I was told to come to the Nether Court, venture up into the mountains and locate the information. I've been coming in for the past month or so, in and out to avoid being seen. Until her."

He nodded at Odella, who pulled a face back at him, her arms folded tight across her chest.

"How did you get in through the wards?" Sannar asked.

Lorens shrugged. "I skip. I've always been able to. The nether doesn't seem to flow around me like it does others."

Demi and Taz exchanged a look but neither commented any further on that.

"How close are the Forgotten to getting what they need?" she asked.

"I can't rightly say. The person I deal with has a female voice, strong and demanding. She was excited when I mentioned being found here though, not what I expected.

Then they sent me here to be a decoy and I'm right in the middle of a fight."

Sannar huffed. "You seemed pretty keen to fight alongside them, even against people who weren't fighting you."

"I did what I had to."

"Why?" he pushed.

Demi let him, her eyes fixed on Lorens the whole time.

"The whole thing is about getting access to somewhere. The woman I speak to is obsessed with it. I figured getting her on side would bring me more opportunity for the future than the information alone. I do what I need to survive."

Sannar noticed the pink tinge leaping to Odella's cheeks, no doubt powered by the thought of what could have happened to her. When he slid a protective arm around her waist, she sank against him.

"Well, this is all interesting," Demi said. "But nothing more than confirmation of what we suspected. Nothing more than pretty words that could mean anything and nothing. Come along."

Lorens reached out to grab the bars, almost wobbling off balance.

"What are you going to do with me?" he asked, his voice demanding.

Demi strode to the door with Taz at her side before turning back and giving him a smug smile.

"I'll unfreeze everyone and you can all have a little chat about what you've told us. Won't that be nice?"

Sannar rushed to lock the cell again, then he clenched his arm tight around Odella and swept her along beside him as they hurried after Demi and Taz. He stopped to lock the door behind him even though it was pointless with the huge hole in the wall. He would have to get someone to come and rebuild that part immediately.

By the time his shaking hands had managed it the others were already waiting by the trundle. Memories of Odella helping him lock the cells danced in his head, but he made no move toward her as the four of them got into the trundle and he set the latch to take them up to the exit. He wanted fresh air and the courtyard. Perhaps if he was quick he could escape to the kitchen or his room before anyone collared him.

Since when do I shirk my duties because I'm tired? He bit his lip. *I should also see Odella back down to town as well. It must be the middle of the night now.*

"Is there anything you need before I try to make sure everything is calm again?" he asked, his tone weary.

Demi glanced at him, no doubt taking in the wan complexion and the sheer dogged tiredness zapping his attempt at a smile.

"We should discuss this but maybe waiting for morning is best. You look like death, no offense."

Sannar chuckled, relieved. "None taken. 'Della tells me that on a good day, and today has definitely been one I'll want to forget." He glanced at Odella. "The last part of it anyway."

She gave him a weary look and turned her head away. Panic thrummed through him when he realised it sounded as though he was blaming her for getting him into the mess in the first place.

Technically she did, but if we hadn't been there the whole thing could have been so much worse.

He tried not to imagine the chaos spilling into the court for a second time, but he couldn't shake the image from his head. Even as the trundle stopped and he let the others out, dodging around them to lead the way to the courtyard on weary feet, he was plagued by what could have been.

He almost didn't notice the unexpected sound of raised voices in front of them as they exited the mountain onto the fringe of the courtyard.

"There you are!" Lady Aereen's voice screeched through the air. "What is going on? All we hear are rumblings from the mountain, then I go down to see you admitting a flow of captives into our dungeon!"

Sannar stared back at her, speechless. She had her hair still done, although the wispy white strands were escaping fast, and he guessed she hadn't bothered unravelling her finery after the day's events before going to bed. Perhaps she'd expected another round of arguing with the queen, but then her words registered and his heart sank.

She thinks I had something to do with it.

He saw Arno lurking at Lady Aereen's elbow and guessed that he'd been sneaking around and run straight to her to tattle.

"I didn't notice you attempting to stem that flow," Demi said, her voice frosty.

Lady Aereen hesitated, caught out. Sannar couldn't stop staring at her, the dagger of bewildered treachery digging deeper into his chest.

She automatically assumes I was letting them in. Not even questioning it. Everything I've done for this court, every extra stupid task...

He flinched as Odella's fingers wrapped around his hand. She nestled against his side, moving his arm behind them so that nobody in front of them would see. So nobody would know that he was an inch from breaking.

But she knew.

"I was trying to hold them back. I did my best," he mumbled.

Odella's grip on him tightened as the queen shot him a sympathetic look. Pity from someone he'd hoped to seem strong in front of.

All the wild, fleeting fantasies he'd had in the last day or so of Demi seeing his worth and perhaps even asking him to transfer to her court and finally earn a name for himself seemed laughable now. He'd made his lowly bed at the Nether Court by being useful, and now he would live and no doubt die in it.

"I have no doubt of that," Demi told him. "I won't dance around my words, but your lady does you a *serious* disservice by doubting you, let alone making random assumptions."

Lady Aereen drew herself tall, towering over Demi by at least a head and possibly even topping Taz by a centimetre or two. Her dark eyes flashed with the fury of someone who'd lived long in her entitlement.

"He isn't supposed to be in the Keep. He's supposed to be up here managing my court. Is it any wonder that the Flora Court had to wait to be served and that half the brothers are in uproar because nobody has arranged the space for their research yet?"

Sannar wanted to scream. He wanted to scream that he had arranged the space but half of them had turned their noses up at it. He wanted to scream that he was beyond done with her and her stupid court, and if breaking the oath he took to serve killed him, so be it. Only Odella's hand around his kept him from raging, because who would see her safely back to town if he was pulverised on the spot?

Then he took a look at Odella's face and almost stepped away in alarm. Her cheeks were bright pink and her eyes had narrowed, extra bright behind her glasses as her lip curled with disgust.

"That's pathetic," she snarled. "Is it any wonder he had to take some time away when the court can't cope without him for the space of an evening? You expect him to be everyone's errand boy, yet he's the one keeping this place running, making sure everyone has what they need, hosting *your* guests! Oh, and don't get me started on the wardings."

"Odella, leave it," he begged.

"No, I won't!" She turned that acidic glare on him next. "You do everything around here, and who ever heard of an entire court being solely protected by the wardings of a seventeen year old boy?!"

A pin dropping could have set off an avalanche in the resounding silence that followed. Her breathing was coming in ragged huffs and Sannar had no idea how to calm her.

He didn't care about the lady's reputation and Demi already knew the situation. But Odella looked like she was about to start hyperventilating, so he did the only thing he could think of to calm her down.

He grinned. "I would prefer young man, but your heart's in the right place I guess."

He thought she might slap his face for a moment, but then she dropped his hand and folded her arms, scoffing in disgust. The entire routine was like heaven to him because he'd succeeded in bringing her back to her normal, charming self.

"You're an idiot," she muttered.

He nodded. "Also quite possibly true. But as I owe you for back there, I'll let it slide."

"That's three favours you owe me."

"Actually it's one big favour, then one more normal one I now owe you."

She glanced at him warily. "What if I wanted three normal favours?"

"You sound like you know what you want already."

He tried not to let the intrigue show on his face because if he did, she would automatically refuse to tell him out of the principle of making him either squirm or beg for it.

"Maybe."

Lady Aereen seemed unable to speak, perhaps rendered silent by the insult to her leadership. Demi and Taz were both grinning though, and Demi sauntered toward them with a chuckle.

"You two can finish whatever this is later. Sannar, go to sleep, queen's orders. I don't mind where. Don't get up early tomorrow either."

He nodded. "I will once I've walked 'Della home."

He took a step away expecting Odella to follow him, but Demi shook her head.

"We'll see her back safe," she said. "She and I need to have a quick chat."

Odella froze, her eyes wide. Sannar searched her face as she gave him a helpless look like a frightened rabbit. Demi recognised his hesitation and rolled her eyes.

"I give you my queenly promise she will be returned home safe, and here safe tomorrow morning. Oh, assuming you actually need to come back up here?"

Odella was still looking at Sannar for guidance and he nodded, a wordless invite. The lady would probably be down on him like a banshee the moment Demi was out of sight, but if he was lucky he might get his rest first. A queen's promise wasn't to be snuffed at, court lady or not.

"I'll be fine," Odella told him. "Go rest, you look like crud."

He nodded, both to the looking like crud part and the

242

resting part. She wasn't exactly fit for company either, the normally shiny brown tresses of her hair a tangled mess with one side hanging down and the other still tied behind her head, her face streaked with what looked like dust and her clothes caked in muck.

She was without a doubt the most beautiful woman he'd ever seen.

And she was staring at him. With that tiny little furrow between her eyebrows that said something along the lines of 'okay, why are you still staring at me like some weirdo?'

Sannar almost burbled random words of gratitude when Taz appeared beside him with a quiet hand on his shoulder, turning him around and leading him away.

As they walked toward the brothers' quarters, Sannar glanced back to find Demi and Odella standing close together with Lady Aereen still glaring daggers at them.

"I'm an idiot," he muttered. "She's right about that. And everything else."

Taz snorted. "They always are. Total pains in the behind too. But we love them."

Love. Is it too soon for that? Sannar turned at the door to the building before walking through it, taking one last look at Odella. *Oh, orbs.*

CHAPTER TWENTY
ODELLA

Odella was too furious to be truly awed or afraid of the queen wanting to speak to her. The only thought in her head the moment Taz led Sannar away was marching a few steps across the courtyard and strangling his lady with her own stupid hair.

"We'll leave you to manage your court, Lady Aereen," Demi said, her tone laced with warning. "I would advise you to leave Sannar be. No disturbances, no getting others to run to him with problems on your behalf, no sneaky noises or dramas to bring him to you."

Lady Aereen sniffed, her body permanently set in a rigid haughtiness. Without a word, she turned away and stalked across the courtyard to her building. As Demi watched her go, Odella eyed the door that Sannar was now disappearing through and closing behind him.

I'm furious. And I know why I'm furious. Stupid feelings. I hate when Mix is right. Hate hate hate the lot of them. Except him. But that's the problem.

"Better out than in," Demi said. "Taz makes me want to throttle him at least ten times a day, but I find venting to someone helps."

Odella rubbed her hands over her face, bending over with an agonised laugh.

"You're a queen. I can't moan about my love life to royalty."

She transferred her hands to her mouth in alarm. 'Love life' sounded scarily real.

"Ah, so it is a love life thing." Demi grinned. "Yay, that means Taz owes me a doughnut. Anyway, they've not been treating him very well here, have they?"

Odella straightened up, the residual fury pounding in waves.

"No. He's been managing the whole court himself. Then I found out he's been warding the whole place himself without any proper training because nobody else would bother. He even came to town tonight to see... well I don't know if it was actually to see me. I think he wanted to see our old friends as well, but it ended up being me and him, and I egged him on to come up here, which I know is basically worth being punished for but it's too late to word-tangle about it now. He didn't want to though, frustratingly dutiful, so I snuck up here and he came down to the Keep and found me. Is he going to be in trouble?"

Demi shook her head. "No, not if I can help it, and I will. He held back a whole horde of Forgotten on his own at the risk of exhausting his gift completely. I'm not sure if we actually have some kind of award for this sort of thing-" She hesitated and scrambled in the pocket of her jeans, pulling out a sparkling white mini-orb on a keychain. "Note to Milo: find out if we have any kind of award system. If not, invent one."

Odella nodded. She liked the idea of that. Sannar of all people deserved recognition.

Demi replaced her orb in her pocket and smiled.

"My friend Milo insists on running my court for me. He gets really excited about it so this whole new award idea will be like a present for him. He's weird like that but we love him. Now, I wanted to speak to you about you."

Demi glanced around, no doubt looking for any lurking ears. When a bubble of protection surrounded them as a hazy rainbow, Odella couldn't hear the subtle sounds coming from the court anymore. Before Demi could say a thing, the words tumbled out.

"I want to help," she said. "I don't know why Lorens was targeting me, Sannar thinks because of my gift. I can basically manipulate rock, like mould it, soften it, break it away. He thinks that the Forgotten will want me to open whatever this flow of origins thing is. But I hate them."

Demi raised her eyebrows. "Hate is a strong word, but I appreciate the sentiment. We would essentially ask you to do the same thing if the time ever came for it, but also I'm trying to make sure that anyone who wants to advance in various areas of Faerie can do it without needing to be entitled. Or titled. Or even pure Fae."

"Yeah, we get that message loud and clear." Odella risked a grin. "A lot of people are on your side, at least around town they are. And my dad sails a lot so he meets other people from far away and most of them are for you as well."

Demi rubbed a hand over the back of her neck, and Odella stared to see the queen of Faerie blushing awkwardly.

"That's nice to hear," she admitted. "Scary as anything, but nice. If you were to help us though, you'd have to be sworn to a court."

Odella grimaced. "Really? I doubt the lady would accept me after what I just said to her."

She wondered then if Lady Reyan might consider accepting her. They'd spoken once before and she seemed kind enough to consider it.

Demi's expression cleared. Now that Odella was standing in front of her without anything exploding around them, she realised that Demi's gaze never fully met hers, always flicking up to her face then diverting elsewhere.

"There are other courts," Demi reminded her, amused. "I would be happy to welcome you into mine. You could stay here in town of course, except for when you needed to help. Or if you fancy adventure there might be a position at Arcanium, but you'd need to apply and earn it like anyone else would."

Odella's pulse took flight. The queen of Faerie was choosing her, *her*, to be a part of the royal court. Or an FDP if she wanted to apply. Perhaps she could be a mentor, although she guessed she might not have the patience to excel at that.

I would have leapt at the chance for this a day or so ago. She eyed the building that housed the brothers' quarters. *I only just started being friends with him again. What do I do?*

"Do I have to decide right now?" she asked.

"No, but I'd appreciate an answer in the next couple of days. If it takes longer, we might not have the upper hand over the Forgotten anymore."

Odella nodded. "I never considered myself ever being important enough to be sworn to a court."

If I really could choose any, would I?

She thought about the other courts, ticking them off and discarding each one. The Flora Court were known to be nature mad, which was fine but she couldn't imagine holing away in a greenhouse like the nether brothers did in their research rooms. The Court of Revels would be fun but they travelled a lot and she enjoyed having a place to call home. She'd heard that the Illusion Court was wholly underground and the Court of Words was stuck high in the snowy mountains somewhere. The Fauna Court sounded like fun with all the animals, but her dad had once met a man who said there was a lot of anatomical inspection that went on, and she didn't like the sound of having to do mostly note-taking.

No, if I was to pick a court, the queen's would have been my dream. Or here so I could be close to home.

She also didn't want to risk being at a court's mercy for the rest of her life, especially when she remembered how Sannar was tied to his duties and used like a dishrag by his entire court.

Demi grinned at her. "Go talk it over with him. He'll probably still be awake."

"I can't go creeping into his bedroom!" Odella whispered, scandalised. "What if someone saw me? It'd get back to my parents and they'd have… okay they'd be overjoyed actually. They've always been fond of him but they'd tease me forever, and you said he needed to rest."

"He does, but I'm sure he'd be happy for a bit of a chat beforehand. Think of it like a bedtime story."

"What would people think?"

Demi giggled. "Well I'm not going to tell them."

She looked up and an expression of withering resignation crossed her face. Odella followed her gaze and bit her lip to hide her laughter as Sannar came creeping out of the brothers' quarters with Taz tiptoeing on equally sneaky feet behind him.

"I swear, if one person takes me seriously one day, I'll die of shock," Demi muttered. "Excuse me."

Odella had no intention of excusing her like an equal or being excused like a subordinate, so she kept a few paces behind as Demi broke the protection around them and stormed across the courtyard.

"Going somewhere?" Demi asked.

Taz turned but Sannar flinched three feet in the air.

Guess that sound-cancelling bubble made us invisible too.

Odella caught his bewildered eye and struggled to keep the grin off her face.

"We were sneaking to the kitchens," Taz admitted. "We haven't eaten in about two hours, and Sannar said that his chef might have some *kaprike* left, and I haven't had that since I was a kid."

The subtle whine in his voice was probably for dramatic effect, but Sannar inched around him and sidled toward Odella, no doubt hoping Demi might forget he was there.

She gave him a smug smile as he reached her.

"Not doing what you're told?" she teased. "I'm shocked."

"I'm a grown man," he muttered, perhaps still sore about the 'seventeen-year-old boy' comment. "If I want to take the king consort to the kitchens in my own court, I can."

Odella tutted, then realised that Demi and Taz had vanished.

"Huh." She searched the courtyard but it was empty except for the two of them. "I'd watch your words though. She has this magic bubble that makes whoever's inside inaudible and invisible."

Sannar's shoulders lowered, his entire body seeming to dribble into his usual slouch.

"I've heard of people who can summon those. Blanket wardings they call it. Can I ask what she wanted to talk to you about?"

Odella nodded. "You can ask."

She waited until he rolled his eyes.

"Fine. What did she want to talk to you about?"

He walked to a nearby bench and slithered onto it. She

sat beside him, mindful to leave a respectful gap between them. No sense cosying up to him, not when she wasn't sure what his feelings were or what her court decision would be. But Demi had told her to talk it over, and Sannar was somehow the person she trusted most in all the realms of Faerie.

"She asked me to help them," she explained. "I said I would before she asked, but that's what she wants. She did say I'd have to swear to one of the courts first though and that she'd be happy to have me in hers. Ideally she wants my answer in a couple of days."

Sannar tensed beside her, his shoulders going rigid again as he sat up. She wished she could read his mind then, but his eyes were fixed on the stone under their feet.

"That's a very high honour," he said, his tone wooden. "To have the queen herself offer you a place in her court."

He sounded like she'd told him his favourite family member had died.

Is he in shock? She frowned. *Or is he wondering why Demi asked for me and not him?*

Her emotions froze before twisting painfully in her chest. The memory of that day four years ago rushed back. Sannar had started being nice to her, but it didn't automatically mean that his thoughts about her lack of importance or court status had changed.

No. He's not like that. He's never been like that, except for that one day which he admitted he regrets. But surely it can't be just because he's going to miss me?

She didn't dare hope, but he huffed a weary chuckle and shook his head, still staring at the floor.

"The Revels Court is all about having fun," he said. "But you might find it chaotic. They travel a lot too. The Flora Court is meant to be breathtakingly beautiful and they are peaceful, but you wouldn't get to travel much at all, if ever. Lord Kainen and Lady Reyan might take you, but I reckon she would want to adopt you as her friend and have you making renovations to their court's halls for the rest of your life."

Odella bit her lips together to snare the smile creeping up. Even when he mentioned the virtues, he sounded like he was announcing a death sentence.

"Court of Words I don't know much about, or Fauna," he added. "I guess Demi might let you speak to each one if there's time. Then of course there's this one, but you'd still need someone to speak on your behalf before being sworn in."

She chuckled. "That's one off the list then."

He lifted his head, and the bewildered sadness in his eyes gave her emotions a swift, breath-stealing punch.

"I'd speak for you if you did want to choose the Nether Court. But would you want that? It's not necessarily interesting work. The queen's court has all the benefits."

She shrugged. "It would make sense though. My family are here, my friends are here." *You're here.* "What would being sworn to this court involve?"

He bit his lip, but she recognised the subtle increase in animation as he twisted to face her, his eyes brightening.

"Well, you'd be given a role to undertake. I could likely help with that and set you up alongside your mum if you wanted, or in the kitchens or the research rooms. Anywhere really. We're fed well and if you wanted to go down to the town you could. You'd probably have to take a room here, but I could see if they'd let you live at home. I mean, it has been done before I think, and I'm sure if I misplace some paperwork nobody would notice anyway."

She started laughing as he smiled. Somehow, him

smiling made the whole world seem right again, as if they could face the Forgotten a million more times without a sweat.

He was halfway through taking a breath, no doubt to go on about potential manipulations of his copious duties to convince her to choose his court, when he noticed her laughing.

"What's so funny?" he asked.

She shook her head and leaned sideways to nudge her shoulder against his. As she did so, her hand brushed his thigh and he jumped.

So skittish. She grinned. *I'll need to think about it properly, but the queen's court has prestige and adventure, while the Nether Court has home, family, friends and him. At least I only need to pick from two.*

"You. You're funny. It almost sounds like you *want* me to stay here, to choose the Nether Court."

His cheeks flushed, barely noticeable in the firelight, but as he shrugged she fought the urge to wrap her arms around him and see if that made him even more flustered.

"It's your decision though," he said.

She decided to take that as a yes, not that she needed confirmation. She was almost certain he'd come to town earlier to see her as much as face Sammy and Mix again. She also knew he could have backed out of going with her to the meadows alone, and with a somewhat romantic picnic. She didn't intend to make that realisation easy on him though.

"Sorry to intrude."

Demi materialised in front of them before Odella could think up a way to tease him more.

Sannar groaned quietly. "That's okay, you've saved me from what I'm guessing was about to be some kind of teasing offensive."

Odella flicked him a sarky look. *Smarty know-it-all.*

"Oh, then I really am sorry." Demi grinned. "But I've been thinking and giving you only a couple of days to decide your future really isn't fair. So, I have a counteroffer. I'll take you as being sworn to my court for six months. After that, you'll be free to resume your normal life without any obligation, as long as you stay loyal to me and my court for those six months, and of course loyal to the good of Faerie thereafter."

It was an amazing offer. Nobody could ever dispute that. But as Odella tried to smile, she had to face the ugly truth that she'd been all but ready to choose the Nether Court. Now, she'd be a fool to walk away from such a wonderful offer.

She blinked as Sannar's fingers slid over her hand, clasping tight. She looked up at him, baffled to find him smiling.

"Six months isn't so long," he said. "You'll barely have time to miss anyone."

She squeezed his fingers, pulled her hand free and stood up.

"Can I take until morning to think it over?" she asked.

Demi glanced around. "It is morning almost, but yeah, take today to think it over."

"Thank you. I'm going to go home, sleep, talk it over with my mum and see if I can get in touch with my dad as he was due to leave last night. But it *is* an amazing offer."

Sannar stood and she knew he was fully ready to walk her home. But Demi stepped between them, a symbolic gesture almost.

"I'll translocate you back," she offered. "Sannar needs his rest and I'd like to see your town before it gets too busy."

Odella stared at the hand Demi held out then gave Sannar a helpless look. She couldn't quite read the smile he gave her in return, but she wanted to believe the carefree expression really was hiding emotions underneath.

She took Demi's hand along with a deep, steadying breath.

Time to make some sensible decisions.

One of which was picking up her jewellery bag, she realised, or Demi might not get her bracelets after all.

CHAPTER TWENTY ONE
REYAN

The bedroom door banging back on its hinges wasn't the way Reyan expected to wake. She blinked in the glare of the bright sunshine filtering in through the window, reminding her they were still at the Nether Court.

They moment Demi had dismissed everyone from the Keep the night before, they'd seen themselves back up to the courtyard and found it in chaos. Even Kainen's charm had no effect on Lady Aereen's dramatic screeching, but the moment the mountain stopped shaking and they saw Demi and the others come out, Kainen had insisted on leaving the situation to those in charge. Exhausted, they'd crashed into bed without more than a couple of mumbles to each other, the sound of the chaos quietening outside audible through the open window.

Reyan struggled up in a swamp of blankets, blinking blearily with one hand raised as though she could actually defend herself if needed.

Kainen leapt to his feet, which would have been way more effective if he hadn't been still clinging onto her hand, and she choked down the urge to laugh as Demi strode in.

"Sorry, would have knocked this time but after last night my brain's fried."

Demi pushed the door shut behind her, pressing her back against the wood and eying them warily.

Kainen sank back onto the bed with an undecipherable grumble. Reyan slid herself sideways toward him, using the movement to hide their clasped hands under the blankets. Demi knew their relationship was a ruse and the last thing Reyan needed was questions about whether she was getting in too deep with believing in it. She wasn't titled to the Illusion Court in reality, and wouldn't be, but she had enough trouble sorting out her own mind without Demi's gentle but inevitable prying into her feelings.

"The Court of Illusions often wakes late," she said, aware of Kainen still not showing his usual charm.

You are so not a morning person, she teased, sending her voice into his head.

He gave her a 'really?' look. *Not unless the wake-up is a good one, no.*

"I've had to move the plan forward," Demi added, not waiting for them to finish mind-speaking. "After last night, I'm going to have to ask you to help move people to the Forever mountains if you can."

Kainen's sulkiness disappeared. "How many?"

"Thirty in the cells. I've got FDPs moving them already, but there's one I want a bit of special treatment for."

"And you trust me to do it?" Shock echoed in his voice.

Reyan squeezed his fingers then wished she hadn't as his thumb started rubbing back and forth over her knuckles, leaving a zingy warmth.

Demi's smile was wistful, her body remaining pinned to the door as though she could fade through it if she had to. Trust was a hard thing to earn in Faerie and almost impossible to re-earn, but Reyan frowned at the thought there was still doubt between them, and that it might never entirely fade.

"I do." Demi nodded. "You have skill with compulsion and I'm also out of time. Turns out Sannar and Odella went wandering last night and managed to dig up a few useful bits of information. Emil's been mentioned as having access to the Prime Realm, or a contact there at least. No idea how or who, but it's worrying. We need to get as much information as we can, and this Lorens bloke seems to be able to get into all sorts of places to overhear things. Oh, and Taz is waiting for you in the courtyard, Reyan. He said something about gift training?"

Reyan had forgotten about her transmutation gift but memories surfaced of her inability to use it while fighting during the night.

She nodded. "Transmutation."

Demi eyed Kainen. "Your doing?"

"Yeah, she needs to be able to protect herself if I'm not around. I figured she's also a good choice for transmutating stuff to defend against *metirin* iron if we have to fight it."

Reyan didn't miss the hint of belligerence in his tone, as though he expected to be told off for it. She guessed Demi had noted it too as her brow lifted momentarily.

"Good idea," she said. "The Flora Court will be hosting a revel which I'll need you both to attend. It won't be straight away but soon, so keep your calendars flexible. Until then, go meet Taz out front for now and I'll come get you both when it's prisoner transport time."

She swept out of the room without waiting for any agreement, pulling the door shut behind her. Reyan sagged.

"She's determined not to act queenly, isn't she?"

Kainen grinned. "I don't know about that. She seems quite happy issuing orders. I'll go back to the court and check in while you get changed and ready."

He let go of her hand and swung to his feet with a groan.

She stayed on the bed, a smile tugging at her lips as he looked back at her before vanishing in a cloud of glittering black smoke.

Unwilling to keep a king consort waiting, Reyan scrambled off the bed, grabbed a change of clothes and dipped into the bathroom. As she freshened up and pulled on the stretchy black trousers and her comfiest long shirt, she let her mind spool through everything.

Demi was worried even though she tried to hide it with sweeping about the place issuing orders and being generally unqueenly about it.

The Forgotten were searching for the entry to the Prime Realm, for what purpose it wasn't entirely clear.

But Kainen was worried about her. Not just as the fake lady to his court either, because if that was the only reason he could have convinced, compelled or coerced her to stay at court. But he wanted her to be able to protect herself, to the point he was giving her a gift that he knew someone else could help her hone.

He'd also willingly accepted Betty into their fake family as easily as Betty had taken to him, a definite positive sign.

Without Betty's warning last night could have been so much worse.

She wondered if that was what Belladonna wanted a shadow-snake for, to sense people approaching or generally feel out areas. But thankfully Betty was safe now with them instead.

She tied her hair back and patted the spiky end of the stubby ponytail.

And I'm apparently safe with Kainen, for now at least.

He cared about her and she didn't have the faintest idea how to process that or what to do about it. But hovering in the sanctuary of the bathroom wouldn't solve anything.

She walked into the bedroom to find him lounging on the bed.

"Are you going to be okay with this?" she asked.

He turned his head, frowning up at her. "With what?"

"If Taz is throwing shots at me to practice with or something, will your whole court protective thing cope?"

She didn't want to upset him by bringing it up again but she couldn't exactly dance around it either. That wouldn't help anyone.

He stood up and rounded the bed toward the door, holding it open.

"He's not going to risk hurting you."

She had to take that as reassurance and walk past him, but the subtle growl in his tone suggested it was as much Kainen promising her that Taz wouldn't have the opportunity as it was his trust in Taz's ability not to hurt her.

The sunlight drenched the courtyard in heat and Reyan had the urge to curl up beneath it and snooze the whole day away. Unable to do that, she approached Taz who standing with his wings outstretched and flaming in the sunshine. His smile slipped ever so slightly as he looked past her, but she knew he and Kainen had a less than cosy history.

"Don't trust me with members of your court, Kainen?" he called.

Reyan glanced over her shoulder in time to see Kainen's expression shutter. He shrugged, hands in his pockets.

"Call it curiosity. Actually, call it whatever you orbing well like. This is training, not sparring, got it?"

Taz grinned, a flicker of Fae-like wickedness crossing his face.

"Clearer than the murkiest pool at the bottom of the *Faraerian* seas. So, Reyan, let's begin."

Reyan smothered a snort. Even she in her cloistered court-bound existence knew that the *Faraerian* seas were an almost impenetrable mass of weed-water with toxic depths that birthed the weirdest and most dangerous of sea creatures.

Taz held up a hand and pressed his thumb to his fingertips, snapping his fingers open to summon a cup.

"The first step is to go through how to transmutate. Luckily I already knew someone who told me how it felt, and that was about the extent of my training, but it helped. It's like using any other gift, you sense the matter of the substance and believe you can change it's state."

Reyan frowned. "So like calling my shadows, or shaping them."

"Exactly." He stepped closer so they were right in front of each other. "Try focusing on the liquid in this cup first. No trying to attack it though because Kainen looks like he's going to decapitate me if anything happens."

Reyan ignored the burning embarrassment on her face and drew her connection together. She focused her gaze on the cup but then closed her eyes to visualise it instead.

The energy of the cup felt colder than the liquid inside it. Like the mountain that held the *Maladorac*, solidness containing something still but active that could move at any moment.

"You have the ability to turn the liquid to solid," Taz said gently. "Slow it down until it matches the matter around it."

She focused, her brow furrowed and her fists clenching at her sides.

"Don't fight it or try to convince it. You have the ability now to change anything you choose to, but you need to believe you can. Make it obey you."

Reyan bit her lip. The gift was right there at the front of her consciousness, tugging at her will, urging her to shift the liquid into solid matter. But somewhere inside her head doubt lingered.

Doubt that swayed with instant submission to the familiar voice that echoed in her head.

It doesn't have feelings, sweetheart. It's not like controlling a person. It's why I chose transmutation and not compulsion for you, because you're too sweet for your own good.

The affection in his tone was veiled by a healthy dose of amused taunting. As if he knew exactly what to say to rile her, to put her on the defensive. He gave her the reassurance she needed to do what she had to do.

She let the gift run free, wordlessly commanding the liquid to solidify. When she opened her eyes, she felt as though she'd run a marathon. Huffing in a breath, she leaned forward to peer into the cup.

"A bit smooshy still, but basically a solid," Taz announced. "Great for a first go!"

She guessed he was being nice about it and flinched as something warm and firm slid over her hip.

"Using a new gift drains your energy," Kainen said, his arm now tight around her waist. "That's enough for now. Practice with tiny things whenever you can."

Taz nodded. "Agreed. Let me know if you have any questions though. The secret to gift-use is knowing that the magic doesn't take sides. It goes where the power of mind is, but it's up to us to wield it wisely."

Was that directed at Kainen or me?

Kainen sighed. "Was that directed at her or me?"

Taz shrugged, smiling faintly. He glanced around and even though he probably spent every spare minute of every day with his girlfriend, his face lit up when he saw Demi walking toward them.

I wish I had that. Reyan resolutely refused to look Kainen's way. *I need to get a grip on the problem, not start mooning around after someone I probably can't have.*

Demi glanced around the courtyard as she reached them and a subtle hush settled. The courtyard continued going on around them, but the sound had disappeared and a faint haze of rainbow light domed around them.

"Can't risk anyone hearing this," she said. "I've made an exorbitant deal with the prisoner in question, but we need to keep up appearances."

"Deals are a necessity in Faerie," Kainen reminded her.

Demi pulled a face. "Yeah, but as much as I hate having to pull rank, I hate having to deal with traitors more, yet I have to do it for the 'greater good' which is a ridiculous practice."

Kainen said nothing more, but Reyan caught the flash of discomfort crossing his face.

"So, there's one of the captives that we need to release, but the others can't know we're doing it."

Reyan frowned. "You want us to let someone go but pretend it's an accident?"

"That's the one. His name is Lorens and he can apparently realm-skip at will which in itself is worrying. But that was the deal, his 'accidental' freedom for some information he leaked."

"Is he high up in their chain?" Kainen asked. "The name isn't familiar."

Taz shook his head. "I don't know of him either."

"Maybe it's a fake identity?" Reyan suggested.

"Possibly." Demi sighed. "But the Forgotten seem to have all sworn not to blab any details, and he is the only one we've seen so far who isn't. That likely means he's not one of them, only working for them."

"Or so powerful that they can't control him," Kainen added.

"Again, a possibility. Which is why we need to let him think we don't suspect him beyond being one of their minions. We've pretended to swallow his 'I'm just a go-between' lie and made a deal with him."

Kainen rubbed his hand on his shoulder, his brow furrowed in deep thought.

"Are we transporting anyone else?" he asked. Demi shook her head. "Right, then we make a show of dropping Reyan back home." He turned to face her. "I'll say that, then you insist you need to drop in on your father. We don't have to go in, but we stop in the village and give him time to vanish."

"What if he doesn't?" she asked.

"He will," Demi added. "It was part of the deal."

Reyan nodded. "Okay, that we can do. If you say in front of him that we're going straight home after our duties are done here, I'll ask to be taken back to my father's. We don't have to say why, but I'll figure out a way to word it."

Kainen smiled then, his worried expression softening.

"I'm sure you will. The second we land there though, warding up, okay? Promise me. The last thing we need is him trying to take the lady of our court hostage."

She nodded. "Promise."

It meant nothing as a word on its own and they both knew it, but she would do as he asked all the same.

"Right, I need to go and find Sannar." Demi grinned, a flicker of wicked amusement lighting in her eyes. "I get the feeling he might not be very happy with me right now. The man you need is in the corner cell furthest from the door, short brown hair, very chatty and always looks exceedingly pleased with himself."

Sounds from the courtyard filtered back in and Reyan realised they'd been completely stuck in a protective secrecy bubble. She watched Demi and Taz walk off toward the mountain entrance that led to the tunnels further up.

"Still baffles me that she's a queen marching around like a normal seventeen-year-old," she said.

Kainen nodded. "She'll never be a 'normal' queen, and that's probably what Faerie needs. Come on, let's get this done then I'm taking you home. Is there going to be any more nonsense about needing to come back here?"

He wouldn't meet her eyes, hiding his hope behind haughty lordliness. She bit her lip to veil a smile.

"I don't think Demi has anything left for me to do here or she'd have said, not until we need to make an appearance at this Flora Court revel or whatever it is. I could do with going home for a rest."

He didn't crow about it or tease her, but she recognised the pleased swagger in his step as she followed him across the courtyard. They stepped into the shadows of the tunnel and she took comfort from their cool presence as they gathered around her, focusing her new gift on them.

They didn't cower or slip away when she let them feel the gift's energy gathering. She held out her palm as Kainen guided her into one of the unbroken carts and pulled the lever to send it rumbling downwards.

"Ah-ah, no gifts right now." He grabbed her outstretched hand, running his thumb over her shadow-cloaked palm. "There'll be time to practice later but we need to get this done first."

She stuck her tongue out at him. "I was just testing it."

"And on any normal day I'd let you. But I don't trust this man even if Demi has made a deal with him. We need vigilance and all our wits."

Reyan glanced around even though they were the only two in the cart rumbling downwards.

"Shh! Nobody's meant to know that bit. Also, wits? You?"

He smiled. "Ouch, sweetheart. But you're right, we need to be the epitome of secrecy. What would I do without you?"

"Go back to your messy sock-strewn-floor ways probably."

He might have goaded her back but the cart came to a juddering halt and he opened the gate.

"Don't engage with any of them," he warned. "Don't speak to anyone. Don't make prolonged eye contact either. I'll do the talking."

As they walked down the long hall toward a cluster of guards, Reyan slid her hand into his.

"It'll be fine. Do your lordly thing and I'll chip in about stopping somewhere."

He nodded and they hesitated while the guards unlocked the door.

Demi will have told them to expect us, he whispered into her mind. *Warding up and allow yours to merge with mine.*

She took a deep breath and visualised her warding firm and strong around her, the hint of shadow doming until it knitted with the subtle spark and tingle of his.

He smiled as though the act of sharing a protection made him feel stronger and threw open the door to the Keep.

CHAPTER TWENTY TWO
SANNAR

The pile of blankets that were set aside for readers who used the upper levels thudded into the wall of the corridor. They fell with a muffled thump, but Sannar didn't bother to pick them up right away. He simply grabbed the next pile and threw that instead.

He'd not managed to sleep a wink, so conflicted about the situation with Odella's choice and also his place at court. Then the lady had called him into her office and insisted he was demoted to cleaning duty until he earned her favour back. Even worse, Arno was crowing about being promoted to the Chief Aide position to anyone who stood still long enough to listen.

He sighed, toying once again with the idea of reporting it, to Demi, but what would be the point? He could also be mad about Demi choosing Odella and not him, but he wasn't.

No, what he was furious about was Demi taking Odella away before he'd even had a chance to admit how he felt about her.

"Stupid queen," he muttered. "Being kind and ruining my chances to have 'Della around for good."

He didn't even care if Odella fancied him, not really, although that would be the sort of things his deepest dreams of late were spun into.

No, I just like her an awful lot and want to see her every day, find ways to make her smile and laugh and constantly prod me about things.

He didn't notice the shadow lurking in the doorway, his mind still distracted as he stormed through cleaning and clearing the blankets by lobbing them against the wall to de-dust them.

"*'Stupid queen'*, I wish I could say that's a new one."

Demi's amused voice filled the room and he almost died of shock. He stayed where he was, half bent over with an armful of blankets against his chest, as if keeping still might mean she wouldn't be able to see him.

"Don't worry, I'm not offended," Demi added. "I've had way worse hurled at me in my short life, and I did kind of offer to steal your girlfriend."

"She's not my girlfriend," he muttered.

"Oh. Why not?"

Why not? Because I don't know how to tell her. Because she might freak out if I do. Because I thought I'd have time and you ruined that!

He couldn't say that to a queen so instead he settled for dropping the blankets and forcing himself to face her.

Demi fixed him with a determined look.

"What do you think Odella should do?" she asked.

A good question, one he'd not stopping thinking about despite his tantrums.

"Honestly? I want her to choose the Nether Court, of course I do, but yours would open far more doors for her. She's strong-willed but her heart is the purest I've ever known and she's brave. Foolishly so more often than not, but you'd never regret taking her on."

Demi's lips twitched as she leaned her shoulder against the doorframe.

"I get that impression," she agreed.

He sighed. "I've told her it's her decision either way. Six months is a long time but it will pass all the same. If she chooses your offer then she would be creating great contacts for a future for herself, and I can't be the reason she misses out on that."

Demi watched him for a long moment of silence but he held his nerve. Where Odella was concerned he was apparently fearless, even in the face of a queen he'd just basically insulted who could incinerate him on the spot.

"Good." Demi nodded, her lips turning up happily. "That's settled then. I've asked your lady- well, actually I demanded, but still. Lady Aereen is going to lend me your services for six months. Seemed happy to get rid of you, so it'll be fun to see how the court fares in your absence. Either way you'll both be coming with us as we go a-hunting for the enemy's secrets."

Sannar's jaw dropped. A thousand possible answers flitted through his head, but he couldn't grab any of them. Demi sidled up to him with a laugh.

"You say thank you," she suggested. "Then you run after Odella and tell her what's happening before she does anything dim, like going to your lady and asking to swear to the Nether Court instead."

That thought shot through Sannar's head with alarming clarity, encompassing all else.

"Oh, orbs!"

Ignoring Demi laughing and the fact he was for the first time in his court-sworn 'career' leaving a job only half-done, he pivoted in the direction the trundles and took off down the hall at speed.

She can't choose the Nether Court, that would be sheer stupidity after what Demi's offered her.

He puffed into the trundle, aware his lack of sleep and the exertion from the fight with the Forgotten was going to be the death of him. Or more likely Odella was going to be the death of him. He grinned and sent the trundle downwards. He would get to her in time. He had to. She'd spend time talking it over with her parents, then she'd go to Sammy and Mix. He'd approach her at her house and tell her the queen wanted him to, make it sound like an adventure.

She wouldn't be dim enough to choose the Nether Court.

Unless… No, she isn't infatuated with me like I am with her, she can't be. Intrigued maybe, but that's not the same.

He shook the thought from his head and burst out of the trundle, picking up a laboured jog as he passed the startled guards at the mountain's entrance. He ignored Lord Bryson hollering after him as he skidded into the kitchen, narrowly missing the frying pan that the chef hurled at his head. Lindy's tutting echoed behind him, but whether she was berating her husband for attempting to maim her favourite nether brother or him for interrupting them, he didn't wait to find out.

He tumbled down the steps curling around the edge of the mountain, holding onto the rickety banister. Once he almost hit a turn too fast and tumbled into the water below, but he righted himself with a gust of his gift and hurried on.

Several townspeople stared at him as he panted past. His feet skidded on the cobbles but he was moving so fast he barely touched them, whooshing by the bakery and almost tumbling down the wrong lane in his hurry.

He hadn't even bothered to change his dust-stained clothes from the fight when he collapsed into bed, then he got summoned to his lady's office first thing, so the locals probably thought the court was about to come raining down on their heads given the state of him.

He didn't care.

He stumbled up the path to Odella's family's cottage and halted, doubling over to catch his breath. He had no hope of presenting himself well in this state, but being able to speak clearly would be a must.

"…wait for you." Odella's mother's voice floated out of the open window.

"*Muuum*, that's not even a thing."

He grinned to hear Odella grumbling, not sure what they were talking about. But he'd caught her in time. A few more moments catching his breath and he'd be able to knock on their door. He didn't want to get caught eavesdropping.

"You know the saying, 'Della," her mother replied. "If their love is swift and true, they will always wait for you. Make this choice based on what will make you happy. It's yours to make, and you can't let anyone else influence you."

Sannar froze.

Isn't that what I'm doing though? I tried to influence her last night to choose the Nether Court by promising her I'd get her a good position. Now I'm trying to convince her to come to the queen's court with me instead. What if she wants to stay with her family, but thinks going with the queen is something she 'should' do?

He took several steps backwards until he was on the street once more. The plan had been to approach Odella, but he started walking through town instead toward the bridge that led out to the meadows. Going back to the court didn't appeal to him in the slightest, and if Odella did want to choose the Nether Court he didn't want to know. Not until he could gather himself enough to pretend to be happy for her.

Demi was doing him a kindness in pulling him from the Nether Court, but he was a sworn-in nether brother; he couldn't refuse to go if Lady Aereen sent him.

After the previous night's fight and then his mad dash down from the court, his legs were all but failing to keep him moving. He ambled through the flowers, resisting the urge to kick them as they sang their tune at him like his heart wasn't breaking. Like it didn't matter.

It's six months. It didn't matter. *If she stays here, I'll come back to her.* He would, but she might have found someone else by then. *If I lose her, I don't know what I'll do.*

He sat on their rock but the memory of their date-that-wasn't-a-date swelled and he lurched back onto his feet. With a handful of stones, he started chucking them at the water with no finesse whatsoever.

He'd gone four years without her, but now he was struggling to imagine a day without seeing her face or hearing her laugh at him over something stupid.

I hate being good. I hate that I can't bring myself to influence her, but she has to make the choice herself.

He stiffened as shoes crunched over the stones behind him. With a deep, ragged breath, he turned and dropped his arms to his sides as Odella approached. She kept coming until she was right in front of him, mere centimetres between them. She tilted her head back until he could look right into her grey-blue eyes.

He took a deep breath, preparing himself for the worst. *This is going to hurt.*

"I'm taking the queen up on her offer," she announced. He froze.

She's doing the right thing, the sensible thing. But she doesn't know that I'm going too.

His mind rioted over the possibilities. She'd given him tiny hints she might like him, at least a little more than friends, and she was doing the best thing for her future, which is what he wanted for her.

She frowned when he didn't reply.

"It's only six months," she added. "Then I'll be back to fray your sanity to your last nerve, don't worry."

He swallowed a catch in his throat. He should tell her his news and see her reaction but her face was so close to his, so mesmerising. The sparkle in her eyes, the way her lips curved as she smiled; he was besotted.

"I also decided that I can't stop my future from happening," she finished. "But I can control it somewhat by my actions."

He tensed as one of her hands landed on the back of his neck. Her eyelids fluttered closed and her other hand touched his chest, but he had no time to react as she guided his head down and sealed her lips over his.

His insides exploded with flutters, and he imagined that somewhere in the magic of Faerie and the nether, a swear-word of absolute joy- no, a string of swear-words, an entire *tome* of swearwords, were invented.

So bewildered by her kissing him, Sannar forgot to kiss her back. But when she dropped her face away from his with a frown, he woke from the astonishment and wrapped an arm around her waist to pull her back to him.

Where her kiss had been determined but momentary, he summoned every ounce of emotional fire and longing he'd suffered, his fingers splaying over her back as his other hand caressed the soft tangle of her hair. When he finally pulled back, and only because it was that or fall over, her cheeks were bright red and she lifted a hand to her lips with a soft laugh.

"Well that was somehow unexpected," she said. "I'm not sure what I expected. Maybe I wasn't thinking."

"Not in your right mind? Nether feeling off today?" he asked, not letting her go.

She bit her lip, her eyes darting shyly down to fix on his chest instead of his face.

"Yeah, that must be it. I'm going to swear to the queen's court for the six months but I wanted to give you a kiss to see if you'd still be here when I get back. Of course you don't have to wait for me, I'm not expecting you to or anything. But I couldn't go without at least having a chance-"

"I'd wait forever for you."

He said it without hesitation, interrupting her babbling. She looked up at him, her expression breaking into the most beautiful ray of sunshine.

Overwhelmed and in the mood to laugh and roll around on the floor simply because he couldn't think of any other way to celebrate, other than maybe parading her through town and telling everyone else she was taken, he wrapped both arms around her waist as she pushed her glasses up her nose with a pleased huff.

"The queen's borrowing me from the Nether Court as it happens," he announced. "Six months with her. So you might have to face putting up with me after all."

She stared at him, eyes wide. "You're coming with us?"

"Yep, wherever that will be. Couldn't let you have all the fun. Is that okay? I don't want to cramp your style."

She rolled her eyes but he thought he saw a traitorous shine at the corners as she wriggled to get both arms free of him so she could throw them around his neck.

"Sammy and Mix are going to *freak* about this. Oh orbs, Mum's going to be unbearable. She always loved you. Dad too, he'll have you signed up to help on the boats the minute we get back."

He grinned but noticed her stilling against him. With the rather wobbly hold he'd had on her, she'd been swinging her dangling feet, but now she lay draped against him again like a backwards cape.

"You know, I think our queen is rather sneaky when she needs to be," she said.

Sannar grinned. "Ah well, she's got my vote either way given that I've got what I want now."

"Oh you have, have you?" Odella dropped out of his arms and pushed a hand against his chest. "Don't be so presumptuous."

"You kissed me. You asked me to wait for you. I'm telling everyone you're my girlfriend."

She sniffed. "Even your court brothers?"

"*Especially* my court brothers. We'll get matching t-shirts," he teased.

Her eyes sparkled up at him as she grinned and stepped close enough for him to hug her again. She let him, her hands pressed against his chest.

"Eww, no. No cheesy stuff. No matching t-shirts. No awful nicknames."

"Pickle."

"Absolutely not."

"Petal."

"No!"

"You can pick one for me too you know."

"Idiot?"

"Okay that's mean!" He grinned. "How about I stick with Squish?"

She nodded. "I can cope with that."

He smiled down at her, his heart racing.

I cannot be this lucky. Although after four years of servitude, maybe the powers that be finally wanted me to have something amazing.

"Thank Faerie the nether was off that day you decided to talk to me," she murmured. "I know we're going into the unknown, but I'm glad we'll be together for it."

"Me too. I can't imagine a day without you, which is probably not the coolest thing to say when I haven't even taken you on a proper date yet but it's true."

She flushed, her gaze darting downward with coy amusement.

"We may not have much time for dates where we're going," she said with a sigh.

It was true, but he planned to enjoy every single second of having her around, whether the Forgotten were looming to fight more battles or not.

"But that's not for a few days at least, is it?" he asked. "I can take you out today. I kind of ran out of the court without telling anyone where I was going, so it may have exploded by now anyway and I'll have all the time in the world."

She lifted her face to his.

"Are you going to kiss me again then?"

He grinned. "Are you?"

So she did.

CHAPTER TWENTY THREE
REYAN

Kainen led the way into the Keep and Reyan kept close beside him as they surveyed the seven grown Fae still standing in the cells, three in one, three in another, and one man with the far corner cell to himself.

That was the man they needed, short brown hair and an air of extreme smugness floating around him, but Reyan's instincts prickled with foreboding. He looked so unremarkable with his hair shorn short and a basic Fae face, pale, ageless and unmarked by any sense of individuality or striking features. His clothes weren't fashion or anything befitting high-Fae either, simple fabric in hues of brown, grey and green.

Perfect for blending in. Too perfect, which means he definitely has something to hide.

"Ready for a one-way ticket, Lorens?" Kainen demanded.

One of the guards unlocked the cell for them but Kainen blocked the way out. Reyan tried not to show any fear, although her nerves where leaping as she held Kainen's hand.

Lorens grinned the kind of indolent smile Kainen usually wore around his courtiers, relaxed and cocky.

"Whatever you say, court lord," he said. "Oh, hello beautiful."

Reyan tensed as his eyes flicked over her, up and down with exaggerated slowness. Kainen's fingers tightened around her own but his eyes, although narrowed to angry slits, were still brown.

"Let's get this done," she said. "Don't forget we need to stop at… you know, as well."

She kept her voice full of secrets, amazed at how easily the haughty tone came along with it.

"Well, that's me done." Lorens clapped his hands eagerly. "I bid you all farewell, my comrades, as my next future beckons."

He bowed low but while Kainen was glaring at him, Reyan noted one or two of the other captives weren't muttering or rolling their eyes. They were dipping their chins, their eyes sharp.

A sign of respect. Why would they if he's not one of them?

Kainen's suggestion that the man was more important than they guessed filled her head and she turned her focus to their shared warding, holding to it with everything she had.

Kainen gripped Lorens' wrist in one swift move, the black smoke already swirling around them. Reyan twisted to see if the other captives made any more telling gestures but the purple grey nether swallowed them before she could glimpse anything more.

The familiar high street of her childhood home formed around her, cloaked by evening and disturbed by a brisk wind. She shivered after the warmth of the Nether Court, but Lorens was already taking in his surroundings and stepping back.

She expected him to vanish, but his face froze in momentary confusion before he started to laugh.

"Smart, court lord. Compelling me before I can flee, very smart. But you can't compel anything out of me that the young queen hasn't already dug up from the dusty recesses of my mind."

Kainen smiled, wicked and dark. "Oh, I don't need information. I trust the queen will have taken what she needs from you. I also know she's made some kind of deal to let you go, and I don't care what that is. No, before *I* let you go, I'm going to protect what's mine."

He blew a breath of black smoke that glimmered in the firelight from the streetlamps burning nearby. Lorens' face contorted and a moment later Kainen chuckled dark and devilish.

"Ah-ah," he sang. "Say it out loud, her name included. Swear it for the whole of Faerie to hear and hold you to."

Lorens clenched his jaw before his lips parted.

"I swear I will not hurt Lady Reyan of the Court of Illusions, or make any effort to harm or destroy her, or have any others do it on my behalf."

Reyan froze. She'd expected some kind of hostility between the two, or perhaps Lorens vanishing without a word, but Kainen was mad if he thought any kind of Forgotten follower would abide by a promise like that. They might not be able to lie or go against a sworn promise, but there were many other ways to take action without acting personally. She wasn't actually a lady either which would probably nullify any actual promises worded that way.

"How kind of you," Kainen said. "Now you may leave."

Lorens took a step back and Reyan felt the sudden thrum of Kainen's entire power gathering around them. She sank into it, taking comfort from him beside her. He knew what he was doing and although she wasn't actually his lady, perhaps while she was pretending to be she would be safe from one enemy at least.

"One court lady won't make a difference to me," Lorens

said, the subtle growl underlying his carefree tone the only sign the promise had rattled him. "I'm sure someone else will target her before long, pretty little thing she is. Perhaps they'll make it hurt and make it last. Once the Forgotten have the location they need and the keys to get through to it, they'll be unstoppable."

Kainen's hand flew toward Lorens' throat. Lorens darted back, a gleeful grin lighting up his face.

"Remember your allegiances, court lord, because vendettas cast long ripples. After all, look what happened to your mother."

He vanished as the puff of black smoke engulfed the spot he'd been standing in.

Kainen roared and the smoke spiked, a roiling mess of darkness and spite.

"Hey, enough of that." Reyan grabbed his arm and pulled. "We're in the middle of the street in front of everyone."

He glowered at her. "So?"

She wrenched herself free of him, drawing his attention onto her and away from thoughts of their escapee as his smoke dissipated.

"So, if you want me to pretend to do the lady thing, you have to learn to listen to me when I'm doing it. We can't make a scene here or people will ask why. Take me home, then you can scream and stomp around all you want."

She wanted to ask what Lorens had meant about his mother. He'd said it as a taunt but even though she'd been part of the court for years, she'd never heard one word mentioned about Kainen's mother, not even in the hushed whispers or kitchen gossip. Lorens had also let slip a confirmation about what the Forgotten were after again, a location and also keys, plural.

Kainen grabbed her hand without warning and skipped them to the Illusion Court right into his study. She pulled her hand free and folded her arms again, facing him down as he dropped sulkily into his seat.

"My father killed my mother."

The words filled the already tense space, enflaming the air between them. Reyan's stomach dropped and she crossed the room, settling to sit on the edge of the desk facing him.

"Do you want to talk about it?" she asked.

"I'm not sure."

"Try. If you want to stop you can at any time. Was he-did they…"

He nodded. "He forbade anyone to ever mention her again after she was gone and the court obeyed. Meri remembers her, and she saved me a bunch of stuff in secret that my father insisted was burned. I've never had the bravery to look at it though."

Reyan reached out and took his hand, running her thumb over his knuckles as he'd done to her before.

"That would take *a lot* of bravery for anyone, let alone when it happened in a bad way."

He sighed, dropping back against the chair. She had to lean forward or release his hand and for a moment she thought she'd end up in his lap. He opened his eyes, realised and sat up again, but she didn't have time to face her unexpected disappointment.

"We were very much his and hers kids, Di and me," he said. "She loved our mother but she was my father's child. Smart enough to realise that smiling and batting her eyelashes while hiding her intelligence was the best way to fool him into not focusing on her too strongly. But of course, I was the oldest, the son. I was to take over the court from him, although he actually spent more time in his Mage of Nightmares house with his mistresses."

"Do you still have it?" she asked. "The house I mean?"

"No, I had it torn down when I inherited after he was removed from title. Sold the land and put the money back into the court. Demi dissolved the Mage of Nightmares position but let me keep the court, even after everything I did to her."

Reyan frowned. "Most of that wasn't your choice from what I remember."

"Most of it, maybe. But I wasn't ever a 'good' person. I treated her horribly and I feel sick when I think of who I was then. I thought my father's world and way of thinking was all there was. But seeing Demi suffer back then, the guilt was unimaginable, like my own mind-control gift had turned the very worst of itself on me."

"You regretted it?"

"Instantly. It was like waking up. I tricked her into my father's house and locked her up. Back then it was a game to me, a bit of Fae manipulation that I was used to from others, one she'd learnt to play along with eventually. The sheer arrogance of it, I feel queasy now just remembering."

Reyan shook her hand free of his and poured two cups of *Beast Lite* from the decanter on the table.

"Here. Go on, you were guilty and feeling sick."

He sighed again. "The next time I saw her, she was in the Old King's dungeon. Same situation, different cell. I didn't have a key to get her out but I figured if she gave me something information-wise, I could convince the Old King that he should spare her life at least. But she was defiant to the last and I've never known shame like it."

"She's definitely stubborn."

"To the last nerve. I almost managed to dodge out of the

Battle of Arcanium but they had Diana with them, and I knew they'd hurt her to get at me if I showed weakness. Then the moment came to walk away and I did. I wasn't brave enough to become a traitor to the Forgotten, but I managed to compel a few of them to flee or fight each other on the way out."

"So you were already beginning to change your mind?"

He nodded. "I was scared. Too scared to risk fighting for the right side, but I knew I couldn't support the Forgotten anymore. When the Oak Queen hauled our family in after that battle and I tried to barter for Diana's safety, she offered me a deal. Become part of her court. Work for her. Prove I'd changed and she would name me my father's successor. She'd ensure Diana remained safely at Arcanium and we wouldn't be tainted with our father's reputation."

"That's when the Forgotten started flocking here with those Apocalyptians, then Demi came and everything exploded?"

"Yeah. Demi still struggles to be around me and I don't blame her."

Anguish twisted in her chest at the broken resignation in his voice, his gaze fixed on his hands limp in his lap.

"She understands though," she insisted. "Demi knows you're on her side now, even if she still can't relax totally around you. That will take more time. Orb her now and tell her what happened with Lorens. Especially the bit about the location and the keys."

Kainen waved a hand over the large black orb on his desk and Reyan twisted so she could see it too.

"Queen Demerara," he announced.

The orb swirled and Demi's face burst up in front of them, a startled vision in pearlescent grey.

"He escaped," Kainen said, his voice flat. "Said something about remembering my allegiances because the Blood and Bone Court will never forget a vendetta. He confirmed as well that they're looking for a location and keys."

Demi snorted loudly. "The Blood and Bone Court, that's original. Forgotten Court would have been way cooler. Okay, then we move onto our plan to hold a revel at the Flora Court next. You'll receive an invitation but I'll send someone in person with some requests beforehand."

Kainen nodded, lifting his hand to disconnect, but Demi wasn't done.

"Thank you both for fighting alongside us by the way. I do appreciate your court's loyalty more than you can ever know." Demi smiled and her gaze flitted to Kainen briefly. "Both of you."

She disappeared and Reyan got to her feet before awkwardness could take hold. They hadn't discussed anything personal yet and she wanted to keep it that way, at least until she figured out how she felt. Kainen was sinfully attractive and twice as fun to flirt with, but if the almost kiss in the Nether Court tunnels were anything to judge by, he might be confusing his feelings for her.

He did it with Demi by his own admission. The last thing we need is for him to assume I'm her replacement for his affections simply because I'm kind to him. I want more than that.

"You need to take some time off or something," she said.

Kainen raised his eyebrows, a surprised laugh huffing from his lips.

"Time off? Court lord's don't get time off. If we're the right sort, we can take advantage of our reputations enough to enjoy revelry and intrigue, but we rarely ever get a proper break."

Reyan grinned. "You know, I don't think you're the right sort at all. You pretend to be because you have to, but you're soft as sugar deep down."

He folded his arms and she breathed a tiny sigh of relief to see his shoulders lowering.

"You think you know all about me now, sweetheart?"

She shrugged. "Enough. You can be kind and thoughtful when you want to be. You're fighting on the right side now too. You protect me even though I'm not really... well, you know."

His face shadowed and for a moment she thought she'd triggered another brooding sulk-fest.

"I won't tolerate people taking shots at you," he muttered.

"I can take care of myself, and apparently we have Betty as a warning system now."

He looked up at her. For long moments they hovered in tense silence, until his lips started to curve up, his eyes beginning to sparkle.

"Of course, but there's no harm in being over-prepared. With that in mind, I've decided I'll train you in combat myself. Until you get another assignment from Demi or we're called to go to the Flora Court, we're training non-stop. Starting right now."

He stood up and shucked off his jacket, prowling around the desk toward her. With a sweep of his hand, he sent the desk sliding neatly against the wall, opening up the floor space.

Reyan faced him, relaxing her hands at her sides. She was no stranger to combat training from her time at court and she could move easily enough with or without her shadows after her time spent dancing.

When Kainen summoned a wooden pike in hand, she flicked out her hand on instinct letting her adrenalin power her gift as she turned the wood into gloopy liquid. It dribbled over his fingers and onto the floor with a quiet splat.

"I really need to work on that," she muttered.

"You'll get there." He grinned. "Okay, first of all, ground rules."

"This is Fae combat. There aren't any rules. Are you sure you can handle me?" she taunted, amusement mingling with trepidation.

Kainen's grin widened with delight, black smoke glittering at his fingertips.

"We'll see won't we, sweetheart. Time to have some fun."

ACKNOWLEDGEMENTS

Huge thank you to every reader who took a chance on the Arcanium series and also to those now diving into the Courts of Faerie series! To those who've shared on social media, done ARC reads or just given me compliments about the book to keep me going, you make this all worth it.

To my family and also my writing family as always, your support means everything to me – Anna Britton, Debbie Roxburgh, Sally Doherty, Marisa Noelle, Emma Finlayson-Palmer, Katina Wright, Alison Hunt, the amazing ARC readers (who have caught so many printing blips it's not even funny...) writing Twitter and BookTok, everyone who joins #ukteenchat, the WriteMentor crew, libraries and schools who took a chance on this series, shops that are still stocking these books and giving this indie author a chance to reach more readers, and to the readers who will find these books in the future:

THANK YOU!

ABOUT THE AUTHOR

While always convinced that there has to be something out there beyond the everyday, Emma focuses on weaving magic realms with words (the real world can wait a while). The idea of other worlds fascinates her and she's determined to find her own entrance to an alternate realm one day.

Raised in London, she now lives on the UK south coast with her husband and a very lazy black Labrador who occasionally condescends to take her out for a walk.

Aside from creative writing studies, an addiction to cake and spending far too much time procrastinating on social media, Emma is still waiting for the arrival of her unicorn. Or a tank, she's not fussy.

For the latest news and updates, check the website or come say hi on social media:

www.emmaebradley.com
@EmmaEBradley

Ingram Content Group UK Ltd.
Milton Keynes UK
UKHW041807040723
424552UK00002B/8

9 781915 909077